UTTERLY

PAULINE MANDERS

Copyright © Pauline Manders 2015
All rights reserved.

Pauline Manders has asserted her right under the Copyright, Designs and Patent Act 1988 to be identified as the author of this work.

This book is a work of fiction. Names, characters, places and incidents either are the products of the author's imagination or used fictitiously, and any resemblance to actual persons living or dead, business establishments, events, or locales is entirely coincidental.

Cover design Rebecca Moss Guyver.

ISBN – 13: 978-1517523633
ISBN – 10: 151752363X

Also by Pauline Manders

Utterly Explosive (2012)

Utterly Fuelled (2013)

Utterly Rafted (2013)

Utterly Reclaimed (2014)

To Paul, Fiona, Alastair, Karen, Andrew, Katie and Mathew.

ACKNOWLEDGMENTS

My thanks to: Beth Wood for her positive advice, support and encouragement; Pat McHugh, my mentor and hardworking editor with a keen sense of humour, mastery of atmosphere and grasp of characters; Rebecca Moss Guyver for her boundless enthusiasm and inspired cover artwork and design; David Withnall for his proof reading skills; Dr Mary McGinty and Dr Tim Howes for their specialist knowledge in Respiratory Medicine; Paul Davies and Geosphere Environmental Ltd for their knowledge and experience with Japanese knotweed; Sue Southey for her cheerful reassurances and advice; the Write Now Bury writers' group for their support; and my husband and family, on both sides of the English Channel & the Atlantic, for their love and support.

CHAPTER 1

Matt squeezed both brakes as the front of the scooter shook violently.

'What the…?' he shrieked as the wheel tilted and slewed.

He pitched his weight sideways and wrestled the handlebars straight. It was impossible to steer.

'Oh no-o-o-o.' He released the front brake. Seconds stretched as the rear brake eased the Piaggio Zip to a ragged halt.

His legs gave way as he dismounted. He hung on to the handle grips. It was as if his plump hands were fused to them. He leaned on the scooter like a duck on crutches and gasped for breath. What the hell had happened, Matt wondered, and kicked down the parking stand.

A puncture? He hadn't seen anything on the road as he'd ridden under the low railway bridge out of Needham Market. Glass? A split can? He sank to his knees. It was easier to see the small front wheel from that level. His hands felt stiff as he flipped up his visor. Something gleamed in the afternoon light. It spiked the tyre as it protruded between the worn treads.

'Shit.' His fingers brushed over a metal shard impaling the front tyre. Clearly there'd be no limping home from this. It would be nothing less than a roadside repair or rescue. Eighteen months of riding his scooter and this was his first puncture. He was totally unprepared.

'Aint yankin' that out,' he breathed, as a vague memory surfaced. He'd read somewhere it would be an easier puncture repair if he left it in place until help arrived.

The cold struck up through the damp grass as he shifted from his knees and sat on the verge. He pulled his mobile from his jeans pocket and checked the time. 15:04. Without really thinking, he pressed Nick's automatic dial number. If a good mate of three years wouldn't come out, who would?

He eyed the tyre with distaste as he listened to the ringtone. Nothing - just the hollow despair of his pulse as the automated voice gave instructions to leave a message after the tone. Anxiety chased frustration. Why didn't Nick answer?

A chill spread from his buttocks and nipped at his bladder. The sudden urge to pee was overwhelming and he scrambled to his feet. He glanced beyond the rough grass, scanning for suitable cover. Low brambles and scrubby hawthorn offered a sparse screen. This'll do, he thought as he pushed through the vegetation, his discomfort growing. A few more steps and a clump of dead stems blocked his path. Straight, brownish-grey and densely packed, they stood well over a metre high. Some had broken and lay on the ground, but most were like spears driven into the soil, no leaves, still upright and menacing. Funny place to see bamboo, he thought and skirted around them.

At last shielded from the road, he faced the cane-like stalks and peed, lost in relief as the urine flowed. A distant noise carried through the air, not quite rushing water but more of a rumble.

The rumble exploded into a gusting wall of sound.

'Flamin' shit!'

A train thundered past, a few metres away. Matt staggered sideways.

'The Norwich express,' he hissed and closed his eyes, as if that could shut out the sound. He forced himself to picture the train timetable – Norwich, Diss, Ipswich, Manningtree, Colchester, Liverpool Street - a protective impulse born of a photographic memory. While the slipstream growled and swirled, he swayed on his feet and read station names.

The train raced further along the track, its trailing force spent at last. He opened his eyes. Before, the brownish-grey stems screened him, now they hemmed him in. Had he staggered deeper into the clump? The train had disorientated Matt and he struck out at the dead canes. They bent and fractured like hollow papery reeds. He forced a path. He needed to get back to the road and his scooter.

'What the…?' His foot slithered and sank.

He froze as his weight pushed down into something. An initial glance told him leaves, earth, twigs…. He looked again, his brain struggling to make sense of the shapes and colours. Was it a bird's foot, its talons curling? But the skin was wrong, the size too large. Could it be a clump of roots?

'Oh God.' Now he got it.

Small, oblong forms morphed into a clearer outline.

'Those aint claws,' he whispered, but his mind refused to accept.

He forced himself to focus. Slowly, he traced the shapes with his eyes. The fingernails became obvious, the fingers unmistakable. They curled, as if clutching the air. It was a hand, palm up.

'Shit,' he gasped.

Instinctively he raised his foot. A putrid stench rose from the ground. Dank rotting leaves stuck to the sole of his trainer, lifting away as he moved. He stared, transfixed by the sight of dead earthy flesh. The force of his imprint split the skin. Lifeless tissue showed through. No pinks or reds, just the dull fawn-grey of disintegrating meat. Tendons, pale and string-like stretched beyond the palm. The hand was joined to something.

'A-a-ah!' He'd trodden on someone's arm. 'Christ Almighty,' he yelled.

Horror and revulsion erupted from his stomach. It tore at his chest. The damp cold air reeked of death and his vomit. He ran.

'Norwich, Diss,' he breathed as he collapsed on the grass near his scooter. 'Ipswich, Manningtree, Colchester, Liverpool Street.' But the timetable couldn't drive away the decaying hand. Or the smell. He reached for his mobile.

•

Matt sat on the grass, his backside numbed by the January chill permeating up from the ground. He watched the uniformed policeman approach. All around, Scene of Crime Officers moved like shadows of the living, dressed in pale jumpsuits with ashen hoods and booties. Cordons of blue and white plastic tape boldly proclaimed, *Police Line - Do Not Cross.* A large hooped tent, a confused mix of globe and cube, was pegged to the ground somewhere near the decomposing hand.

'We'll need your trainers, Mr Finch,' the policeman said.

'What?'

'It is Mr Finch? Matt Finch, that's what you said your name was, right?'

'Yeah.'

'A student at Utterly Academy, Stowmarket. Computing and IT. And you say you stopped because you had a puncture and then went for a pee.' The policeman flipped forwards some pages of his notebook. 'Remember you told us you'd stepped on an arm?'

'Oh God.' Matt relived the sensation; his foot slithering and pressing until the tread cut into the rotting flesh, then the resistance of underlying bone.

'And of course your footprints will be all over the place. Your trainers, Mr Finch. I'm afraid we need them.'

'But what will I wear? How will I get home?'

The policeman frowned. 'You could have a pair of plastic overshoes. There's bound to be some spare in one of the vans. They'll stop your socks getting muddy.'

A hooded figure in a white all-in-one approached. Matt couldn't help noticing the blue well-fitting latex gloves encasing a pair of dainty hands. He reckoned there was a good chance a girl was inside. He shifted his gaze and focused on the bunch of plastic evidence bags. They flapped as she walked.

'For your shoes,' a clear voice cut from behind her mask. She proffered a bag while Matt yanked off his trainers, trying not to touch the soles.

'Thanks.' She turned and murmured something to the policeman before handing over another evidence bag.

'What's this for?'

'If you could just be sick again, but into the bag this time?'

'What?' Matt stared at the policeman.

'The SOCO,' he nodded towards the hooded figure, 'says it'll help to exclude you and your vomit from the crime scene.'

'You're kiddin', right? Can't I just say what I've been eatin'?'

'Only if you're sure you can't vomit up some more for us.' Her voice was crisp, the tone matter-of-fact.

Matt groaned, his insides almost touching with emptiness.

The policeman grimaced. 'OK, you think about it.' He turned and spoke quietly to the SOCO. Matt didn't even try to catch their words, just watched as the policeman stepped closer to the girl. They seemed to talk as if he wasn't there. Matt cleared his throat, hawked up some mucous and spat into the plastic. His feet were cold. He felt wretched.

'Good,' she said and held out her blue latexed hand for the bag. She scrutinised the miserable offering of spit for a moment before returning it. Rejection.

'But I aint got nothin' left to puke.' Panic stirred. Would she want him to pee into a pot next, just to exclude his urine from the scene?

'OK,' the policeman muttered. 'Let's get you into one of our cars. But keep the bag with you in case you come over queasy. The DS wants to ask you some questions.'

Waiting for the police to arrive had seemed an eternity to Matt, and now they were everywhere as he picked his way in socks and plastic overshoes to the car. At first he'd been tempted to ride away rather than hang around for them, but the metal shard spiking his front tyre was a decider. He was trapped between a rotting corpse and his broken down scooter. There'd be no escape. And so he'd lingered for an age, alone but close to the Piaggio, wondering if the arm was attached to a body.

'Oh God,' he breathed as he realised it could have been worse. Imagine slipping on putrid guts? Or stepping on a decaying face? He hugged his stomach while his thoughts raced on. Was the hand flung from a passing train? The dismembered limb cast away in an act of crude disposal? One thing was certain, he was glad he hadn't taken a longer look.

'Norwich, Diss, Ipswich, Manningtree, Colchester, Liverpool Street.'

There was nowhere for the police and crime scene vehicles to draw onto the verge, so they clogged the road. Matt followed the policeman. He supposed the normal traffic must have been diverted to avoid the blocked route under the low railway bridge. When someone finally held the door of a patrol car open, he was grateful to get in. He sat on the back seat and clutched the evidence bag close, as if it could transmit some warmth or bring good luck.

'DS Stickley will be with you in a moment, Mr Finch.' The words were tossed in as the car door shut with a clunk.

'DS Stickley?' Matt queried to the closed door. The name sounded familiar. Wasn't he the detective who'd visited the Academy a few months ago? The guy with a voice like a cheese-grater? Matt closed his eyes in an effort to focus on something other than the rotting hand.

'Keeping you from your sleep, are we?' The abrasive voice ricocheted across the back seat, as a young man dressed in a taupe-coloured windproof looked through the open window.

Matt flinched. 'What?'

'Enjoying the comforts of our deluxe rear seats, Mr Finch? It's DS Stickley, in case you'd forgotten. Just a few things I need to ask.'

'Yeah?'

'I know you've already spoken to the uniformed police,' the DS rasped as he opened the door.

A cold blast cut through the flimsy plastic overshoes protecting Matt's socks. He wiggled his toes inside the puckered material.

'Bleedin' shower caps.'

'What?'

'On me feet. An' I got a puncture an' all.'

'Is that's why you stopped?'

'Yeah, nearly came off me scooter. They've taken me trainers. I didn't set out like this.'

There wasn't much to tell, but the DS wanted to hear it in painstaking detail, and then his age, where he lived and how often he rode that way.

'So do you have breakdown recovery?' Stickley asked in metallic tones.

'I...,' Matt's voice drifted. For a moment he was a kid again and struggling to understand, not a plump twenty year old with a stubbly ginger beard and a plastic vomit bag for evidence. Was the DS asking about traumatised emotions? The after tremors of a grisly shock?

'Your scooter. You'll need to get that tyre fixed.'

'What?' And then he got it – Stickley meant scooter breakdown, not the nervous kind. He felt foolish, but at least there'd be no mumbling of words like distraught and shattered while he watched for a nod of approval. He took a deep breath. He needed to remember he was king of the keyboard, a star student in Computing and IT now.

Matt squared up. 'Flamin' right. Dirty great piece of metal sticking out of it.'

'I'll ask one of the uniforms to get it dropped off at a tyre place for you.'

'Thanks mate.' Perhaps Stickley wasn't so bad, Matt decided. Voices could be misleading.

'And we'll get you home. Tumble Weed Drive, did you say? Stowmarket?'

'Yeah. So is it just an arm, you know, or is stuff attached?'

'Apart from the hand, you mean?'

'Yeah.'

The DS looked at him for a moment, as if sizing him up. 'It's a complete body, as far as we can tell - that's if you discount the animal damage.'

'Animal damage?'

'Nibbling. Pecking. You know the kind of thing.'

A picture of carrion crows jabbing and tearing at dead flesh slammed into Matt's mind. He swallowed back the bile and changed subject.

'D'you still work with Clive Merry?' he asked, trying to appear in the know. He'd met Clive a few times. He'd even had a few drinks with him, but only because he'd shared a workbench at the Academy with Clive's girlfriend. That was before he'd changed from Carpentry to IT.

'The DI doesn't get back till after the weekend.'

So was that a yes or a no? Matt couldn't tell.

'I'll pass it on that you mentioned him. I'm sure he'll be thrilled to find your name amongst all this on his desk, first thing Monday morning.'

'Flamin' hell,' Matt murmured, and rested his head against the seat as exhaustion overtook and dusk began to fall.

'Well, that about wraps it up for now. Time to get you home.' The voice seemed to soften, but Stickley had opened the door and his words were directed towards the grass verge as he got out.

A gust of cold air chilled the car's interior, leaving Matt alone. Yes voices played tricks, he decided.

So how long had the body lain there? Matt shivered. He didn't want to think too hard about it, and screwed up his eyes in an effort to shut out the ideas he'd conjured – but a carrion crow flashed into his mind. Its head grew. The beak thickened, then curved.

'Norwich, Diss....' It wasn't going to work. He tried an older trick from his childhood. He concentrated on the silky black feathers. He forced his mind's eye to soften them to mocha-charcoal, then speckle them with browns and beige. The head ballooned, transforming into a magnificent eagle. It became a creature born of his comic-strip books, Mega Eagle. It would soar in his imagination and transport him from the mundane sepia of the page to a fantasy world beyond. As the police car bumped and rocked over the rutted verge, Matt rode the eagle in his mind. The car suspension complained, but the magnificent wings didn't miss a beat as he swooped under the low railway bridge and glided on thermals above the old road from Needham Market to Stowmarket. From high in the sky the world seemed smaller, his problems manageable. He forgot the hand. He was flying. He didn't even hear the text message *ping* in his pocket.

Crack! Static spat and snapped on the police radio.

Bang! Mega Eagle took a shot to the chest. Matt spiralled with the bird. Down he came.

'OK, Mr Finch. We're here now.'

'What?'

'Is it this one?' The police car drew up outside a modest semi-detached bungalow. Tired paint crazed the door and flaked from frames surrounding windows that gaped dark and lifeless.

'Just dropping the witness off... yeah, the Flower Estate... where d'you say? ... we'll be on our way,' the policeman muttered into the radio receiver.

'Yeah, that's where I live, but can you collar me out the car? It'd help with me street cred.' The Suffolk accent coursed through Matt's vowels as he shook off sleep.

'Now Mr Finch, if we're talking street cred, take a look at your feet. Let's live down the shower caps first, shall we, sir?' The policeman handed him a name and number scribbled on a scrap of paper.

'What's this?'

'It's the details of where your scooter'll be taken. And look on the bright side, the light's fading. No one'll see you now. So, out the car – we've got an urgent call. Goodbye, Mr Finch.'

CHAPTER 2

Chrissie bumped her front door closed with the sole of her leather boot and wheeled the small suitcase further into the narrow hallway.

'Would you turn the central heating up now we're back,' she called to Clive as he strode ahead. She watched him pause, as if picturing her thermostat and timer before heading for the kitchen. She supposed mastering the vagaries of someone else's heating system only came when you were freezing or considered it yours as well.

She likened her end of terrace cottage to a cocoon. It might be cramped, quirky and, for the moment glacial, but it had been her home in Woolpit for the best part of twelve years.

Her wheelie collided with Clive's rucksack, discarded on the floor where he'd shrugged it off his back.

'Oh hell,' she shrieked.

His luggage label twisted. She caught the faded writing: *Lavenham, Suffolk, UK*. Was he intending to make the final ten miles of his journey back to his own home this evening, she wondered.

'Are you OK, Chrissie?'

'I've just wheeled my case into your backpack. The bowl - I've probably smashed it,' she shouted to the nippy air.

'Oh no.' He sounded distracted.

For a moment she wasn't sure if he was talking to the central heating controls or to her. They'd tramped halfway around Paris and most of a flea market carrying the bowl in his pack. She reckoned it should have raised a fruitier expletive than *oh no*, and bit back *if you hadn't left it in the middle of the hall I wouldn't have run my case into it*. There was no point. He most likely hadn't heard her, and she didn't want to add a sour note to the end of the trip.

She thought back to the long weekend they'd spent in Paris. The Eurostar had whisked them through the Channel tunnel, their ears popping as they ploughed the subterranean depths. He'd held her hand as they'd gazed at the base of the Eiffel Tower, the great superstructure lost that day in misty cloud. Rodin, the Mona Lisa – it had been a whistle stop tour. They'd scurried into the Musée d'Orsay for warmth, lingering there until Clive eventually dragged her away from the Art Nouveau furniture displayed somewhere in the upper floor galleries. And the small shallow bowl, more like a chalice? A find in a flea market, le marché aux puces de la Porte de Vanves.

'Marché aux puces,' she murmured, the French words wistfully melodic as she opened his rucksack.

'Right, that's all set now,' he said as he reappeared in the hallway.

'Thanks for doing that.'

'Whatever's the matter? Why are you scrabbling around in the…?'

She didn't bother to answer as she pulled at the tatty French newspaper and scraps of old bubble wrap.

'Of course, the bowl.'

Ever the great detective, she thought as she muttered, 'I think your socks saved it.'

'What?'

'And maybe the sweatshirt. Small collision with your backpack.'

'What? You're a liability, Chrissie. Will you be OK left on your own?'

'And if I said no?'

'I wouldn't believe you.'

'Because you forgot to add resourceful to liability?'

'Something like that.' He crouched to look at the pale clay chalice. 'You know, it reminds me of the whitish bricks round here. It's the same colour.'

'I hadn't thought of it like that,' she said and ran a finger over the glazed surface.

'Is it OK?'

'I think so.'

He sighed, almost a low breathy whistle, his habit when luck dealt a surprise.

'Sorry Chrissie, but I'm going to have to get moving. Monday morning tomorrow, I'll be back in the thick of it at the station. No doubt there'll be something grim waiting on my desk.' He stood up, as if suddenly weary.

'Oh for goodness sake. Monday morningitis already? The weekend isn't over yet.' She got to her feet and kissed him.

'Hmm... it's all right for you. The worst thing you're likely to face tomorrow is peeling veneer and a bit of woodworm damage.'

'I don't know,' she murmured. 'The coat stand might have tried to murder the tallboy, and the only clue is a broken cabriole leg hidden in the linen press.'

Clive laughed, and gave her a hug. She squealed in protest as he almost crushed the bowl.

'Careful.'

'I hate it when holidays end. Bye, Chrissie. I'll give you a call when I get back to Lavenham.'

He scooped up the rucksack straps and hoisted them onto his shoulders. She watched him, top flapping open and socks poking out as he headed for the door. She couldn't help noticing how his crop of short auburn hair looked dark against the weathered blue canvas.

'Bye. Hope your car starts,' she called, determined not to admit she missed him already.

'Of course it will. Mine's a modern car.' He tossed the words over his shoulder as her front door swished, then clunked.

'Bloody cheek.'

Her TR7 might be thirty years old, but it filled a special place in her heart. Admittedly she'd held her breath while the fuel pump clicked and the starter motor whined in the car park, but the trusty two litre engine only took a moment to shake and splutter into a throaty roar. What's more, it had lazily burbled around the M25 from Ebbsfleet International in Kent and back into deepest Suffolk.

'He's right, of course,' she sighed. He wouldn't have given his Ford Mondeo a second thought after he'd tossed in his rucksack and slipped the key in the ignition. But reliable and dull were almost interchangeable in Chrissie's mind, and she was anything but humdrum.

She strained to catch the smooth murmur of the modern engine as he drew away from his parking spot outside her cottage. It was a signal. The weekend break was truly over, and she needed to fight the cloud about to descend. Action, she thought. It was the only way.

'Unpack,' she muttered.

Chrissie glanced at the bowl-like chalice still cradled in her hands. Perhaps the unpacking could wait, she thought as she headed to her small kitchen. She placed it on her narrow breakfast table, flipped her laptop open and pressed the on button. She was curious about the object. It stood about seven inches tall on the old scrubbed pine and had felt light in her hands. So was it porcelain or earthenware? The glaze seemed transparent, bathing the underlying clay in colours of honey, but allowing the blues, greens, browns and orangey-yellows of the delicately moulded decoration to show through. When she'd held it up to the light earlier, there'd been no translucency. So not porcelain then?

It conveyed mixed messages; the detailed embellishments looked fragile, but the short wide stem merged into a large pedestal base and gave an air of stability and sturdiness. She guessed it must have helped it to survive relatively undamaged.

'Survive?' It struck her as a strange term to use. It implied age and the passage of time. Was it an antiquity? She hadn't a clue, but something about it felt old. Where to start, she wondered as her laptop jingled into life.

Makers' marks and stamps seemed the obvious place, and she turned the object upside down and studied the base. Nothing.

She carried it over to the sink where a single light hung low and scrutinised it again. Even tilting it and running a finger delicately over the surface – still nothing. So, what next? If this was made of wood instead of clay, how would she assess it? Surely her years of carpentry training had taught her something. She almost heard Ron Clegg's voice as she pictured him in his workshop. He'd identify the type of wood, the tools used in its construction, the nature of the joints, glue and nails, and of course the style. He'd work out its age and origin in no time at all.

While the kettle boiled she tried to translate the process into pottery. What type of clay, firing and glazes? Had the clay been turned or pressed into a mould, and the style – continental, eastern or…? Except she knew nothing about these things.

Five minutes later she sat at the pine breakfast table, a mug of steaming tea to one side of her laptop and the mystery chalice to the other side. She guessed she had hours of background reading ahead and for the first time since returning with Clive from her Parisian break, the empty, end of holiday feeling in the pit of her stomach started to wane. The strikingly-coloured object next to her computer filled the void for the moment. She sipped her tea and read about the three major pottery types – earthenware, stoneware and porcelain.

'Better check my emails,' she murmured, ready at last to embrace the life she'd left behind for three days. She waited for her mail to load.

'Matt?' What did he want? He usually communicated by text message, but of course she'd been abroad. She idly clicked on his first post.

F ing awful day – puncture and then trod on dead hand. Police crawling everywhere. Scooter out of action and can't raise Nick.

'What? A dead hand? Nick's dead hand?' It hit like a blow. She read it again, searching for something she might have missed. She checked the date. He'd sent it two days earlier. Friday.

'Christ,' she hissed and savagely clicked the computer. All thoughts of Paris, Clive and pottery flew out the window as her eyes scoured the screen, hungry for the next post.

Still 0 from Nick. Collecting scooter this pm. Will ride over to Barking Tye if still heard 0.

That had been Saturday. There'd been no communication since. She chewed her lip. Was no further news the same as good news? Angst mingled with despair. Why couldn't Matt flesh out his words?

'Trod on dead hand? What the hell does he mean?'

Exasperated, she ran her fingers through her short blonde hair, almost tearing at the roots, as if that would help. There was nothing for it but to ring. She knew him well enough. They'd shared a workbench at Utterly Academy.

'Matt?' Her voice rasped, even in her own ears.

'Oh hiya, Chrissie.' He sounded surprised, and a bit sleepy.

'I got back from Paris an hour ago and I've only just opened your emails. Are you OK? Is Nick OK, have you found him? And whose hand is it? You said something about a dead hand.'

'Oh yeah.'

'Oh yeah? Is that all you can say? Stop drip-feeding information. Expand. Tell me more.'

'Well I dunno his name.'

'So it isn't Nick. Nick's OK, then?'

'Yeah, but the bloke near the bridge aint. He's dead. Very dead.'

'Who? Who is dead, Matt?'

'It didn't half hum. Reckon it may not be easy to say.'

'Then try. Tell me what happened.'

The Suffolk tones and phrases grew impenetrable as Matt relived his Friday afternoon. At times Chrissie hardly believed her ears as she strained to catch the meaning.

'Frawn a cold?' she echoed, as her head started to throb.

'Yeah, it wuz rafty. I dint fare a mucher.'

'What? What are you talking about?'

'I wuz frozen an' it stank. Puked up me guts. What you think I said?'

'I wasn't sure. That's why I asked, but I'm getting the picture now. Slow down.'

For a moment she wondered if it would have been easier in French, but as his words sank in, she shivered. She'd always thought those scrubby verges near the low railway bridge out of Needham Market exuded an air of menace and danger. She'd even noticed something spooky a few months earlier when she'd taken a narrow lane doubling back from the low bridge. An old brick shed with MORTUARY chiselled into the stone lintel above its door stood about fifty yards from the railway track, almost hidden from view. She'd thought it looked Edwardian, no longer in use but nonetheless scary. Even the nearby waters of Needham Lake, chilly and serene, had reflected a glassy stillness. It felt eerie at the time and she pictured it again.

'Are you OK, Matt? I mean, really OK?' She softened her tones.

'Yeah, yeah, yeah. It'll be easier over a pint.'

'Tomorrow then, at the Nags Head. Usual time?'

'Yeah, an' Nick can say his self where he disappeared to, if he aint still freshy.'

'Freshy?'

'Yeah, pissed.'

'But–'

She bit back the questions tripping from her tongue. She needed to digest Matt's news. Nick would have to wait.

CHAPTER 3

Nick massaged his temples. It had been one hell of a weekend. He winced as the gremlin chipped at the inside of his skull with an ice pick. Earlier it had been the crushing jaws of a vice, but now at least there were moments when the pressure let up.

'Ahh.' Here it came again, the sharply insistent pick. So at what point had someone spiked his drink or slipped him some drugs?

He was usually very careful when he sang at gigs with the band, always taking a bottle of spring water on stage. And afterwards he generally only drank lager or beer straight from a bottle or can. Had Friday been any different? He struggled to remember.

Colours swirled in his mind as the daylight dazzled. It had been a new venue. A bistro in a barn renovation belonging to the Rattlesden vineyard and winery. The band had been asked to play at a birthday celebration for the new manager, a private party for a twenty-nine year old. He remembered the aromatic tones of the white wine. There'd been a toast. 'Bacchus,' the manager said as he raised his glass. Nick thought it was a request for something classic. They'd played *Whiter Shade of Pale*, the keyboard evoking Bach organ tones while Nick's voice floated across warm atmospheric vibes. Later, Jake the guitarist told him the toast was to a variety of grape, but Nick didn't care. The riff had caught the mood and the number went down well.

There'd been a girl, but then there were always girls at gigs. He remembered her scent, something musky and the hint of alcohol on her breath. She'd called over a bloke, Brett or Jett, or some such name. They talked about music and then someone handed him a glass. He'd felt hot and everything grew louder.

'It must have been then,' he groaned. 'But why? Why slip me something?'

He rubbed his eyes. Vague memories floated past: a black ink marker, the sensation of a pen tip moving across his skin, vodka chasers, insects crawling up his legs, demons flying from his chest, the world spinning faster and faster.... He must have tripped on a drug from hell, some kind of psychedelic speed.

There was something scrawled on the back of his hand. Numbers. He tried to focus. He'd noticed them earlier but they'd seemed unimportant, just the mad scribbling of a crazy evening. Now, as the hammering slowed with his pulse, he looked again.

'Of course, the girl,' he murmured and breathed a hint of musk. She'd written her number for him. He spat and rubbed at his skin but the ink didn't fade. She must have meant business if she'd used something permanent.

'Oh God.' Realisation struck. She was the bait and worked with that guy. She'd made the initial approach, eyeing him up, and standing too close. More than likely it was her job to casually introduce her target to the dealer. She probably reckoned a couple more parties, or following him to a few more gigs would get him well and truly hooked, and then she'd leave him to the dealer. Except he'd reacted badly. It was one of the oldest tricks in the book and it came with the territory of playing with a band.

'Shit.' How could he have been so stupid?

There were big holes in the weekend, of course. He guessed there would always be blanks for part of the time, but he remembered his mate Matt appearing on Saturday, or maybe Sunday, and making him drink loads of water. Matt had wanted to tell him things, but Nick kept drifting off and losing track. Something about a rotting hand? He reckoned the memory must have been conjured by the drugs and had nothing to do with Matt.

It was only now, as he sat in a Monday morning queue of cars and massaged his temples that the cobwebby recollections resurfaced.

'Matt said something about taking a pee,' he murmured as he noticed the police cordon. But even Matt couldn't have caused all this.

A single line of cars waited to file past the closed entrance to a small lane. He knew it led to the low railway bridge out of Needham Market and he took his time when it was his turn to drive past. Police scene of crime vans blocked the way beyond the temporary barrier. A dog handler led a black labrador on a lead.

Thank God it's not my route, he thought to himself and headed on. Five minutes later he turned off the road and drew up alongside a fence enclosing the secure parking for Willows & Son. He sighed with relief. Against the odds he'd made it to work, despite the gremlin inside his skull and the aching nausea in the pit of his stomach.

'Morning, Nick,' Dave called. The portly carpenter had just arrived. He stooped to slam his car door, but paused as he watched Nick.

'Hi.' Nick tried to disguise the gravelly tones in his voice as he half stumbled out of his car. His throat felt dry, his head throbbed.

'Are you OK?'

'Yeah, of course. Why d'you ask?'

'You look rough.'

'Yeah I–'

An engine revved about fifty metres away as a clanking thud shook the ground. The sound jarred his senses. Still edgy, Nick spun in the direction of the commotion.

'What the hell are they doing? I don't remember seeing anyone working there on Friday.' He pointed to a mechanical digger. It clanged as the bucket-shaped excavator hit the ground, the metal teeth cutting into the solid earth. The engine noise changed as the hydraulics flexed the arm and then dragged the bucket back, lifting lumps of soil.

'They're clearing the waste ground behind Willows. You know, before you get to the railway line.'

'Is it something to do with the police swarming near the bridge?'

'Don't think so,' Dave replied. 'I'm probably not supposed to say, but everyone knows about the Japanese knotweed. It's been growing there for years. They were injecting the stems last August. Now they want to get on and build some industrial units on it, so they'll have to clear the ground first. And that means digging down maybe three metres or more.'

'Why?'

'That's how deep the rhizomes can grow. At least that's what I've been told. I've got a friend with knotweed problems.'

'Rhizomes? So what's that?'

'It's a kind of swollen stem. It sends off new shoots and roots. You know, like an Iris. If you don't get it all out, it keeps growing back.'

'Aren't the injections enough? It'd be a damn sight quieter.'

As if on cue, a low pitched engine spluttered into life. The sound of a dumper truck rumbled and rattled as it tipped a load of excavated earth onto a pile.

'What the hell are they doing now?' A discordant clatter drowned Nick's voice. He guessed he stood about as much chance of being heard as a frog in a barrel and gave up.

'Come on,' Dave mouthed and together they walked past the wire mesh gates, and alongside the Willows single story workshop. The customers' entrance and showroom office were at the front of the building and they headed through the works side door.

'So what happens with that pile of digging?' Nick repeated as he sank onto a plastic stacker chair. The restroom doubled as an office for the carpenters, with filing cabinets squeezed along one wall and shabby armchairs vying for space with a desk table, an old electric kettle, and a stainless steel sink and drainer. Around him, the air was heavy with stale tea, sour sweat and the scent of wood dust.

'Don't take it as gospel, but I've read they heap it on a membrane so it doesn't get everywhere, and then take it away for special disposal. Dig and dump. I guess it could be something like that.'

'It's going to take months,' Nick groaned and rested his head in his hands.

'Now liven up, Nick. If Mr Walsh sees you wilting all over the place like this, it could go badly for you. At the moment you're likely to be taken on here when your apprenticeship ends in the summer. Don't mess up.'

'Really, Dave?' He gaped at his trainer. 'That would be–'

'Mornin' all.' Tim, one of the carpenters, walked into the restroom. A fraying rollup dangled between his lips. He took a final drag, and then pinched the wizened cigarette between finger and thumb before squeezing all life from the lit end.

'Good morning, Tim,' Dave said as he filled the kettle.

'Have you heard the news? They've found a body near the railway line. Could've been there for weeks. Caught it on the radio as I drove in.' Tim slipped the rollup into his shirt breast pocket.

'One of these days you'll set yourself alight, Tim.'

He patted the pocket. 'Waste not, want not. It'll do for later. Two sugars in mine if you're making, Dave.'

'What else did they say about it on the radio?' For a moment Nick forgot the ice pick.

'It's a bloke, and they haven't named him yet. Don't know how he died. Could've been killed there or just dumped.' Tim shrugged as if that was the end of it.

'Probably want to inform the relatives first,' Nick mumbled. He glanced from Dave to Tim and wondered if he'd be so indifferent when he reached their age. Perhaps it was the throbbing in his head or the ache every time he moved his eyes, but if this was how it felt at twenty-three, he definitely didn't want to reach forty. And then he remembered the dead man and shivered. Perhaps it was better to suffer the aftermath of a bad trip than lie rotting, perhaps murdered before your time.

'Are you alright?'

He looked up to catch Dave studying him.

'Yeah, I reckon so.'

Dave sipped his tea. 'Hmm, I think I'll ask Mr Walsh if you can come with me to Rattlesden today. It'll do you good to get away from here for an hour or two, and besides, I could do with some help measuring up. Got some work at the turkey farm.'

•

Nick swayed with the Willows van as Dave took the corners at speed. G forces yanked and jerked him against the seatbelt, reversing any restorative properties of his morning mug of tea. The pick wielding gremlin stirred and skewered his temple.

'Ahh,' he groaned.

'So what were you really up to this weekend?' Metal grated on metal as Dave dropped a gear and accelerated hard.

'Good gig. Bad trip.'

'I thought you didn't do drugs.'

'I don't. Somebody slipped me something in a drink.'

'Why? Why'd they want to do that?'

'I don't know. A joke. To get me hooked.' The skin on the back of his hand prickled as he ran a finger over the indelible ink. Perhaps he shouldn't have rubbed so hard when he'd first noticed it in the car. He traced the numbers.

'Shit!' He caught his breath. 'It's mine.'

'What's yours? What're you talking about?' Dave swung off the Needham Road and into a roundabout, saw his exit and floored the accelerator.

'It's my mobile number. Someone scribbled it on the back of my hand. But why? Unless....' He patted his pockets. Dug his fingers into his anorak. 'It's gone.'

'What's gone?'

'My phone.' The ice pick struck. His stomach lurched.

'So when did you last see it?'

Nick struggled to think. He remembered finding a couple of missed call alerts on his mobile late on Friday afternoon. He'd sent Matt a text but Matt never got back to him, and then it was time to meet up with the band. He'd switched it to silent mode just before the gig, and hadn't used or seen it since. He reckoned the barn venue in Rattlesden must have been the last place. So was it something to do with the girl?

'She must've taken it. But it doesn't add up. If she wanted me to ring her, why didn't she write her own number?'

'Who? Who's this she? You're not making any sense, Nick.'

'A girl at the gig. Friday night.' The musky hints mingled with new fragments of recall. Long hair, honey blonde with platinum streaks, creamy skin and wide cheekbones. A sudden anger flared. She'd messed with his mind and taken his phone.

'So are you going to ring her?'

'I'll have to. I mean, I've got to phone my own number if I'm going to have any chance of getting my mobile back.'

'I wonder if that's what it's all about. Entrapment.'

'Shit.'

Stowmarket looked damp in the cold morning light. Nick stared through the windscreen as Dave followed Station Road to the west. It threaded past the old flint church and timber frame buildings bearing painted pebbledash and sash windows. Soon they left the main centre, and newer houses, thirty or fifty years old, lined the route. A quarter of a mile on, the building thinned out, leaving spaces to view hedgerows and earthy fields. The ground seemed to rise on either side as the road followed the shallow valley cut by the Rattlesden River.

'Where are we going?' Nick asked. He didn't really care. He was too stunned by what the girl may have done.

'Turkey farm, just before we reach Rattlesden.'

'I should think it's their quiet season. After all, we've had Christmas.' The words came automatically as he struggled to remember if she'd ever said her name.

'Yeah, I expect that's why they want the work done now.' Dave yanked on the steering wheel.

'Hey!' Nick yelled as the van slewed across the road and onto a narrow track. 'Did you say Rattlesden?'

'Yeah, why?'

'Rattlesden. That's where we played the gig. It was a barn renovation, belongs to a vineyard and winery. If we stop off there I can ask if my phone's been handed in.'

'Yeah, OK. But after we've visited the turkey client.'

'Thanks.' He could have kicked himself. What was wrong with his brain? It was as if it was mired in treacle. Nothing in his head seemed to connect without effort.

The van rocked and swayed over the uneven track. Sections of gravel gave way to rough tarmac. Ahead, the hillside sloped gently upwards and a wide terrace of vines snaked across his eye line. Dark knobbly trunks sprouted wiry branches that crept along cables. Not a green leaf in sight. Must be south facing, he thought, but there was little evidence of sunshine. It felt cold and damp, but then it was January.

The track forked. A notice, shaped like an arrow and pointing to the right, announced TURKEYS in bold letters.

'Bleak,' Nick murmured.

Dave grunted and swung to the right. The ruts hollowed into potholes at the junction, but then the track widened and the surface improved. It took them alongside a narrow field as they traced the base of the hill.

'Is that it?' Nick pointed to a couple of long single-storey structures, a cross between sheds and prefabricated hangars. There were no windows, but ventilation ducts jutted out at intervals, like big black limpets clinging to the sides.

'Must be where they keep the turkeys.' Dave turned into a concreted yard and slammed on the brakes. A Nissan 4x4 was already parked in front of a small prefabricated office.

'Right, well we'd better see if we can find Mr Core,' Dave muttered.

The cold air chilled Nick's face as they got out of the van. He pulled his anorak closer and glanced around. An old farmhouse with thatched roof and sagging walls looked down a slope from about fifty yards away. A stable block bordered the yard, its hayloft leaning perilously towards the concrete. Work must have already started on it, judging by the scaffolding, but Nick couldn't see any workmen.

A man in wellington boots and overalls strode from a small door cut into a large sliding panel in the front of the closest turkey shed.

'Hello. You must be Dave from Willows & Son,' he called. The tone was friendly, if not quite welcoming.

'Yes, good morning. Are you Mr Core?' Dave asked, and when the man nodded, Dave turned to appraise the stable block.

'I'm afraid we've had to stop work on it,' Mr Core said behind them. 'You can see the roof's about to cave in. We wanted to keep the old timber and beams, you know, preserve the character of the place, but when our builders removed one of the internal walls last week....'

'Yes, I can see. A roofslide. Graham's already contacted us. He says one of the main supporting beams has rotted and some of the trusses have gone. We need to have a look and see what wants replacing. I'm hoping we can source some old salvage beams. Even if we have to modify them a bit, it'll still be cheaper than using new wood.'

'Good.'

'And it keeps the character. I assume Graham is still doing the work?' Dave turned to face Mr Core again.

'Yes.' The word came quickly, almost too quickly.

'Good, we've worked with him before. Well, if that's all, can we have a closer look?'

'Of course.'

'Bring the long tape measure, Nick. And while you're fetching, better bring the laser one as well.' Dave tossed the words back as he started to walk across the yard with Mr Core.

Nick felt relieved to have a few moments to steady himself. He tried to focus on the job while he collected the items from the van. He even remembered to tuck a clipboard with paper under his arm. If he hadn't lost his phone, he would have been able to take photos as well, but the reminder made the ice pick strike again. He struggled to rein back his annoyance and shifted his thoughts to

Graham. It seemed they'd be working with him. Nick couldn't remember much about the builder apart from him being a bear of a man.

While Nick scribbled down measurements and held one end of the long tape measure for Dave, he couldn't help wondering if the roofslide had been the result of bad luck or poor judgement. The further they clambered over rubble strewn floors and gazed up at the gaping hayloft boards, the more confused he became.

'Most of the beams look sound,' Dave muttered.

'They're heavily wormed.'

'Yeah, but there's plenty of strength left. They'll be fine once they've been treated. This old wood is as hard as iron.'

'But some of the tie beams are missing, right Dave?'

'Reckon so. The loft and some of the roof are probably going to have to come down, and carefully. Then we'll put it back together like a puzzle, and replace the missing timbers.'

They climbed down from the scaffolding and Dave looked back up at the roof.

'When those pan tiles come off it'll be easier to make sense of it all,' he said, as if that closed the matter.

'Hmm.' Nick wasn't so sure. 'What's it going to be used for?'

'Mr Core said an office and shop. Come on, let's get back to Willows.'

'I still don't really get it. Hey, don't forget we're dropping in at the barn on the way back.'

'What?'

'My bloody phone. You can't have forgotten.'

'Oh yes, your phone.'

'Yeah, my bloody phone.' The ice pick pierced, and this time twisted.

CHAPTER 4

'So was your phone there?' Matt mumbled before swigging back the last of his lager.

Matt already knew about the gig and the bad trip, but this phone business sounded weird. It was also kind of cool. He glanced towards the bar, torn between refilling his pint and hearing what Nick was going to say next.

Bass notes thudded from the jukebox, racking up the tension. It was still too early for the air in the Nags Head to be charged with the full mix of alcohol and rank body odour. Give it a couple more hours, he thought, and it would feel like a normal Monday night.

'Go on, Nick. What happened?' Chrissie prompted, leaning forwards.

'Yeah, tell us, mate.' The pint of lager could wait, he decided.

'It wasn't there. It hadn't been handed in.'

'Bot! So you rang your number, yeah?'

'No, Matt. I....'

'Didn't Dave lend you his phone? Here, use mine.' Chrissie rummaged in her bag.

'Yeah, ring now.'

Nick seemed to hesitate.

'What's the matter, Nick? Don't you want to find out what's happened to your phone?'

'Of course I do. But what if she's a stalker?'

'You mean a kinda creepy fan?' Matt mumbled, still confused.

'Yes and not drug bait working for a dealer like I'd assumed. Think about it, Chrissie. If I use your phone, mine will recognise your number and caller ID. She'll get your name and number. She may even think you're my girlfriend. Remember she's weird. She could be dangerous.'

'Well I aint your girlfriend. What about usin' my phone? Long blonde hair, did you say?' Matt didn't have any qualms about an attractive bird ringing back.

He dug into his jeans pocket and fished out his mobile. He watched as Nick keyed in the number. A flutter of excitement caught at his chest as he waited, willing the mystery blonde to answer.

'Put it on speaker,' Chrissie hissed.

While the ring tone pulsed, nothing else existed for Matt. Time slowed in anticipation as the Nags Head, with its beams, rough wooden floorboards and quarry tiles near the old fireplace, paused in freeze-frame mode. Even the jukebox faded to mute.

'Hello?' a reedy voice answered, shattering the moment.

'Hi, I think you have my phone. It went missing on Friday.'

Matt shifted closer, but all he could hear was a breezy sizzle. The jukebox burst into life. The opening riff to *I don't like Mondays* drifted into the void. Matt held his breath and glanced at Chrissie.

'Please say something. You're still on the line, I can tell.' Nick's tone sounded softer, coaxing even.

'Hello?' the feeble reed fizzed. 'Speak up will you. The battery's going.'

'You've got my phone. I need it back. Please.'

The voice seemed to hesitate. 'It'll be at your next gig.'

'But who are you? What's your name?'

The line went dead.

A Bob Geldof harmony chafed across a piano refrain as the jukebox thundered on.

'Who the hell picked that track?' Nick almost spat the words.

'Don't look at me, I dunno. So was that a bird talking?' Matt asked.

'Oh for God's sake! I know there's a bloody racket in here, but–'

'He's got a point, Nick. It could be someone pretending to be the girl. Anyway, when's your next gig?' Chrissie stared into her glass of ginger beer as Bob Geldof continued to not like Mondays.

'Saturday.'

'Hmm. I could ask Clive to come with me. He could flash his card and warn her off, if you like. That's if I ever get to speak to him before then. Seems he's up to his eyes working on Matt's find.'

'What, the stiff with me footprint?'

'Yes, if you must call him that. Anyway, I think they've identified him now. Apparently he's not from around here. Are you OK, Matt?'

'Another pint'd help ease the pain,' Matt mumbled and glanced at his tatty, holed trainer as he waggled one foot. 'Yeah, Maisie an' me could come Saturday, Nick. Might 'ave me trainers back by then.'

•

Matt opened his eyes. A tiny butterfly niggled in his stomach. Was it hunger or anxious anticipation, he wondered. He focused on the wall, pale grimy blue, the colour of Mediterranean smog. He reckoned the ache behind his eyes had to be something to do with that final pint in the Nags Head the evening before. Better not swivel the orbs, he reasoned - just keep looking straight ahead. It was less painful that way.

Things had changed over the past few months. Take his duvet cover. Maisie said the printed design wasn't cool, so he'd turned it inside out.

Now the side of the fabric showing only hinted at a faded Spiderman. The comic-strip hero was hidden, forever trapped against the polyester hollow fibre duvet beneath. But Matt reckoned at least he'd got twice the use out if it before it was due for its next wash.

His thoughts settled on Spiderman. Why had Maisie sniggered a few days earlier when she'd spotted his collection of comic-strip books? He couldn't tell if she'd thought them funny and cool, or just plain sad. He'd told her they were collectors' items from the past, might be valuable one day, and pushed them out of sight under the bed.

And only yesterday, after Nick left the pub to get an early night, Chrissie had spent forever telling him about some old bit of pottery she'd found in a Parisian flea market. Surely comic-strip books were more *now*, awesome and exciting than old clay?

He rolled onto his back and contemplated his bedroom ceiling and then the day. The butterflies stirred again.

'Bot,' he groaned as the morning alarm buzzed under his pillow and interrupted his thoughts. He reached back and fumbled for his phone, extracted it and killed the sound. Only a couple of hours left before his appointment with Mr Smith.

He'd already decided he was going to wear his new tee-shirt, a surprise present from Maisie. It had a techie theme, and he reckoned it was lucky on all counts. He knew Maisie was bedazzled by anything to do with Computing and IT, and he hoped Mr Smith, the department head would be likewise impressed.

The tee-shirt was still folded. He opened out the grey-green cotton and read the bold print emblazoned across its front.

THE GENIUS OF COLOUR

Another line, but in smaller lettering, was written beneath.

Color: rgb(35, 102, 93)

The small line was the bit he particularly liked.

It was for people in the know. HTML computer speak in American spelling for a particular shade of green. Type it into HTML programme coding and you'd have a screen background or text in the exact shade of the tee-shirt. At least that was the idea.

'I just love bright things,' Maisie had squealed when she'd seen him looking on his laptop at a website of HTML colours.

A week later she'd come back with the specially printed tee-shirt. Genius. He just hoped Mr Smith would think the same and the green Maisie had chosen wasn't too far removed from the HTML command.

He tugged the grey-green cotton over his head and ignored the sudden stretch as a thread snapped and a seam almost gave way. The new material held its fold lines.

Knife-like ridges framed the front of his chest, and then smoothed out across his generous midriff.

'Neat,' he murmured and ran a plump hand along the line of HTML.

So what did Mr Smith want to see him about? He'd mentioned a job, but that was last week and the meeting wasn't until this morning. Delays only spelt ambiguity for Matt.

'Why wait till today?'

He struggled into his jeans and grappled with yesterday's socks. Satisfied with the result, he shoved his feet into last season's trainers. They were dog-eared and stained, but at least there were no body remnants in the tread. Chrissie had said they looked distressed. He shrugged and turned his attention to his hair. A quick finger-rake over his head and he'd calmed what was rapidly becoming a dark sandy mop.

'Haircut,' he muttered. It was on his list.

'Bye, Mum,' he called as he lumbered along the narrow hallway. She didn't reply. He guessed she'd be sleeping off a late shift or watching daytime TV. He still didn't understand why the virtual umbilical cord had withered and died with such finality from her end.

Once outside the bungalow, he zipped up his field jacket, a past find in a Stowmarket charity shop and slung his backpack over his shoulders. The Piaggio started first turn of the ignition key, but the wind chill on the ride froze his arms and struck through to his chest.

'Phishing hell,' he yowled twelve minutes later when he pulled up at the Academy motorbike stands. He pumped and banged his hands together.

'Found more food for worms?' a first year car mechanic shouted from the bus stop shelter, less than twenty metres away.

Word must have got out. He might not make celebrity status, he thought, but at least he'd be known for showing an awesome edge to riding a scooter, and that gave a certain zing to the notoriety he was gaining with the recent find. Respect would have been nicer.

He ignored the *food for worms* comment and stowed his helmet under the Piaggio's seat. His cheeks felt numb as he followed the car mechanic through the Academy's main entrance door. By the time he'd trudged up the wide staircase to the canteen, his skin was on fire beneath his stubbly ginger beard.

•

Mr Smith's office was on the third floor of the Utterly Mansion. Matt remembered Chrissie telling him the rooms up there had once been servants' accommodation, with lower ceilings and smaller windows than in the rest of the old building. Matt couldn't imagine fifty years ago, let alone over a hundred. All he knew was that it made his own faded bedroom feel like a claustrophobic hell, or in comic-strip imagery, the innards of an empty vending machine.

'Ah good,' Mr Smith said, looking up from the computer screen on a sleek glass topped table. A fan whirred, cooling the central processing units sprawled on the floor near the wall.

'You said you wanted to see me 'bout a job.'

'Yes.' Mr Smith leaned back in a chrome and faux leather office chair. Chrissie had once described him as aspirational. Matt had no idea what she meant. He thought him a poser.

'What year is it, Matt?'

'It'll be on the bottom of the screen.'

'No, I meant – because of the year, what important sporting event is about to happen?'

'Snooker? The Masters tournament starts in a few days' time. That's up in London.'

'No, think of the world stage.'

'Melbourne? The Australian Tennis Open. It starts in a few days' time.'

'No, Matt. The Olympics.'

'Oh yeah. Thought you meant this month.' He stared at his foot. The canvas had split. It must've happened when he'd parked his scooter and caught the width of his trainer against something. He wiggled his toes. They'd been too numbed by the cold to notice he'd bashed them at the time.

'This year the Olympics are being held in London, but one hundred years ago, in 1912 the Olympics were held in Stockholm and Sir Raymond Utterly–'

'Won a medal?'

'Not exactly, but his cousin was in the clay pigeon shooting team.'

'Gold?'

'No, they won silver. But it's given me an idea. I want you to design an app. A computer game or a quiz for a phone or tablet. Something like... I don't know... you could call it *The Utterly Olympic Silver* based on Sir Raymond's Olympics a hundred years ago. What do you think?'

'I....' A stinging pain throbbed along the side of Matt's foot.

'I'm sure you'll get plenty of help from our library's archives. Just think of the prestige, the exposure.'

'I'm getting paid, right?'

'There's no money, Matt. Think of it as an opportunity.'

'But I thought you said a job.'

Mr Smith didn't speak for a moment. Instead he gazed at Matt's chest.

'I suppose *genius* comes in different guises. I like the HTML, by the way. A thoughtful touch. No confusing the colour. Red and green look the same to me.'

Matt wasn't paying attention, his mind ran along a different track.

'Is the app goin' to be a free download, Mr Smith?'

'I hadn't... yes I suppose it'd be an opportunity to raise some funds.'

'An' I'd get a percentage, right?'

'Possibly. Look, I'll ask around. There might be some money from one of our benefactors, but I can't promise. Now don't let me keep you any longer. I'm sure you've lots to be getting on with. Oh yes, I meant to ask. Are you OK? You found that dead body didn't you.'

'Yeah, s'pose so.'

'They said on this morning's news he was from London.'

'London?'

'Can't think what he was doing near the railway line in this part of the world.' Mr Smith turned his attention back to the screen.

'Maybe he was lost?'

Beep-itty-beep! Beep-itty-beep beep!

'No! Don't answer it in here. And close the door after you.'

Beep-itty-beep! Beep-itty-beep beep! The mobile was insistent in Matt's pocket. Dismissed and deflated, he limped from the office.

He needed a job. He needed the money. All he'd been offered was a project he couldn't refuse and a heap of unpaid work. Without really thinking, he reached for his mobile.

'Yeah?' he grunted.

He heard a slight rustle, then the caller cut off.

He looked at his phone screen. The number was displayed with the subtext, *unknown*. Who the hell was ringing him, he wondered. He pressed ring back and waited.

CHAPTER 5

Chrissie waved. Clive hadn't spotted her as he hurried through the low doorway into the Plume & Feathers. She'd only just arrived herself and was standing by the bar waiting to order. She thought he looked preoccupied, his mouth tense and unsmiling, and with the hint of a loitering frown.

'Over here,' she called and waved again.

He paused as he swept the bar with a fleeting glance.

'Hey, Clive. I'm over here. Do you want a half or a pint?' She turned to catch the bartender's attention, sensing Clive had seen her at last.

'Hi, Chrissie. A pint of whatever Adnams they've got on tap, please. I've just about got time.' He bent and kissed her cheek.

'What? I thought you weren't working this evening.'

'So did I, but something's just come up. I got a call driving over here.'

Chrissie bit back her disappointment. She knew the deal. He was in the middle of a murder case. She sipped ginger beer from her brimming glass before it spilled down her hand. Without another word, they pushed past the other drinkers standing at the bar and headed across the worn flagstones to a small table in the corner, Adnams and ginger beer slopping as they walked.

'I'm sorry, Chrissie, but you know how it is.'

'You could at least tell me what it's about.'

'I won't know myself till I get in and interview the witness.'

'Can't it wait till tomorrow morning?'

'The man's got a ferry to catch. We can't hold him. He's a witness, not a suspect.'

'Ah. I suppose it's about the railway line body, isn't it?'

'Hmm.' Clive lifted his glass and drank.

'Do you know how he died? I mean, are you sure he was murdered?'

'Oh yes. Forensics are still testing, but we've got the main picture. His skull was fractured. And also the plastic bag tied over his head and his face smashed in, were a bit of a clue.'

She ignored his wry tone. 'So how long ago do you think he was killed?'

'The weather's been cold, but the pathologist reckons that judging by the decomposition and insects, the body must've been there for at least three weeks before Matt stumbled on it.'

'So sometime before Christmas.' She gazed into her glass. 'He was from London, wasn't he? I'm sure I heard it on the news.'

'He used to run a children's home there. It seems he was in the process of moving up to Ipswich.'

'Oh God, Clive. A children's home and now dead like this – I hope it isn't anything to do with kids. There's so much in the newspapers these days....'

'You can't jump to conclusions like that. And we don't want a press feeding frenzy, so not a word of this, Chrissie. We're keeping some of the details back for the moment.' He caught her eye. No smile, just the incipient frown and tense face.

'So where did this witness pop up from?'

'He was visiting his elderly mother. She lives in the old folk's home as you drive out of Needham Market. Last time he'd visited was just before Christmas. He saw the notices today and remembered seeing something.'

'Well let's hope it turns out to be useful. Where are you interviewing him? I mean how far have you got to drive now?'

'Ipswich. It's on the way to his ferry. He works from Felixstowe. I think he comes over to see her every three or four weeks.'

It was obvious Clive had to go. Delay wasn't going to help the case, she told herself. Whatever the man wanted to report was already three or four weeks old, and another high wind on the North Sea might only blow more holes in his memories. She swallowed the last drops of her ginger beer, resigned to an evening alone.

'You'd better get going, Clive.' She determined to be upbeat. 'Catch him in Ipswich. You don't want to end up on a ferry with a load of containers heading for Holland.'

'Too right, I don't.' He followed her gaze to the *Specials* written in chalk on a blackboard.

'*Pheasant casserole with parsnip mash and seasonal vegetables*. It looks good, doesn't it? I am sorry, Chrissie. I've really messed up this evening. We'll come back on Saturday, how's that sound?'

'Ah, I need to tell you something about Saturday.'

'Sorry, it's going to have to wait. Tell me later, OK? I'll ring you when I'm done. Bye.'

He leaned across and kissed her. Before she had a chance to say anything, he was on his feet and striding towards the door.

So what now, she wondered. Delicious aromas wafted from the kitchen. The bouquet of shallots and herbs cooking in red wine sent tendrils of flavour straight to her nose. She was hooked. She glanced up at the *Specials* board again. Was it to be a drive straight home and a quiet evening in front of the TV? A lonely wait for Clive to phone? Not likely. She had a life as well, and besides, if she'd felt hungry before, she was ravenous now.

The Plume & Feathers was already gearing up for the evening rush, and she scraped back her chair as she hurried to place her order at the bar. When she sat down again, she set her newly filled glass next to Clive's empty pint. It was like sitting next to his footprint. The only proof he'd been in the pub that evening and a reminder of his absence. A sudden shaft of loneliness and irritation punctured her armour. She didn't want to admit it still smarted, even after one of the bar staff picked up Clive's empty pint glass to make room for her casserole.

Thirty minutes later, Chrissie made her way through the old pub door feeling soothed by her dinner. The cold air nipped her face as she paused to stare up at the night sky. Across the road, the sound of water flowing under a tiny bridge added a sense of timelessness. For a moment she imagined a railway line and the body lying undiscovered. A secret only the killer would have known. She shivered. It would have been cold, just like this. She hurried to her TR7, parked close to an old brick wall near the bridge.

'Of course Clive had to go,' she told herself, but it didn't mean she had to like it.

The road curved away from the small River Brett as she headed to Bildeston and then followed smaller lanes cross-country to Woolpit and home. By the time she threw her car keys down on the narrow hall table, she felt happy to spend the rest of her evening snug on the living room sofa with a mug of coffee in her hands.

•

She woke with a start, a rick in her neck and the corner of a cushion pressing into her nose. Footsteps advanced along the hallway. She froze.

'Hiya,' the familiar voice called.

'Oh thank God it's only you, Clive. You frightened the life out of me.' She blinked away the remnants of sleep as her heart pounded.

'Well who else was it likely to be? I rang you before I left Ipswich, but you didn't answer. Are you OK?'

'Yes, of course. I must've drifted off.'

'At least it's not as late as I'd expected. It's only just after ten thirty. Is there a beer in the fridge?'

'If there's any left, it'll be down on the bottom shelf.' She smiled, pleased to see him.

His irritation and tension were obvious. He clearly wasn't ready to sit and relax. She waited, listening while he rummaged and clattered in the kitchen.

'So how was your witness?' she asked when he reappeared with an opened bottle.

'Flimsy.' He swigged the beer. 'On the face of it he sounded reasonably plausible, but I don't know, maybe it was because he was a nervous type, but I couldn't decide if he didn't want to remember or just wasn't very good at it.'

'Didn't want to remember?'

'Perhaps that's too strong. He said he saw a van parked at the side of the road. He was irritated because most drivers would have drawn off the road and into the parking for Needham Lake.'

'So what was so special about that?'

'Nothing very much. He just says it may have been a wine delivery van, or at least may have had pictures of grapes on the side. And he can't give a make or colour. His excuse is that it was dark. He reckons about seven o'clock.'

'That's hardly unusual before Christmas. It must be their busiest time. I'm surprised he thought it important enough to remember.'

'Exactly. It was the Friday before Christmas. December 23rd. He can't recall anything about the driver, but he says the passenger was wearing a tartan anorak.'

'Had you described what the dead man was wearing in your appeal for information?'

'Oh yes. And of course the fact he was wearing a tartan anorak in this part of the world might have made him stand out like the fairy on the top of the Christmas tree.'

'So were they behaving suspiciously?'

'Apparently not. I'm just not sure if he's a reliable witness. He could just be an attention seeker.'

'Wow.'

'Exactly.' He settled next to her on the sofa.

•

The radio alarm leapt into life.

'And later we shall be hearing from....'

Chrissie pulled the pillow over her head. Was it time to get up already? Beside her, Clive stirred. She knew he'd be instantly awake, even now restless and ready to face the day. She felt the movement as he swung his legs out of the bed and sat up. Cold air billowed under the duvet.

'Morning, Chrissie. I'll be in the shower.' The pillow lifted, as if by magic.

She groaned and grabbed it back, but not before he'd kissed her.

By the time she'd summoned the energy to get out of bed, Clive had already showered.

'Where'd you like to go for the meal on Saturday?' he asked as he towelled his hair dry.

'Can we eat before the gig?'

'What gig?'

'Remember I said I needed to tell you about Saturday?'

'Oh yes.'

She caught his expression. He wasn't listening and his mind was miles away, probably already at work. This wasn't the moment to explain about Nick's crazy groupie with sticky fingers and a penchant for mobile phones. Instead she headed for the shower and left him to hurry down the narrow pine stairs to snatch a mug of tea and a bowl of muesli from the kitchen. By the time she emerged from the bathroom, he was striding through the hall, ready to leave for work.

'Did you say you'd found out something about our flea market find?' He tossed the words up to her as she paused at the head of the stairs.

'No, but I might take it with me to show Ron this morning.'

'Good idea. I thought you'd said something about it. Bye,' and with that, Clive opened the door and was gone.

'But I didn't say….' She was talking to thin air. If this case wasn't solved soon, it was going to be a difficult few weeks. She took a long deep breath.

Thirty minutes later she was dressed and driving to work. The flea market find was parcelled in bubble wrap and safe on the passenger seat beside her. Grey light over flat earthy fields heralded sunrise as she turned onto a road bordering Wattisham Airfield. She slowed, as if on automatic pilot. She didn't need to read the notice: *Ron Clegg. Master Cabinet Maker and Furniture Restorer*. It was as familiar as the rutted access leading to the workshop itself.

She swung the TR7 onto the track. It bumped and jolted over potholes and stones. She braked, trying not to launch the pot into the footwell, and drove at crawler speed.

'*Suffolk County Council is set to freeze council tax....*' The radio announcer's voice blended with the engine as she changed gear. '*Suffolk's ancient woodland is in grave danger from the National Grid's preferred route for an overhead power line....*'

She stopped listening as the last fifty yards brought the barn workshop into view. It faced a rough courtyard and there was an old brick outhouse close by. The barn's dark weatherboarding gave sombre overtones to the morning's first light. Chrissie pulled up and parked next to Ron's old van.

'Good morning, Mr Clegg,' she called as she pushed the heavy door and stepped into the barn.

'Good morning, Mrs Jax. For a while there I wasn't sure who it was. You usually storm along that track as if you've got the devil on your tail. What's up?'

She didn't answer for a moment, but instead inhaled the scent of mahogany as she walked past the panels of a dining table top propped against the wall. Its legs lay on a workbench near Ron.

'I needed to be careful with this.' She held up the bubble wrap bale.

'Whatever have you got there? An empty petrol tank?'

'No, Mr Clegg. Remember my trip to Paris last week?'

'With that nice DI of yours, Mrs Jax?'

'Yes, we found this in a flea market, le marché aux puces de la Porte de Vanves.' The French rolled off her tongue as memories of roast chestnuts, crêpes and strong coffee flooded her mind.

'You brought back some pieces of veneer?'

'No, nothing as useful as that. I fell for this, I'm afraid. I knew I had to have it.'

'Good heavens, Mrs Jax. I've never thought of you as impulsive.'

She caught his expression before he glanced away. The humour in the old eyes, the creases as he smiled. He lifted his mug to drink. She guessed he wanted to take refuge behind its rim.

'This seems to be empty. Any chance of you putting the kettle on Mrs Jax?' he said mildly.

She discarded her duffle coat and slung her hobo-style bag onto a workbench. Five minutes later she set a mug of steaming tea in front of Ron and settled onto a stool with a mug for herself.

'Well?'

'Well what, Mr Clegg?'

'Aren't you going to unwrap it?'

She bit back any comments about not wanting to be impetuous and slowly removed the bubble wrap.

'It's beautiful,' he murmured as the first glimpses of the honey coloured glaze reflected the light.

'Here, have a closer look,' she said as she carried it over to him. 'I don't know anything about it. I wondered if you knew anyone who could tell me more.'

'It's old. Definitely old.' He picked up the chalice-like pot and turned it around in his hands. Old hands recognising old pottery, she thought as she watched his gnarled joints.

'And it's architectural in its design. The way it's been almost constructed. Yes, I think that's the correct term. A bit like assembled metal work.'

'What do you mean, Mr Clegg? I don't quite follow what you're saying.'

'Well it looks as if some of the techniques have been borrowed from a metal worker. And look at the coloured bits, they're almost like inlay or enamel on metal, except they're coloured glazes on pottery of course.'

She didn't want to say, but he'd lost her.

'You were right to fall for it, Mrs Jax. I've no idea if it has any value, but it is certainly old. Several hundred years old, I should guess.'

Silence filled the workshop only to be broken by a helicopter, its rotary engines juddering as it flew low from the airfield nearby. It broke the spell.

'What are you going to do with it, Mrs Jax?'

'I don't have space for a display cabinet. I thought I'd make an Edwardian-style pot stand. I know they're meant for plants, but I thought my pot would look good on one.'

'Make several, Mrs Jax. Take them to the Snape Maltings Antiques & Fine Arts Fair in the summer. Put your pot on one of the stands. You'll soon have the place buzzing, and someone will recognise what your pottery is. You may get lots of opinions.'

'Really, Mr Clegg? Can we rent space for a stall at the fair?'

'Why not? If you're going to work here on a permanent basis when your apprenticeship ends in July, it would be a double reason to exhibit our skills.'

'On a permanent basis? Are you offering me a job, Mr Clegg?' Chrissie could hardly believe her ears. She dreamt of working in a business like Ron's but had never dared to hope. Her life held too many disappointments. Being widowed after eight years of marriage had almost destroyed her emotionally. She'd left her friends and her accountancy career behind in Ipswich and started again. And this? Well this sounded too good to be true.

'Mr Clegg, are you saying there's a job for me?' she prompted.

'Well not a job exactly, Mrs Jax.'

'Then what, exactly?'

'I don't know if there'll be enough money to pay a regular wage. You see I won't be getting apprenticeship subsidies for you anymore. I thought if you were willing to take a risk, something more like a partnership?'

She caught her breath. 'A partnership? Really?'

Chrissie gazed around the old barn workshop. Shelves were crammed with bottles of oils, varnishes and stains fought for space with racks of tools. A band saw and wood turning lathe stood dusty and majestic at the far end. A table saw adjoined a workbench with a router, pillar drill, and sanders. She knew she'd never have the money to set up on her own. Just the pieces of wood salvaged from old furniture and stacked near the cramps would take half a lifetime to amass.

'You don't have to make up your mind straight away, Mrs Jax. And you know I'm not a business man, but I do keep accounts of a sort. You'd be welcome to take a look at them.'

She nodded, almost in shock. 'Yes I'd like to check them through, please.'

'Good. Well that's enough said about that for the moment. How about you start turning a spindle for Mrs Hornsey's whatnot?'

'Whatnot?'

He eased himself off the work stool and limped to an early Victorian stand. It stood on a tilt with one of its casters missing. The rectangular shelves sagged at one corner where one of the elegantly turned wooden spindles had fractured. A remnant of the splintered wood stuck out at an angle like a spear.

'Ah, a whatnot,' Chrissie murmured.

'Yes. A high impact injury from Mr Hornsey's backswing. A number five iron, I think she said.'

'Right. I'll need to take it apart. Then I can use one of the unbroken spindles to make a template guide to use on the lathe.' She hoped she sounded business-like.

'Yes, Mrs Jax. And you may find a caster that'll match if you have a hunt through the old bits of brass in the outhouse.'

A sense of peace settled on Chrissie as she realised that some structure to her life in the future might be a positive.

CHAPTER 6

Nick looked at the drawings Dave had made of Mr Core's stable block.

'So you reckon we can get away with scarf repairs to the bases of those posts?'

'Yes, I've had a chance to speak to Graham now. I still don't understand why he wasn't there on Monday. It would've been a damn sight easier to make decisions with him on site, instead of all this faffing about on the phone.'

'What did he say?'

'He agreed we'd also replace a couple of the ceiling beams rather than try and scarf them into the wall.'

'No, I didn't mean what he'd said about the beams. I meant, why wasn't he at Mr Core's on Monday to talk about what work needed doing?'

They were sitting in the Willows restroom taking their mid-morning break. Most of the other carpenters were out on jobs. Dave had been working on Mr Core's plans, sourcing materials and preparing an estimate. Nick had been in the workshop helping Tim restore a sash window, or rather the upper and bottom sashes of a large bay window from a house in Lavenham. He'd spliced in fresh timber where he could, and ground away smaller areas of rotten wood which he was about to fill with epoxy filler.

'Did you brush the epoxy primer on before your tea break, Nick?' Tim stirred two sugars into his tea as his voice cut across the talk of stable block repairs.

'What? No, I hadn't thought.'

'I've only got you for today, remember and I don't want to waste time while we're waiting for the primer to set.'

Nick swallowed. Tim wasn't much of a talker, but he always managed to make him edgy and uncomfortable. He focused on the drawings instead.

'I've rung round for old beams,' Dave said, without missing a beat. 'They've got what we want, the right size and length in the reclamation yard in Diss. And we're in luck. They can deliver to Rattlesden tomorrow morning.'

'And meanwhile Graham's spent the best part of the week elsewhere,' Tim muttered.

'No, he was working there with his men yesterday and today. I think I might drive out before lunch. If it turns out we need more beams, there's still time to get them on tomorrow's transporter.'

Conversation died as they contemplated their mugs of tea.

'Have you noticed those diggers have gone quiet?' Dave murmured.

A distant rumble announced the fast train to Liverpool Street. It thundered past with a whoosh and a fury, and then it was gone. There should have been clanking and thumping as metal buckets dug into soil and diesel engines growled and reverberated. Nick strained to hear, but there was nothing. Just the gentle hum from the restroom fridge.

'They can't have finished chasing the knotweed already. You told me they'd be digging for months, Dave.'

'It'll be a tea break, more like.'

Tim really was in a sour mood, Nick decided.

'So you reckon we'll start work on Mr Core's stable block tomorrow, do you Dave?'

'Yeah, Friday, Nick.'

Not much else was said and he downed the rest of his tea and hurried back into the workshop. It was an open and airy space, like a small warehouse with the roof structure and supporting RSJs exposed. The wide, roller shutter door at one end was locked down. It led to a small goods delivery area outside and the secure parking for the Willows vans. Noise from the knotweed extraction work had cut through the metal structure like hailstones through an open window all week, but now there was peace. It felt almost ethereal.

'Do you want the door opened to let in some air, Tim?'

'Nah. They'll be crashin' and bangin' again in a moment. Get on with the epoxy primer.'

The day passed rapidly as Nick worked on the sashes.

'Don't forget to clamp pieces of Plexiglass over the wet epoxy filler,' Tim called from his workbench. 'It'll give you a nice smooth surface once it's hardened and you've taken the plastic off.'

The lunch break was snatched. Tim had little to say, and without his mobile phone, Nick wasn't tempted to spend time reading and sending text messages. His sandwiches were unpleasantly cold from sitting in the fridge all morning, but hunger helped him wolf them down, toss back some water and gulp tea. None of the other carpenters were about, so while Tim went outside for a smoke, Nick headed back into the workshop to cut mortise and tenon joints for shutter frames and cross rails.

'They seem to have stopped digging the knotweed,' Tim said when he returned, the bitter cloying smell of smoke and nicotine still thick on his breath.

57

'So are they packing up and leaving?'

'Can't tell. Just a lot of standing around in huddles. Yeah, and there's a police car over there. I couldn't see much from this distance. Can you start sanding these panels for me?'

Tim didn't want to talk more, so Nick swallowed his curiosity and focused on work.

By four o'clock he was exhausted. It was time to start clearing away. After he'd swept up and binned the wood shavings, Nick ambled to his car. Something odd was happening on the waste ground behind Willows. He stood and stared.

In the distance the heavy diggers and earth movers stood like dead silent creatures, frozen in time. A tent had erupted from the ground and reams of tape cordoned a whole section of the site near the railway line.

'Oh no.' A sinking feeling pulled at Nick's stomach. He'd seen something like it before, except it had been down the road near the low bridge. Police cars and vans. People in overalls and overshoes, gloved and masked. And these ones were setting up arc lamps.

'Oh God. What've they found?'

He spoke automatically but he knew he needn't have asked. It was a logical certainty. Nobody made this amount of a fuss over a buried cat.

•

The news officially broke on Friday morning. Nick sat in the Willows van as Dave swung out of a roundabout, accelerated through Stowmarket and headed for Rattlesden. His stomach churned with each swerve and jolt as a jingle trilled on the radio.

'Radio Suffolk - bringing you the news across the region. The remains of a badly decomposed body were discovered,' announced the newsreader.

'Oh God,' Nick groaned as the smooth voice continued.

'... while digging on waste ground near....'

'I knew it was going to be something sick. I could've told you as much. It was obvious yesterday when I was leaving Willows.'

'Probably means they've only got bones if it's taken this long to hit the news,' Dave murmured and changed gear.

'Then why don't they just say bones?'

'Don't know. Guess they don't want to give too much away.'

'This is the second body....'

The image of a hasty, shallow grave drove a sudden chill through Nick.

'A police spokesman cautioned that it was too early to say for sure if a serial killer....'

'It'll have scuppered the knotweed clearance. They can say that for sure,' Dave muttered cheerfully.

'Won't they have to dig it all up anyway to check there are no more bodies buried?'

'Probably. But they'll have to go a damn sight more carefully, and someone may have to sieve the earth they excavate. Now that's going to slow them up.'

Nick almost smiled, despite his horror. He hummed along to a jingle on the radio, but there was no need. His breathing was under control. There was no risk of hyperventilating.

He caught Dave's sideways glance. 'What?'

'Have you got your phone back from that crazy groupie yet?'

For a moment Nick had to think what Dave was talking about.

'Oh yes, I mean no. She's going to return it at tomorrow's gig.' The sudden frisson of excitement surprised him. Perhaps it was just because he was on edge.

'Oh yeah?' Dave grunted.

'Well, I'm expecting a policeman in the audience.' He wasn't going to explain it was Chrissie's boyfriend, or that he hadn't actually spoken to Clive about it yet.

'Watch out Dave!'

The van lurched as Dave spun the wheel. A bump and a bounce and they were on the narrow track. They rocketed over the deep rut near the sign to the turkey farm and moments later parked in the yard next to a battered pickup truck.

'Well that's more like it,' Nick said as he took in the scene.

Two men were lifting tiles down from the stable block roof. A cement mixer sputtered and grated somewhere out of sight. A large waste skip had taken residence in the yard and a radio blared from the scaffolding.

'Where's Graham?' Nick asked.

'I expect he'll be inside, somewhere. Come on. No point in sitting in the van. Bring the drawings with you.'

They found Graham levelling a wet concrete floor with the edge of a board. At the other end of the stable block a series of adjustable steel posts jacked up a ceiling beam where part of a supporting wall had been demolished.

'Mornin', Dave.'

'Hi, Graham. Do you want us to start on this one first?' He pointed to an oak post. Its base had been eaten away by damp and worm. The rotten wood had crumbled, showering dust and decay where it had once rested solidly on the ground.

'There's another one rotted up from its base in the same wall. See there. We realised in time so we've left some supporting structure. Mr Core wants this opened up and the two oak posts left as a feature.'

'Well if you've got enough jacks, can you get on and get the second one exposed for us then?'

While Dave talked to Graham, Nick watched. He was curious. He guessed the builder was well into his forties, but whereas Dave sported a paunch, Graham hinted six-pack abs. His naked scalp glistened sweat and his face looked surly with dark stubble. He exuded an uneasy mix of fitness and slob, charm and belligerence.

'We'll get on with scarfing that first post while we're waiting for the beams to arrive on the transporter.'

It didn't take long to carry the tools from the Willows van.

'Let's hope that handsaw is good an' sharp because this old oak will be as hard as iron,' Dave said as he poked at the rotten wood with a screwdriver. 'Ah, this is better. I think we're into sound timber here. Hey, hand me a pencil and I can mark it.'

'Can't I use the electric saw?' Nick asked.

'We're cutting it off in position. And we want a nice V-shaped end to rest into the new section of base. I'm afraid it's a hand saw, lad.'

'Frightened to use a bit of muscle, hey?' Graham grunted as he swung a mallet at the brick infill across the room.

Something in the sneering tone hit a raw chord. Nick's edginess exploded.

'And that's from someone who brought half the roof falling down by using muscle instead of his brain, and didn't even turn up on Monday?'

'Nick, that's enough. Watch yourself.'

'What?' Graham lowered the mallet slowly.

'I said–'

'I heard what you said. For your information I wasn't here on Monday because I was using my brain. So don't ever say I don't use it. Right?'

'So how's that?' Dave asked mildly.

'I was over at the winery. Strad Kell, the owner, saw my van here and wanted a quote for some building work. Couldn't make a potential customer wait, now could I?'

'I suppose they'll be neighbours. We noticed the vines on our way out here.'

'But…,' Nick caught Dave's warning look. He bit back the comment about duty to current customers. Instead he mumbled, 'The winery? I played a gig at their restaurant shop last week. Well it's actually a renovated barn.'

'Yeah?' Graham's manner and stance altered. He pulled out a loosened brick as if they were all mates again.

'I tell you, that Strad Kell's onto a good thing. He gives troubled youths work experience. The girl hanging around when I was there looked really tasty. I wouldn't be surprised if he gets to pick them.'

'Girl hanging around?' Nick echoed.

'Well she was probably meant to be out tending the vines, but I don't know, she seemed too ditzy to be much use. Well, for that sort of thing, anyway.'

The words ditzy and troubled made Nick's stomach lurch. Musky hints assaulted his senses.

'Did she have long blonde hair?' He didn't mention the wide cheekbones and creamy skin. That would have made him sound sad. Like a loser.

'Aha. Now you're interested. Now I've got your attention. Have you met her then?'

'Might have. At the gig. She stole my phone.' He felt his cheeks fire.

'Ha!' Graham whooped and slapped a thigh.

'Come on, enough chatter. Nick get sawing.'

It was shoulder burning work, but Nick put every ounce of effort into the action as he followed Dave's pencil line. It helped to numb the humiliation. He worked until a diesel engine rumbled, heavy tyres crunched, and the transporter arrived from Diss.

CHAPTER 7

Matt stared at the computer screen. He felt uneasy. Three days ago Mr Smith had tasked him with creating the Olympic Silver App. It was Friday already, and so far he'd only managed to come up with more questions than answers, and a load of fat squids for ideas.

He'd toyed with the notion of designing a game in which the player was a member of the 1912 Olympic clay pigeon shooting team and fired at a disc launched across the screen. It wasn't very original, but neither was designing something like Snap where two cards were simultaneously turned. He supposed the cards could display in a random order pictures of: clay discs, lead shot, steel pellets, medals, and marksmen. It would be easier to code. Another idea was an app linking to the official Olympic website and simultaneously displaying the results from the two Olympics, Stockholm 1912 alongside the up-to-the-moment results of London 2012. That might be neat, but more complicated.

'Ideas to match feasibility,' he murmured. Design speak and buzz phrases made him feel more in control.

He rocked onto the back legs of his chair as he scanned the wall of bookcases on the other side of the library. He couldn't help but wonder why Sir Raymond Utterly had built such a massive room. Stone divided windows and oak floorboards might have been all the rage one hundred years ago, but they certainly weren't to Matt's more modern taste. Even the bank of computer stations couldn't drag it into the twenty-first century.

'If I had....' Matt made a gun of his hand and aimed along his finger at some books on a top shelf. '*Pow*!' he whispered as he fired the imaginary trigger.

'No shooting of firearms in the library.'

'What?' Matt rocked forwards. The front legs of his chair reconnected, *bang*, with the floor.

'And silencers should to be fitted at all times.' The words sounded progressively stifled as the voice rose musically.

He swung around, almost falling sideways from the chair. Rosie, the library assistant flanked his screen.

'Hi, Matt.'

'Hey, how long've you been standin' there? An' stop laughin'. It aint funny.'

'I know. You nearly killed yourself. Shouldn't play with guns, it's bad for your health.'

'Yeah, yeah. I got all that.' His cheeks scorched under his beard as students, who moments earlier had been glued to their screens, now seemed rudely curious about him.

'I heard you're a celebrity,' Rosie continued, glancing at the audience. She swept back wisps of auburn hair and tucked them into her loosely tied ponytail.

'Yeah well....'

'What do you think about them finding the second body?'

'What? What second body?'

'Hey keep your voice down. Haven't you heard? It was on the news this morning.'

His throat went dry as curiosity wrestled with flashbacks.

'Here, let's have a look.' She leaned across and quickly keyed in the Eastern Anglia Daily Tribune site, followed by the library's membership number. The air was laced with floral hints of her scent as seconds later the newspaper's front page displayed on the screen.

Matt read out the lead. '*Second Body Discovered Near Railway Line In Needham Market.*'

Rosie reeled off the next line. '*Knotweed clearance specialists uncovered a gruesome find yesterday on waste ground near the railway line.* Look, I'll leave you to read the rest yourself, but don't go without telling me what you think.'

He barely glanced as she crossed the library. Normally he'd have ogled her tight jeans, or rather the outline of her bottom and thighs, but he was too distracted by the news. His eyes gravitated back to the screen.

He skimmed along the lines. The phrase *badly decomposed* leapt at him. He supposed it was code for just bones because the next sentence said something about the skeleton being male. The reporter suggested damage to the skull could have occurred after death, but *the results of further examination are awaited.* Was it a reference to the knotweed specialists and their spadework?

'Age and cause of death?'

He scanned the columns again. Now he saw it – *awaiting further analysis* and, *difficult to be exact about the length of time the body had been buried before discovery. Toxicology testing may not be possible.*

'Bones,' he breathed. 'That's all they'll have. Frag.'

The body, he read, but he assumed they meant bones, *hasn't been identified.* However it was the next sentence that freaked him out. *The police are unable to say at this stage if the death is connected with the murder of Mr Victor Pack, the man discovered only 200 yds away last week.*

'Victor Pack?' Matt murmured. The corpse with an imprint of his trainer now had a name?

It was almost too much to take in. He felt queasy as images bombarded his mind. Was there a serial killer out there? Someone lurking near the railway line and waiting to pounce every time a bloke took a leak?

Without really thinking, he typed Victor Pack into the Eastern Anglia Daily Tribune search box. A moment later, a one paragraph report from the previous day's edition opened on the screen. *Man Found Near Needham Market Railway Bridge Named.* It gave his age as sixty-three, his address as a South East London postcode, and of course his name. There were no further details.

Beep-itty-beep! Beep-itty-beep beep! Matt's mobile burst into life.

'Wild,' he hissed as he recognised the caller's number displayed with the subtext *unknown*. Except it wasn't unknown. This was the fourth call. One every day since Tuesday and always the same format. He'd say yeah? And she'd ring off. At least he hoped it was a girl. Thoughts of railway lines, serial killers and a bladder with the capacity of a fuel tank, started to fade.

'I heard you've got long blonde hair,' he whispered, spontaneity bubbling through as part of his mind pictured a hot groupie.

'Where's Nick?' The words sounded distant, reedy and to the point.

He punched the air. He was being cold called by a bird. It was official. There was just one thing he needed to clarify.

'You are a bird, aint you?'

'Pervert!' she shrieked and cut the call.

He pressed ring back, but like the times before, the ringtone died mid *burrh*. Matt glanced up to catch a student watching him from across the library. He'd arrived – celebrity status and nuisance calls, all in the space of one week.

So where did Maisie fit in? She was his girlfriend of course. The first real girlfriend he'd ever had. Pure excitement and desire. But, he reminded himself, just because he had some sweets in his pocket didn't mean he couldn't look in the candy store. He'd heard other guys say things like that. The trouble was he didn't really understand why she was his girlfriend. They'd been an item for a couple of months and most of the time he couldn't work her out. Take his Spiderman duvet cover. He'd turned it inside out rather than getting rid of it as she'd requested. But the other afternoon while sharing a moment of intense passion, he guessed she must've spotted the faint mask-like face behind his shoulder because she screamed. Or was it more of a primordial groan? He wasn't sure.

He'd sensed she was dazzled by his knowledge and he loved the way she came over dreamy eyed when he spewed facts. But he'd have felt more secure if she liked him for his looks as well. After all, he was attracted to hers. He reckoned if other girls thought him cool, it upped his pull with Maisie. And anyway, he liked sweets.

He turned his attention back to his computer screen and typed the postcode into the search box. It was easy to find properties for sale on the house move sites and names on the electoral register could be matched against addresses with the South East London postcode.

'So his house was for sale – yeah and no one else named as livin' at his address. Single? Alone? Now dead?'

Digging deeper or looking at restricted access information was more of a challenge. He needed to pay for searches or join find-your-ancestor sites, and for a fee. Perhaps Rosie could help.

Matt ambled over to the library assistant's station near the entrance door, but it was deserted. It took him a moment to spot her in the librarian's office. The door was open so he wandered in.

'Hi, Rosie. Is Bill away?'

'I wish you students wouldn't call her that. Mrs Wesley would be really upset if she knew.'

'Why'd she be pullicking? He scored more goals for Stowmarket than–'

'Pullicking?'

'Yeah, complainin'.'

'Yes, but she's got a squint.'

'An' that's the point. Never know where she's looking. She'd make a legendary striker.'

He watched Rosie smile. It was his moment.

'Any chance of usin' the library 192 account or a find-your-ancestors site?'

'We don't have one. The Academy office might, though probably not the ancestor's site membership. Was Victor Pack a relative?' She seemed to catch her breath.

'Nah, but I need to trace the British 1912 Olympic clay pigeon shootin' team. For Mr Smith.'

'Then get the IT department to pay. They'll have a department code. Charge it to them.'

'Yeah, right.' He turned to leave the office.

'So what do you think, Matt? Is there a serial killer out there?'

'Yeah,' he grunted, no longer listening. His mind was on access codes and the main office.

•

It was already dark and Maisie tightened her arms around Matt's waist. He liked the way she nestled into his back and held onto him. He made sure the scooter kept tilting as they left the Ring Way and headed into the small roads lacing the old town centre.

'Look out for Frasers,' he yelled back to her. Even at this hour Bury St Edmunds seemed more alive than a typical Saturday evening in Stowmarket.

'Still don't see why we had to come so early.'

'I told you. We don't know when the crazy'll turn up. Need to be here for Nick.'

He felt the sigh.

'There!' Maisie shrieked and pointed at a neon sign spelling out the name Frasers in Mediterranean blue.

'*Bar and Function Suite*,' Matt read.

'Follow the arrow. The arrow!'

At first Matt thought the directions were taking him away from Frasers, and then he got the picture. The bar and function suite stretched between two roads, with the bar at the front and the rest of the building spreading out at the back. Access to the car park and suite were from the other road.

'Yeah, yeah. Follow the arrow,' he muttered.

A turn around the block and he spotted another Frasers sign. The car park was small, more of a drop off and pick up area than parking for anything but a handful of cars. Luckily, the Piaggio could squeeze into most tight spots.

'There's room near the large wheelie bins, over there.' She waved her arm as if to emphasize the size of the space.

'Cool.'

He eased the Piaggio onto its parking stand and pulled off his helmet. The smell of stale pee wafted strongly from a wall behind the bins. It made the place feel edgy. It threatened to bring back memories as he dismounted.

'Watch out, Matt! Don't step in it.'

He stopped dead, almost toppling, one foot mid stride.

'Yuck. That's gross,' Maisie squealed. 'Chilli and rice.'

'Shit, I thought you were goin' to say....' He didn't finish. She grabbed his arm and yanked him back.

'I aint dancing with a guy with vomit on his trainers. Come on, stop messing and put the helmets away.' She turned and her bleached hair took on the blue of the neon sign, excitement seeming to ooze from every pore of her body as she made a demonstration disco move.

'Come on Mais. Now who's messing?' He stowed the helmets and followed her to the function suite entrance.

They stepped into a generous lobby. On one side they could see into the main bar with its tables and sofas laid out for casual eating and drinking. The other direction led through double doors thrown widely open and down a couple of shallow steps into a large room. A bar, DJ station, and square of wooden dance floor gave it a nightclub feel.

'Hi,' Matt called. He recognised Jake, the lead guitarist. He was setting up a couple of speakers. They stood next to a pair of altogether larger ones.

'Bet those big bruisers'll be Adam's. He plays bass,' he mumbled to Maisie.

A funky rhythm pounded as the drummer struck a seemingly random mix of warm up beats. They wandered towards Jake.

'OK, Jason? If you're happy now, can you give me a moment to get my guitar balanced?' Jake shouted.

The drummer grinned and put down his drum sticks.

'Is Nick here yet?'

'Sorry, Matt. Haven't seen him, but he should be here soon. We'll need to do a mic check with him.'

'So when are you playin'?'

'In about an hour and a half, but we need to get set up before people start arriving.'

'I hadn't realised it was so complicated. I guess I kinda hadn't thought about it before,' Maisie whispered as she took Matt's arm and guided him back towards the front bar.

'Yeah, sorry Mais. Nick said he'd be here seven thirty. I didn't think. How's about–'

'We find a pub? It's goin' to be pricey here. We could hide a couple of cans in the Piaggio and nip out the back for them later. How's that sound?'

'Yeah, but–'

'And while we're in the pub you can tell me what the crazy looks like and what the plan is, yeah?'

'Oh frag.' He hadn't got a plan.

'Why d'you keep sayin' frag?'

'Sorry, Mais. Frag… fragment. It's a computer gamin' term. When you shoot somethin' down you fragment them.' He felt on safer ground.

CHAPTER 8

Chrissie felt torn as she stopped outside Sarah's house and tooted the horn. Her TR7's two litre engine idled gently, providing a soundtrack to her restless thoughts as she waited. She checked her watch. The clock on the dashboard was an authentically original instrument, right down to its inability to keep the correct time. No way was it midnight. Usually she liked its quirkiness, but this evening it irritated.

'Come on, Sarah. We'll be late for the gig at Frasers.'

It should have been Clive collecting Chrissie in his sleek Mondeo with its modern in-house sound system, pampering, attentive and soothing. But he was working and her friend Sarah had stepped in at short notice. It wasn't Clive's fault he couldn't come. She understood, but she didn't like it.

'Come on, Sarah,' she breathed and tooted the horn again.

She leaned back against the headrest. 'Poor Clive,' she sighed. He was the one who needed soothing, not her. She pictured his face when he'd told her about the second body.

'It's a serial killing,' he'd said on Friday evening, lines etched into his forehead.

'But you said there were only bones. How can you be so sure?'

She remembered his wry smile, the pretence at humour. 'The plastic bag over the skull was a bit of a give-away.'

'But couldn't he have smothered himself? You know – alcohol, drugs and then a bag over his head?

'But he couldn't have buried himself. That would have shown unnatural determination.'

'Oh God,' she'd moaned.

'Yes, a similar modus operandi to whoever killed Victor Pack. Plastic bag tied over the head and a fractured skull. Turned out the bag wasn't biodegradable, and what the murderer couldn't have realised was that some of the mush inside the plastic might give us something useful to work on.'

'Ugh... too much detail. So both killings have to be connected, right?'

'Right. And for the next week or so we'll be searching the site. Let's hope to God there aren't any more to find.' And then he'd hurried away, his thoughts obviously working along lines of the investigation.

'Of course he has to work overtime,' she whispered. The pressure to find the murderer was obvious. She imagined him at home in Lavenham, stretched out on his sofa, a sheaf of papers slipping off his chest and snoring softly. She should be there with him.

Tap, tap.

'What?' She jumped as the sound jolted her back to the present.

'Aren't you going to open the door then?' Sarah half purred, half mouthed on the other side of the passenger window.

Chrissie leaned across and released the door catch.

'Thanks, Sarah. I didn't want to go on my own but I'd promised Nick.' She slipped the car into gear, pulled away from the curb and followed Mill Lane out of Woolpit. 'I probably should've stayed back with Clive.'

'Oh don't be daft, Chrissie. You said yourself he's totally taken up with the Needham Market bodies. He doesn't need you mooching around because he's too distracted to give you enough attention. Lighten up. This evening's going to be fun. An adventure. Now how does a groupie think? We need a plan.'

'Oh God,' Chrissie murmured. She knew Sarah was right, although sometimes her enthusiasm was exhausting.

'We could be groupies too. Nothing suspicious about that. She'll be where Nick is, and so will we. I've dressed for the part.' She flicked her silky black hair into its well styled bob and stretched her legs into the footwell. The jet glitter in her tights caught the light.

'And no doubt you're wearing sensible chasing shoes as well? Nice combo.'

'I hadn't thought of that.'

Chrissie accelerated onto the A14 and headed for Bury St Edmunds. Perhaps it was going to be fun, after all. Sarah's idea of dancing was a series of fencing moves set to a hip thrusting beat. She supposed it was only to be expected considering Sarah was still a keen member of the fencing club where they'd first met, almost five years earlier.

'How's that fencing instructor? Is he still at the club in Ipswich?'

'Why don't you take up fencing again? Then you could find out for yourself.' She had always been quick with a foil and this was akin to a parry.

'Matt should be there tonight with his girlfriend Maisie. Could be an interesting evening,' Chrissie said, accepting defeat and changing the subject.

They parked in a small side street near Frasers. Narrow fronted terraced cottages built in Victorian times gave a sense of solid quaintness. Their front walls were only a few feet from the pavement, and the yellowy-white Suffolk bricks reflected the street lighting. It felt more dusk than dark.

'Come on, it's eight thirty already,' Sarah said, striding ahead.

Notices announcing *Live Music* were on boards outside the main entrance. The front bar felt hot and busy. They eased their way past tables and sofas, the air loaded with aromas of chilli beef, fast food and beer. It didn't take them long to find the function suite.

While Sarah queued for drinks, Chrissie circuited the room.

'Hey found you,' she called, spying Nick. He was sitting on a stool next to Jake, one eye on the stage and instrument set, a bottle of water in his hands.

'Is she here? Have you recognised her yet?'

'Hi, Chrissie. Nice to see you too,' Nick murmured.

'Can I have your autograph?'

'What? Are you feeling OK, Chrissie?'

'Of course I'm OK. Now play the part and don't break my cover. I'm a swooning fan, by the way. I want big obvious writing on my arm.'

'Can I write on you too?' Jake asked.

'No you cannot. Now let's hope she's watching and this gets a reaction.'

By the time Sarah found them, Nick had drawn a heart and signed his named on Chrissie's forearm. 'How about you Sarah? Are you one of my fans as well?'

'I reckon we need to broaden the fan base. Here, if you sign my bottle of lager....' She turned to Jake, 'and you could.... Are you in the band?'

'Yeah, I'm Jake. Lead guitar.'

'Well then, Jake – a bit of Banksy work on my hand wouldn't go amiss.'

While Nick signed the Stella Artois bottle, Jake worked some graffiti onto Sarah's hand. Meanwhile Chrissie concentrated on adopting a dotingly possessive, star struck expression and scanned the room. There were plenty of expectant drinkers and girls dressed for a Saturday night of dancing and booze, but no crazy long haired blonde. Despite her misgivings, she was gripped with excitement.

'Have you seen Matt?'

'Yeah, he's outside watching the back entrance. He said he'd come in when we started playing.'

An idea started to form. 'Hey Sarah, I'm just going to have a quick word with Matt and then check the ladies loos. I'll be back in a minute. Look after my bottle of ginger beer, will you.'

'You bet. They charged a fortune for it.'

Outside, she found Matt leaning against his scooter and with an arm around Maisie.

'Hiya,' Matt mumbled. 'Any action yet?'

'Not inside. Has she come this way?'

'Nah.'

'Look, I've a gut feeling about this. Did she ever ring back on your number?'

When Matt nodded, Chrissie started to explain the outline of her plan.

'You didn't say you had her number,' Maisie squealed before Chrissie could finish.

'Well Nick borrowed my mobile, didn't he? That's how she got it. It aint my fault she's been phonin'. So I got the number she rings from. So what? See Nick's don't work.'

'And what's she been sayin'?' Maisie set her lips in a hard line.

'Nothin'. Just cuts the call when I say, "yeah?"'

'Can you ring her now?' Chrissie butted in.

'What?' Maisie screeched.

'Give me a couple of minutes to get inside and then ring the number. Hopefully we'll hear it. You may have to ring it several times. We won't stand a chance once they start playing.' She didn't hang around for Maisie's reaction. She was on a mission and the clock was running.

Back in the lobby, she hurried for the toilets. A few striding paces and she spotted Sarah.

'Hey I thought you were sticking close to Nick.'

'Yeah but I needed the loo as well. Reckoned you could hold these bottles while....'

Tinketty-tink-tink-tink! Tinketty-tink-tink-tink!

The door to the Ladies swung and the ring tone faded.

'Hurry. Follow that phone.'

'What?'

'I'll explain later. Just follow my lead. Right?'

Chrissie body-bumped the door into the Ladies. Sarah followed close on her heels.

'Look everyone. Have you seen? I've got Nick's autograph. He's drawn a heart,' Chrissie shouted, and waved her arm for anyone who'd look. She caught her reflection in the mirror above the hand basins. Shades of embarrassment threatened to break her cover. Was she over egging it?

Tinketty-tink-tink-tink! Tinketty-tink-tink-tink!

She spun around to face three closed cubicle doors.

'Here, let me–'

Tinkett–

The ring tone cut.

'That's nothing. Look what Jake's drawn on me. You can tell he's good with his hands,' Sarah crowed. She tilted her head towards the locked middle door and raised her eyebrows.

A hand drier burst into life with the force of a jet engine as a girl in six inch heels thrust her hands under the wall mounted unit. The blast startled Chrissie. She almost missed the sound of the cubicle door catch as it slid from red to green.

'Hi,' Sarah purred as the middle door swung open.

A girl stared out with pinpoint pupils set in sea-green eyes. For a moment Chrissie wondered if she faced a ghost. The pale skin, wide cheekbones, and aura of otherworldliness were haunting. No wonder Nick was mesmerised. The long honey blonde locks had been swept into a large clip comb. Platinum coloured strands hung wisp-like, framing her face. Chrissie guessed seventeen, but she could almost have passed for a child.

'Hi,' Chrissie murmured. 'Do you follow the band?'

'Yeah. Do you?' She frowned, and then added, 'Aren't you a bit old for Nick?'

'I don't think I'll ever wash again.' Chrissie breathed, ignoring the jibe as she held up her arm and ran a finger over Nick's art work. 'So what d'you collect?'

'I collect bottles,' Sarah chipped in. 'Nick's signed this one.'

'I wasn't asking you. What's she collect?'

'Phones. I collect… you know, mobiles.'

'What? Mobiles? Have you got Nick's? Is that what you're holding? Now that's cool.'

'Yeah, really cool. Let's have a look.' Sara lunged with the speed of an attacking foil.

'Hey! Leave off. This one aint his.'

'Is it Jake's?' Sarah screeched excitedly.

'No it's mine, now get off will you.'

'OK, OK. Here,' and she tossed it back. 'Tell you what. I'll do you a swap. My bottle for Nick's mobile. How's that sound?'

The doors to the other two cubicles opened, and the occupants hurried self-consciously to the basins. A few moments later, Sarah and Chrissie were alone with the fragile looking girl.

'Come on, we don't want to miss the first number,' Chrissie said, as they fell into close step on both sides of the girl, hedging her in and moving her towards the toilet door. It felt like a corps-a-corps, an illegal move in foil and sabre fencing. Sarah must have thought the same, because she stepped neatly sideways, held the bottle by its neck, and launched a coup lancé. With a quick thrust the bottle came to rest lightly against the girl's lycra camisole, central chest, virtually over her heart.

'Cool fencing move,' Chrissie mouthed.

'I'll swop this bottle for Nick's mobile. I've offered once. Don't make me offer again,' Sarah said mildly, but her eyes warned a different message.

'Collecting bottles is more direct and personal than mobiles, wouldn't you say?' Chrissie murmured.

'If you hand over Nick's mobile, you can have this signed, personalised bottle.'

'And we all get to leave the toilets.'

'And, we'll catch some of the first number. I think they've started playing,' Sarah finished.

'So what do you say?'

'You're weird.' The words were defiant but the tone broken.

They eyed each other up, Chrissie expecting the door to swing open at any moment and wondering how it would look if anyone walked in.

'OK,' the girl said, breaking the standoff and dropping her gaze. 'But it don't mean he aint mine. You can have his phone, but you lay off him, right?'

'Right.' Sarah kept the bottle poised, just touching the girl's camisole, and still on target for her heart.

'Thanks.' Chrissie held out a hand for Nick's mobile.

The girl slipped delicate fingers into a small drawstring bag hanging around her neck. Chrissie imagined those same fingers deftly stealing a phone, picking pockets or cutting a line of coke. She watched, transfixed as the girl drew out Nick's slim android smartphone.

'Sweet,' Chrissie murmured and took the phone.

'Here – the bottle's yours,' Sarah said.

Without a word, the girl grabbed the bottle, swung the toilet door open and legged it.

'What the hell was she on?'

'I don't know, Chrissie. The important thing is, mission accomplished. Let's go and enjoy the music.'

Much later, after they'd bopped their way through the first set, celebrated their success with Nick and the rest of the band and then exhausted, sat out the second set, Chrissie wandered outside to get some air. She found Matt with Maisie in the car park near the waste wheelie bins.

'Hi,' she sighed. 'Did you get to see her? She was a strange girl. Rather sad, I thought.'

'Yeah, she came out this way a couple of times. I think she was after Matt.'

'Really Maisie? Are you sure? I thought she was fixed on Nick.'

'Yeah, she only wanted to listen to me if I talked about Nick. I don't think she recognised me voice, though,' Matt added.

'Her face went funny when you said Nick was working on a turkey farm, you know, out Rattlesden way?'

'Oh Matt. You didn't tell her where Nick was working?'

'Er, I might've. Is that a problem?'

'I hope not.'

CHAPTER 9

Nick banged his tray onto the canteen table. His cutlery clattered as the bottle of spring water toppled. A deft snatch with his right hand, and the bottle was saved.

'Well, I couldn't have done that last Monday.'

'No. You weren't here last Monday,' Matt mumbled, his mouth full of chips.

'That's not what I meant.'

Nick pulled back a chair and sat down. What he'd meant but hadn't said, was that last Monday he'd felt so rat-arsed unwell he was lucky to have recovered the power of speech, let alone the co-ordination to catch a falling bottle of water. The girl had seen to that. This time at the gig he'd ignored her for the most part, only caught her eye a couple of times and stuck like bonding agent to Jake. Nothing stronger than choice expletives passed his lips all evening.

'I know the release day is every other Monday, Matt.' His mind ran on, 'I hadn't realised how much I missed my phone till I got it back. Thanks again, mate.'

'That's OK. Has she rung you?'

'Don't know. I blocked all calls from the number you gave me.' He spotted Chrissie, and waved. 'Uh oh – who'd have guessed she's a closet fan? Do you know she kept her sleeves pulled down through the teaching session in case anyone saw the heart? Oh yeah, and Jake is thinking of adopting Sarah as a bodyguard.'

He felt unspeakably relieved. The evening had worked out better than he'd hoped. For a start there'd been no nasty incidents with the strange girl. It would have been just the sort of thing to get into the local press; a flimsy drugged-out girl, and him the one taking advantage, the villain of the piece. He'd imagined it all, played out against the backdrop of Frasers function suite. As it turned out, they'd even been asked to return sometime in the summer and his reputation and phone had been saved intact.

Chrissie must have seen them, because she grinned and made her way over with her coffee and sandwiches. She set her cup down on the blue Formica, coffee swilling around her saucer.

'Hi,' Matt muttered between mouthfuls.

'It's mad in here. Nearly tipped my cup over.' She glanced back at the students queuing at the service counter and continued, 'So how's the rock god today? Interesting talk on managing debt in business accounting, didn't you think?'

'A bit scary. To be honest, Chrissie, I'm hoping Willows take me on. I can't imagine issuing claims in a small claims court or using debt collectors.'

'Well, here's fingers crossed for you. Did I tell you Ron Clegg offered me a partnership in his business?'

'Cool. What did you say?'

'I'm looking at the accounts first.'

'Debt collectors? Did I hear right? Is that the kinda job I could do on me scooter?'

'What you, Matt? You don't do intimidation.'

'Yeah, but I need cash.'

An image flashed through Nick's mind. 'I suppose people might pay up just to get rid of you. Not a good look, Matt camped outside your front door. You have to agree, Chrissie, it'd be a novel approach.'

'Give me strength,' she groaned and bit into her egg mayo sandwich.

'So are there many owing?' Matt dangled a chip on his fork.

'Yes, I was surprised. I mean part of it's down to Ron not sending more reminders. And judging by some of the addresses, well they must be flush, so why not pay? Take the wine chap in Rattlesden. He can't be short of a bob or two. Strad Kell.'

'Strad Kell?' Nick pictured the terraces of vines near the turkey farm. They'd looked pretty lifeless the last time he'd passed. 'Grapes are seasonal, so there could be a cash flow problem, Chrissie.' He guessed even vineyards had to diversify to survive. Hence the converted barn restaurant and wine shop.

'But alcohol aint,' Matt chipped in.

'True. So I'm going to send reminders or last demands to most of the people on my list. I suppose I could phone some of them. I might get a better idea of why they haven't paid.'

'You could call it market research and tell them you'll be presenting your findings at the next Academy open day. That'd loosen their grip on their credit cards. Just to avoid getting named and shamed,' Nick added.

The conversation meandered on, and while Matt suggested ways he could earn money tracking nonpayers and embarrassing debtors into coughing up, Nick's thoughts drifted. Was it really two and a half years since they'd first sat down together in the Utterly canteen? It had been decorated differently, but was just as busy back then. Matt had been awkward and totally unsuited to carpentry, and Chrissie raw from losing her husband but still managing to be feisty. And what about him? Nick remembered the pain of an ill-starred romance and shattered confidence after leaving the Environmental Studies course in Exeter. Could he recognise their earlier selves in the people they'd become, he wondered. Had they changed? In those days he couldn't have imagined knowing anything about the small claims track in County Courts, let alone expecting to use one. And a rock god? Well, who'd have guessed?

'What are you smiling at? What's so funny?' Chrissie asked.

'Nothing.' He dug into his spaghetti bolognaise.

•

Tuesday dawned with a frost on the ground and a brisk easterly wind. Nick was eager to get on with the business of carpentry. The chapter with the crazy fan was over. He felt he'd turned a page. Semi-outside jobs suited him fine, and the stable renovation, with half the roof off and a clear view up to the sky certainly counted as part outdoors.

'So did you get much done without me yesterday?' Nick asked, savouring the bite in the cool air.

'Let's just say I managed.' Dave opened the back of the van and gazed at the assortment of tools.

'What are you after?'

'The circular saw. The rough-base floor cement has been down for several days so we've something flat and solid at last. We're working on the ceiling beams today. Graham's men will help slide 'em across into place.'

'But we're cutting to the right length first, and not with the hand saw this time, right? Have his men knocked holes in the front wall?' Nick reached for the long tape measure.

'You should've been here yesterday. All fun and games, but I must say, Nick, you shouldn't mix work and pleasure.'

'What? What are you talking about?'

'Well, look for yourself.'

'Oh shit.' He caught his breath and ducked behind the van door.

'Yeah, Graham did his best to keep her entertained yesterday. Pecs, six-pack – paraded the lot.'

Nick's guts twisted. 'But you told her I didn't work here? You must've realised she's the crazy groupie? The one who stole my phone. What's she doing here today?' It had to be a nightmare. One pinch and he'd wake up.

'Obviously I wondered if it was her because she looked... so strange. I even asked her if she'd brought you a phone.'

'What? It's more likely she wants to pinch it again. See I got it back, or rather my mates got it back for me on Saturday.'

'That's great. It was stupid to tell her you were working here, though.'

'I didn't.'

'Oh? Anyway, it was Graham who said you'd be here today. I think he's rather taken with her. Does she have a name?'

'What? How'd I know? I already told you she drugged me and took my phone. I don't remember anything more. My mates might have talked to her on Saturday, though.'

'Well just tell her you're not interested and ignore her. You're on Willows time now and we've a day's work to be getting on with.'

'Yeah, of course. But why'd she have to turn up here?' He slammed the van door and followed Dave. He couldn't help but sneak a glance around the yard.

He saw the wind catch her hair, swirling the platinum streaks into loose knots, lifting the honey blonde strands and whipping them across her face. A voluminous jacket billowed freely while a pair of stick-like legs in skinny jeans rooted her. If she hadn't gripped one of the upright scaffolding poles, Nick swore she'd have been picked up and whisked away. A sudden spark of attraction surprised him. This girl was dangerous.

Confusion slowed his steps as he headed to the salvaged beams laid on the ground near the scaffolding. Nick rested the circular saw alongside one of them while Dave put down the extension cable reel he'd been carrying.

'Do you think she'll try to steal the circular saw?' Dave muttered.

'Don't give her ideas. Did you lock the van?'

'Nick....' The reedy tones carried on the wind.

'Better go and tell her you're not interested. Get rid of her Nick.' Dave stood solid, arms crossed against the wind.

The girl stepped back, almost disappearing from view behind the scaffolding. Nick felt his face burn, right to the top of his head as a wolf whistle ricocheted from the staging above. Anger bubbled up. How dare she turn his life upside down? She was nothing more than a common thief; vulnerable, frail and disturbing, but still no more than a light-fingered junkie. And now this was to be played out in front of an audience of the worst type, work colleagues.

'Hey, are you stalking me, or something?' He tried to keep the snarl out of his voice.

'Aren't you pleased to see me?'

'No.'

She seemed to recoil, as if he'd hit her with the bluntness of his reply. It almost disarmed him.

'So, what are you doing here? Are you stalking me?'

'Why shouldn't I be here? I work just across there.' She turned and pointed beyond the turkey sheds. 'At the Kell vineyard.'

'Then why aren't you over there working? What brings you here? Not on my account, I hope, because I don't even know your name.'

'Skylar.'

'Well Skylar, leave me alone. I'm not interested. Got it? Do you really think I'd want to have anything to do with a girl who steals from me? Now go away.'

'But–'

'Go away. There's nothing between us. There never was and there never will be. It's all in your head. And following me around can't make me like you. It's just irritating.' He turned on his heel, breaking their connection. He strode into the stable, reeling from the look she'd unleashed from those bottomless sea-green eyes. His head buzzed with resentment. She had to be mad, or unhinged or something.

'Has she gone now?' he snapped when Dave joined him in the stable a few minutes later.

'Last I saw, Graham was chatting to her.'

'What? Is he trying to encourage her or something?'

'Who knows? Anyway, if you ignore her, she'll soon lose interest. It's much too cold to hang around out there for long. Now grab one end of the tape measure and let's check the span in here. We'll allow an extra hundred and fifty… maybe two hundred mil each end to rest in the walls.'

By the time they went outside to start cutting the first beam to length, the girl seemed to have vanished.

CHAPTER 10

Matt reached for his glass, one arm still resting around Maisie. The jukebox pumped out electropop with frenetic drum beats at ear splitting volume.

'Does this count as a date?' she asked, jiggling one foot to the rhythm.

'Well it aint your home or mine and we're out, so yeah, technically it's a date.'

'But the Nags Head... it aint special. It's not like a real date. I mean, not romantic. You come here all the time so it don't count as takin' me out.'

'I put your favourite song on the jukebox, Mais. Aint that special enough?'

'Yeah, but *Moves like Jagger* don't cut it.'

'Well I aint flush.' He gulped his lager. 'So what you think about debt collectin'? I reckon I'd be good at the tracin' bit.'

'Does it pay well?'

He'd been explaining his idea, or rather the one Chrissie had planted. It had taken root while she'd talked in the canteen the previous day about customers not paying their bills. He'd never thought about it before, least ways not from the administrative side, but as soon as he was back in front of a computer he'd surfed the net. And his conclusion? Debt recovery was big business. He was made for the job. Not the heavy stuff. That was for the tough guys with attitude. But tracking debtors, finding addresses? With his computing and IT skills he'd be a natural. Excitement replaced frustration. If dreary Mr Smith couldn't come up with funding for the app, then tracking debtors was definitely an option.

Maisie rolled her shoulders and swayed to the music.

'So what you think? You still aint said, Mais.'

She sipped her vodka and orange, all the while eying him over her drink. He felt like a curiosity in Great Yarmouth's Sea World. Big, floundering and up against the glass.

'I didn't know you liked nosin' into other people's business.'

He saw the frown, feared her disapproval and groped for what he thought she wanted to hear.

'I don't,' he said, 'but that dead bloke by the railway line, the one I trod on–'

'Victor Pack? Weren't that his name?'

'Yeah – exactly. Victor Pack. Now I know his name I feel kinda connected. Who was he? Why was he killed? Wouldn't you want to know more? How he got there?'

'No. It's sick dwellin' on it. I'd want to forget, move on.'

'But see, I'm ace with computers. It's like a game for me. Instead of quick firin' a trigger or movin' a fighter around and fraggin' a monster, I'm usin' me brain. Findin' answers. I aint nosy, Mais, just–'

'Clumsy?'

'Yeah.' For a moment he thought of Spiderman, Mega Eagle and his other comic-strip super heroes from childhood. Not much different from sophisticated computer games, but instead of fighting on a screen, their action played out on paper. Is that why he slipped into his comic-strip world so readily? In his imagination he'd be a fighting hero, but on screen there'd be a score reflecting his botched trigger coordination. 'Yeah,' he repeated.

'Then do it, Matt.'

'Yeah.'

•

Matt sat in the offices of Balcon & Mora in Bury St Edmunds. It had taken a couple of phone calls and a few days research, but he'd landed himself an interview. It felt discrete, tucked away down a back alley behind the Buttermarket shopping area. He sported the same lucky tee-shirt he'd worn to face Mr Smith across his glass topped table on the third floor of the Academy building only ten days before. The one with THE GENIUS OF COLOUR written on grey-green cotton and with the HTML computer speak beneath. This time he felt nervous.

He glanced around. It was more like a lobby than a waiting room. The stark pint-sized space felt unwelcoming, with its two plastic stacker chairs lined up against a wall and no room for a coffee table or pile of magazines. He ran his sweaty palms across his jeans. What would they ask him? Judging by the last phone call, he guessed he might have to demonstrate his skills. Before he'd had a chance to run through his HTML in his head, the door into the office beyond opened with sudden force. A man wearing a sweatshirt and denim poked his head out.

'Hi! Are you Matt Finch?' His voice was soft and he spoke in a rush.

'Yeah. Are you–'

'Damon. Damon Mora. Come on in,' and with his last word he disappeared back into the office with lightning speed.

Matt stood up, surprised. He'd expected a secretary or girl receptionist, but the man's name suggested he was the boss, the Mora of Balcon & Mora. He swallowed his anxiety and followed the voice into the office beyond.

'Sit down, Matt. Now, tell me why you want to come to work for us here and what experience you have.' Damon looked at him across a trestle desktop. External hard drives and consoles sat in the open framework of both supporting ends.

'Well,' he faltered, 'I need the cash.'

Damon opened his mouth to speak, frowned, and then fixed Matt with an unblinking gaze.

'I mean you pay for work done, right?'

'We pay for results. I give you a list of names. You find addresses, places where the names can be reached. If the contact details turn out to be correct, you get paid. Simple.'

'Right.'

'If you get it wrong, then it costs me in reputation and I lose clients - so it'll cost you.'

'Yeah, I got it,' Matt mumbled.

'You said on the phone you've done this before.'

'Yeah.'

'So have you brought references with you?'

'Ah....' Matt squirmed. 'The thing is, I aint done it as a job before. Not for money. See, I'm good at nosing things out and I'm good with computers.'

Even to his own ears he sounded like a stalker or a lecher. He waited for Damon to say something, but all he got was silence and a deadpan face - tawny eyes set in pale skin and topped with mousey hair.

'I-I can get the computin' course director to vouch for me, say I'm OK if you like? He's asked me to design an app which needs me tracin' the Olympic clay pigeon shootin' team from the 1912 Stockholm games. Told you on the phone I'm at Utterly. Computing and IT.'

'So how'll I know if you're any good?' Damon fired back.

Matt's mouth went dry. 'I could trace a name for you here an' now if you like.'

'But I can't give out names. They're confidential. They belong to our clients. And anyway, how'd I know what you'd do with the information? I don't know if I can trust you.'

'Well, instead of tracing one of your debtors, I could use any old name as a demonstration. Like that bloke found dead near the railway line, Needham Market, a couple of weeks ago.'

'Victor Pack?'

'Yeah. He's not goin' to be complainin' if I look him up, is he?'

'I suppose not. OK then – good choice. So tell me how you'd go about it.' Damon seemed to relax, resting his hands in his lap and leaning back in his shabby office chair. Patches of the leather-effect surface had worn away, and dirty base-weave showed through on the arm rests and seat edges.

'Well first I'd....' Matt felt his confidence grow as he described a typical search, starting with typing the name into a search engine like Google; scouring Facebook and other social media sites; studying electronic newspaper records; checking the Electoral Register; looking up names, addresses and postcodes on sites such as 192.com; checking names on the Companies House registered business site; and sometimes even court records.

'I've never used any of those find your ancestor type of sites, mainly cos I'd have to pay. And the same goes for some of the 192 type of sites,' he finished in a rush.

Damon didn't say anything for a moment. He just sat, as if waiting for more while Matt fidgeted and wondered what he'd missed out.

'I don't use sites I 'ave to pay for, so births, marriages and deaths – I got to rely on local newspaper announcements,' he added, now unsure of himself.

'OK, Matt. Let's see you netsearch for real.' Damon gestured to a poky corner with a cramped table, screen and keyboard. A plastic stacker chair was pushed in tight against it.

'On this computer, yeah?' Matt asked. He eased himself into the space. There was no leg room and his stomach strained against the table edge. 'Frag. Who usually flies this?' he muttered under his breath.

'Now don't get any ideas. We're linked. I can watch every keystroke you make on my screen here. The good news is you'll have the firm's access to some of those restricted sites you mentioned.' The tones stayed soft but the words were clipped.

'Cool,' Matt murmured, picking up the implied warning as he keyed Victor Pack into the Google search box. It didn't take him long to settle into the task. With each keystroke he felt the tensions fall away. The keyboard and screen became his reality, all awkwardness forgotten as he immersed himself in his favourite activity.

When Damon asked why he searched East Anglia newspaper reports, Matt answered easily, as one techie to another, all formality dropped.

'I need the background information, mate. Don't want to confuse one Victor Pack with another. See the Eastern Anglia Daily Tribune says he was *sixty-three years old* and *in the process of retiring to Ipswich from his home in South East London*. I reckon there'll be an old and new address. Let's hope he requested the post office to forward his mail cos he won't have had time to get onto the Suffolk electoral register yet.'

'Yeah, that's neat, Matt.'

'And look, he's retired. I wonder what he did?' he muttered, as his thoughts raced on.

'Yeah, I've got it now. He *ran a children's home*. Now if I search a list of local authority children's homes, and focus on ones in South East London or in easy strike range, then I might be able to find where he worked. An obituary notice might also give me the details of where he'd worked. It may need a phone call, but they should give me a forwardin' address. And if it's the same as the Post Office forwardin' address….'

'There, stop there, Matt. Type Mr V Pack, SE London into the 192.com search and I'll key in our account number to pay for the extended information,' Damon murmured.

'Yeah. Cool, mate,' Matt whispered as his fingers flew across the keyboard. 'Not many Mr V Packs. Right, can I hold that screen while I search the South East London children's homes listed on 192?'

'Sure.'

'Frag! Are there really two hundred children's homes in South East London? Just a minute,' he muttered as he scrolled through the list, 'there's a cluster round the Victor Pack in Driffield Road, SE18. I wonder which one....'

'And the Driffield Road man is sixty-three. Awesome.' Damon punched the air. 'How'd you see the cluster, Matt?'

'Photographic memory, mate. There's some in SE postcode areas 2, 3, 6, 9, 15, 18 and 28. I wonder if there's a local newspaper for SE18 – the Plumstead Gazette, or summut? Local man retires, kind of thing?'

'Not all the smaller papers come in electronic form.'

'Yeah, but I got to try. Frag, what this?' Matt couldn't believe his eyes as he read the headline. *'Limesgrove children's home manager takes early retirement as allegations of improper behaviour resurface. Mr Pack, sixty-three*.... Shit. Did he come out all this way to top himself, do you think?'

'I don't know, but I'm surprised the press didn't splash that across the nationals when the body found at Needham Market turned out to be a Mr Pack. I reckon either the police asked for press silence, or it's a different Mr Pack,' Damon said.

'Look – it's awesome, mate. Limesgrove children's home is in Laureldene Gardens, SE28. On the Google Earth map it's a stone's throw from Driffield Road, SE18. Right, wait a sec, I'll get the Limesgrove's website up on the screen.'

Matt scoured through the official site, but there was nothing. The name Victor Pack didn't appear in the staff directory. Had it been scrubbed, he wondered.

'Hey, look at this mate.' Excitement resurfaced as he clicked back to other Limesgrove search results.

'*Limesgrove Children's Home Wins Rosette for Carnival Float*,' Damon read aloud from his linked screen before adding, 'How's that going to add anything?'

'Yeah, but if you read more…,' Matt scrolled down, 'you'll see… yeah look, *the manager, Victor Pack, praised the enthusiasm, commitment and hard work of the children. "These are amazing kids. They deserve this rosette," he said.* It kinda builds up a picture, don't you think? The manager aint Mr Pack, he's Mr Victor Pack, same name and age as our dead man and the one living in Driffield Road. If he resigned because of allegations and lives really close to the children's home, I reckon it's odds on he'd also want to move house. Get right away.'

'So how can we be sure Driffield Road is, or rather was the contact address?'

'A second validation? Check for a forwarding address, an' if there is one and it's Ipswich, that more or less clinches it.' Matt pushed his plastic stacker chair back from the desk and turned to face Damon.

'All facts match. So what you think?' he mumbled.

'I think we're going to get on. You're hired!'

'Yeah?'

'Yes.'

'Cool.' Inside he glowed. He'd have punched the air if he hadn't been wedged into such a twisted position. 'Who usually sits here then, mate?'

'It'll be you. I'd rather you work from that computer for the first few weeks.'

'But….' For the first time since he'd come into the office, Matt took a careful look at the room. There was only one door, and he'd already come through it from the waiting room outside.

'So where's Mr Balcon's office? Where does he sit?'

'Ah, there's something…,' Damon hesitated, his pasty features pulled into a frown. 'I'm going to tell you something because with your skills, you'd soon find out. There isn't a Mr Balcon. He's an invention. I figured the business sounded bigger, more professional as Balcon & Mora. Better than plain Damon Mora, don't you think? Why not attract more clients and inspire confidence simply because of the name?'

'Right. So no birds? Just you and….'

'Exactly. Just me. And now I've got you on piecework. Debt is a mean crowded market, Matt. Results bring in business, big knockers are a distraction.'

'So….' He was curious. He wanted to ask how long Damon had been running his people tracing business and where he'd learnt his computing skills, but something made him hold back the questions. And Damon's age? At a guess Matt thought about twenty-eight, maybe younger. But he knew he could find all this later, when he had access to more search sites.

'Good. Be here Monday afternoon, about three o'clock. I'll give you your first list of names and you can work through till late. OK?'

'An' when'll I get paid?'

'After the client pays me. Money'll start coming in after the first month, I reckon.'

'Shit.' Matt stood up. It was still only Friday lunchtime and he felt drained. All he'd used were his fingers and brain.

'Bye. See you on Monday, Matt.'

'Yeah, cheers mate.'

If only Balcon & Mora had offices in Stowmarket, Matt thought as five minutes later he put on his helmet and started his scooter.

CHAPTER 11

Chrissie slipped her mobile back into her bag. The soft leather folded and collapsed in a heap on the workbench.

'Still chasing customers?' Ron Clegg asked mildly.

She sipped her tea. Friday lunchtimes always felt relaxed in the Clegg workshop. The end of the week was in sight and Ron was more inclined to chat. Usually he focused on teaching topics, but occasionally he'd stray onto other things. She took her opportunity.

'You know you'd let the accounts slide, Mr Clegg,' she said, slipping into accountant mode. 'The taxman has to be told what we've billed for each year. You know, for the work actually done in each tax year. We can't just fill in a return only declaring the bills paid and ignore half the work we've done because the customer hasn't picked up the tab. That way we can claim for the costs on our losses. And when eventually a late payment comes in, it has to be linked to the year the work was done. If the taxman cares to check, and he finds we'd never declared it....'

'It all sounds very complicated Mrs Jax. You could be stirring up a load of trouble. I've always kept things simple.'

'Hmm... well that was a call from Matt. Would you believe he's just this morning landed a part time job tracing debtors? He needs the cash to fund his computing and IT course. It's been tight for him since he dropped carpentry. He's missing the apprentice wages.'

'You weren't thinking of asking him to work for us, were you, Mrs Jax?'

'Of course not. We know where our customers live. It's just a matter of picking up the phone and making a call. Everyone chases down people who don't pay their bills these days, Mr Clegg. It's normal. Customers expect it. Take Mr Kell, over at Rattlesden.'

Ron closed his eyes. 'Mr Kell.... A small, rectangular wine tray. Mahogany. You don't come across them very often. Regency period. I thought it was possibly a book tray, but I didn't like to say it to him, not with him owning a vineyard. The balustrade around the edge was badly damaged. Worth a bit in perfect condition, I should think.'

'Yes, and you scribbled something about melon feet. Was that a reference to–'

'The wine tray. It was nothing to do with Mr Kell.'

'Because he sounded quite nice on the phone,' Chrissie continued. 'I was kind of expecting him to have a limp or strange feet.'

'Haven't you seen them before? The melon refers to the shape, Mrs Jax. Sometimes they're decorated – reeded melon feet. Cheaper to produce than a ball and claw and they look less heavy.'

Ron's words faded into the background as Chrissie remembered Mr Kell's voice. He'd sounded nice on the phone. She'd suspected he was chatting her up. It had been fun and if she was honest, instead of being offended she'd been charmed.

'Sometimes casters are enclosed in the melon feet....'

She sank into her thoughts. So how old was he, she wondered. Thirty? Forty? He'd sounded young. Confident, but young. Her cheeks burned. What was she thinking? Why should she be interested in his age?

'Obviously you wouldn't have casters in the small melon feet on a wine tray. But something heavy, like a desk....'

Chrissie drifted again. He'd said he'd drop the money round to the workshop, and to make amends, he'd bring a bottle of wine from the vineyard. It was probably all good PR, but his voice, it was hypnotic. Was she a fool to believe he'd pay up? Had she allowed herself to be fobbed off too easily? She decided not to mention it to Ron. If Mr Kell didn't turn up, then she'd spare her embarrassment.

'Have you been listening, Mrs Jax?'

'Yes, yes, Mr Clegg. Cantaloupes for the tray. They're a superfruit.' She reached for her mug of tea, acutely aware she was being watched and grinned at him over the strong brew.

'Quite,' he murmured. 'So I can expect a cheque in the post from Mr Kell. Now how far have you got with applying for Snape Maltings?'

'What?' His question surprised her. 'I wasn't sure how serious you were about exhibiting at the antiques' fair.'

'Of course I was being serious, Mrs Jax. It was more a case of if you'd made up your mind about staying on as a partner.'

'Well, I've checked on their website and we've got another month to get the forms in. I think photos are going to help, so I thought–'

'Better get on with the pot stand, then.'

'Exactly.' She put down her mug and rummaged in her bag.

'So...?'

'I printed this out, Mr Clegg,' she said, unfolding a sheet of A4 paper and deliberately evading his real question. She slid from her stool, and walked over to his workbench. The sudden rumble of rotary engines flying overhead drowned her footsteps in guttural vibrations.

'Ah, you've gone for an Arts & Crafts plant stand, Mrs Jax,' he said, raising his voice to compete with the helicopter.

She watched him run a gnarled finger over the image. It was obvious they'd make good partners in the business and it was time she told him. She'd spent long enough worrying. She'd almost made herself ill with self-doubt.

'This curved bracket and the design cut out of the aprons supporting the legs... it's both Arts & Crafts and architectural. Your pot will look good on this. Nice choice Mrs Jax.'

'So....' The knot in her stomach tightened.

'What, Mrs Jax?'

'I've made up my mind, Mr Clegg. I'd like to stay on as a partner.' There, she'd said it. She just hoped to God she hadn't tempted fate and nothing dreadful happened to Ron. What if she was left in sole charge of the business?

'Good. We've plenty of time to sort out the details.' He nodded, smiled and nodded again. It was just like him to say so little, she thought.

'I'd have to take charge of the accounts,' she said in a rush.

'Naturally. It seems like you already have, Mrs Jax. So, no change there.'

A shrill ringing cut through the scent of oak and pine in the old barn. Startled, she twisted around. 'I'll get it,' she said and grabbed the workshop phone. 'Hello. Clegg Cabinet Makers and Furniture Restorers. How can I help?'

'Ah hi. Is that Chrissie Jax? I'm–'

'Mr Kell? I recognised your voice.'

She feared her cheeks might flare, but committing to the partnership had spent her emotional energy. She felt drained. There was nothing left to respond to a sexy voice.

'It's about settling my bill. Look, I'm really sorry but something's come up and I won't be out your way for a while. I'll put a cheque in the post instead. But I meant it about the wine.' He lowered his voice. 'You must come for a meal in my winery restaurant. Just mention your name and the wine will be on the house. Bring your husband, a guest, or whoever you like.'

'That's very kind of you.'

'It's my pleasure. You know where the restaurant is, don't you? In Rattlesden?'

'Yes... I mean no, but I'll find it.'

'Good, that's settled then. Bye, Chrissie.' He rang off.

She was grateful for the silence on the line while she collected her thoughts. Surely he wouldn't have offered wine at his restaurant if he was wriggling out of paying his bill. Or would he? Was she a fool, she wondered for the second time that day. She made a decision. She'd go there for a meal with Clive on Saturday.

'That was Mr Kell saying he'd put a cheque in the post,' she said as she replaced the handset.

•

'I'll drive,' Chrissie said. 'I won't be drinking much.'

It was Saturday evening and she'd suggested it would do Clive good to take the night off, go out and unwind. He didn't need much persuading. The investigation into the Needham Market railway line murders seemed to have been all-consuming, both physically and mentally. Hours spent on overtime had meant she'd hardly seen him all week, and by the time he finally slumped on her sofa on Saturday afternoon, he'd fallen asleep with a glass of wine in his hands.

'I bet you've been snacking all week. Come on, when was the last time you saw a fresh vegetable? Let's go out for a nice meal and retune your palate. There's a restaurant I want to try, and I've had the promise of wine on the house. If I drive, you won't have to worry about drinking.'

'Sounds nice. So where's this place? And how come there's wine on the house?'

'I'll explain on the way.'

She left him to lock her front door while she started her TR7. The night was cold, with a mean January nip to the air. She switched the heater to blowing full fan. It was only a short journey and she reckoned they'd be half way there before the heater warmed the car. At least her seatbelt pulled her coat closer. For a moment she wondered if it would have been cosier to stay at home, but there was something about Mr Kell that made her want to check out his restaurant. Nick had said the crazy girl worked at the vineyard, but he'd implied it was with the vines. Let's hope she's nowhere near the restaurant tonight, she thought and mentally crossed her fingers.

She talked as she drove, only half her mind on what she was saying as she concentrated on the inky swirl of dampness, almost impenetrable to her weak pop-up headlights. They followed the lane from Woolpit as it cut a straight path across seemingly empty farmland before dipping down into the Rattlesden valley. House lights spiked the blackness, signalling their approach into the village.

'We should pass a cemetery on our right.' She'd looked up the route earlier in the day when she'd phoned to book the table. But now she was in the dark and the landmarks weren't obvious. 'And the vineyard is... well you'd have to head left, back towards Stowmarket. Gipsy Lane, or something.'

'If it's Kell's Vineyard I think one of our sergeants has paid them a visit.'

'Whatever for?'

'Remember I told you someone reported seeing a man in a tartan jacket sitting in what he thought was a wine delivery van, close to where Victor Pack's body was found? It wasn't much of a description - a picture of a bunch of grapes on the side of a dark coloured van. Almost helpfully unhelpful, I'd say, but we've nothing else to go on, so some poor bastard's checking every wine delivery service in the region.'

'Oh dear, well I can't imagine Mr Kell killing anyone,' she said, remembering the softly hypnotic voice. She caught Clive's sideways glance as she turned onto Lower Street.

'So we're looking for a renovated barn?'

'Yes, past the village church and we keep going towards the Felsham Road. It should be somewhere... yes here on the left.' She swung the car into a gravelled parking area and drew up in line with a row of cars.

'This looks nice, Chrissie.'

'And busy. Come on, I'm starving.' She locked the car, cold air catching at her hands. They hurried to the restaurant door, glass in the midst of a massive glassed section and positioned between upright wooden beams.

'Wow.'

She knew as soon as she stepped inside she'd made a terrible mistake. Perhaps it was the way the girl stood with her back to them, weight on one foot and hip thrust out. But the skinny legs and platinum streaks shimmering in the long blonde hair brought the memories back with a vengeance.

'Oh God, this is embarrassing,' she breathed and grabbed Clive's arm. She pulled, trying to swing him around.

'What? What's the matter, Chrissie?' he said, resisting her.

'I... this could be awkward. I'm not sure if I want to eat here.'

'But we've only just arrived.'

'I know, but I think I've changed my mind.' She looked again to see if she'd been recognised.

'So what's with that girl?' he asked, following her glance.

'I didn't expect her to be in here tonight. She was definitely somewhere else last Saturday. I thought she worked with the vines.'

'She's a waitress. She's wearing an apron, Chrissie. What's got into you? Why can't we stay?'

'It's a long story, but... to cut to the chase, she pinched Nick's phone and... well Sarah and I got it back from her last week. At Nick's gig on Saturday. I thought you'd be too taken up with your murder inquiry to want to know.'

'Well my phone's in an inside pocket. She can't take it here. Look I'm hungry and that sage and rosemary smells–'

'Delicious, I know. But I'm uncomfortable meeting her again.'

'So that's why you wanted me to come to the gig. I hope you and Sarah didn't... no, best I don't ask. Ah, too late, she's seen you now.'

The girl stared at Chrissie, her eyes growing larger as blankness changed to surprise, and then something Chrissie couldn't quite place, but it reminded her of a wild animal, cornered.

'Come on,' Clive muttered, 'time to ask for a table or get out of here.'

'Hi, I'm Mrs Jax. I booked a table for eight o'clock,' Chrissie said, swallowing her discomfort and banishing all memories of a conversation in a ladies toilet.

The girl looked pale as she ran her finger across a page of bookings, her nail almost bitten to the quick.

'I can't see your name,' she mumbled.

'Are you sure? Can I take a look?'

'Is there a problem, Skylar? Can I help?' The sexy hypnotic tones were unmistakable.

Chrissie spun around, focusing on the voice. A man wearing smart graphite chinos and a casual shirt faced her. She guessed he was pushing thirty-five, but where was his hair? Could he really be that bald? She dragged her eyes from his scalp and smiled self-consciously.

'I... I....'

'Chrissie Jax? You see I'm good at recognising voices.' He flashed a smile and then shot a *let me deal with this* look at the waitress.

'I booked a table and–'

'I think you'll find, yes here it is. And look, there's a note saying wine gratis. Skylar is just helping out this evening. Staff sickness. There's lots of colds and flu about at this time of the year. Now if you'd like to follow me....'

He led them past other diners to a table near the wall while Chrissie wondered if nature handed out consolation prizes. A sexy voice for no head of hair?

'I'll bring the menus over. Tonight's specials are on the board. It's nice to finally meet you, Mrs Jax, and of course your husband. Enjoy your evening.'

'Last time that girl saw me, I had a heart with Nick's name drawn all over my arm,' Chrissie said in a low voice to Clive.

'Seems your double life is catching up with you.'

She watched him focus on the specials board, his face relaxed, amusement written clearly across his mouth. She launched into a light-hearted account of Nick's gig, with Sarah and her masquerading as crazy fans and finally swopping a signed bottle for the phone. By the time she'd finished her tale, they were sipping Mr Kell's wine, a blend of aromatic bacchus and fruity pinot blanc grapes.

'Hmm… I'm getting hints of tropical fruit and cut grass,' she said, swirling the wine in her glass. She'd noticed Mr Kell approaching and couldn't help wanting him to be impressed.

'What do you think of our wine?' he said as he set down bowls of steaming winter vegetable soup.

'I'm getting citrus overtones,' Clive murmured as he caught Chrissie's eye.

'It's delicious, thank you.'

'Well, if you're interested, you must come and visit my winery. It's near the vineyard.'

'Gipsy Lane?'

'Yes. Gentle slopes. Chalky boulder clay – it's ideal for the vines. Mother Nature at its best, and an end product that's as ancient as time itself. I find it grounding, therapeutic. That's why I signed up for the scheme to offer troubled youngsters a second chance by working in my vineyard. Thought it might be therapeutic for them too. It's hard graft of course, all that pruning and caring for the grapes. It's backbreaking work while they're on the vine. But there's something at the end of it. A visible product. A reward.'

'Is Skylar one of your troubled young people?' Clive asked.

Mr Kell hesitated. 'What makes you ask?'

'I just wondered, that's all.'

He didn't answer, just moved away, his smooth scalp catching the light.

'Did you notice he hasn't got any hair on his eyebrows either?' Chrissie whispered.

'Did you notice he didn't like me asking about Skylar?'

'Alopecia,' she muttered between spoonfuls, 'and I don't think he liked the way you looked at her, either.'

The soup was both tasty and warming, and Chrissie concentrated on it as she tried to analyse her fascination with Kell's voice. She found her thoughts drifting onto the subject of eyebrows as she savoured the flavours of celeriac and parsnip. Without those hairy dividing lines, the forehead risked extending into the eyelids and facial expressions could be blunted. Is that why his voice had to be so expressive?

'It's funny, but you don't normally think about types of soil, do you?' Clive said mildly.

'What?' Chrissie said, dragging her mind back.

'You know, the type of soil suitable for growing vines. Take the ground we've been digging behind Willows, near the railway line. Gravel on clay.'

'So not suitable for growing vines?'

'Not vines. But it means the knotweed clearance guys haven't had to dig as deep as they'd expected. The rhizomes and their shoots grow in the direction of least resistance, skim along the clay when they meet it, then up to the surface again.'

'But what's your point?'

'The soil is gravelly, easier digging than solid clay. It's made it straightforward for our SOCOs and of course the killer. But my point is you can sieve gravel, you can't sieve lumps of clay, at least that's what I've been told. We've found more than we'd expected.'

'Oh no, not more bodies?'

'No, not yet.'

'So what else have you found? You can't start telling and then stop half way. It's not fair, Clive.'

'Broken china.'

'What? A diner plate or something? Are you trying to say the poor bastard had a last meal of chicken wings served on bone china, or something? You are joking, aren't you?'

'Kind of, but it's not any old bit of china, Chrissie. It's, when pieced together – it's a figure of a boy wearing a bathing costume. It's about this tall.' He held his hand above the table.

'Over a foot?'

'Yes, with a good solid base. Forensics report tiny fragments impaling the plastic bag, the one tied over the victim's head.'

'So are you saying you've found the murder weapon? That's brilliant, Clive.'

'I don't know.' He shrugged. 'He's been too long in the ground to be sure. Forensics say it could have been smashed over his head after he died. Unfortunately what was in the bag was... well let's just say, liquid putrefaction makes interpretation difficult.'

'Ugh, that's horrible, Clive. We're eating. But the broken figure, it must be important.'

'Oh yes. It's bound to be symbolic.'

'And sick. It's weird, Clive.' For a moment Chrissie pictured an egg, its smooth shell fractured inwards, yolk and white leaking like blood and brain. She shivered.

'Talking of china, have I told you I've chosen a design for my pot stand?' she said, feeling slightly nauseous and changing the subject.

Clive seemed to follow her lead and the rest of the meal passed on a lighter note. Rich aromas tickled Chrissie's nose as Clive cut into a steak and ale pie. Hints of sage and rosemary drifted up from her plate as she heaped roast potatoes alongside slices of locally reared turkey.

'We must eat here again,' Clive said when they finally left, overly full and with memories of mouth-watering flavours still fresh on their palates.

They drove back to Woolpit in silence, Clive nodding into a wine infused sleep while Chrissie concentrated on the road. Her thoughts drifted back to Mr Kell as she drew up outside number three, Albert Cottages.

His voice was the lure, she saw it now. But the voice and the person were two separate things. He was probably nice, and certainly generous and thoughtful, but she knew she could never be attracted to the man himself. It was only his voice. In fact it was a relief to know that in any future business dealings there'd be no risk or guilt in finding his voice so sensual.

And then she smiled as a wicked thought struck her. Was Skylar's infatuation with Nick's singing voice so very different from her own fascination with Strad Kell's speaking one?

'Don't be so hard on yourself,' she muttered.

'What? What did you say, Chrissie? Are we home yet?'

CHAPTER 12

Nick looked to see if the coast was clear. All he saw was a renovation site with scaffolding clenching the stable block, and a courtyard turned into a builders yard. He scanned the piles of rubble and rotten timber, but the place seemed deserted.

Thank God she's not here, he thought as he jumped down from the Willows van. Skylar or Hylar or whatever the girl liked to call herself, had been turning up every day, wafting past the stable building and souring the air for him. But on first glance this morning the site was Skylar-free.

'We're OK.' He tapped the van window and signalled a thumbs-up to Dave.

Dave nodded from the driver's seat. 'Apart from Mr Core's 4x4, have you noticed there's no one else here either?' he said as he swung his door open.

'What?'

'None of Graham's pick-ups or vans are here and the place looks deserted.'

Nick checked the time. 'It's not quite nine yet. I know he always cuts things pretty fine, but...,' he let his voice trail, as a battered pick-up swept into the yard. 'Talk of the devil.'

He watched as the pick-up braked, tyres spitting grit and stones. Two of Graham's workmen slid from the passenger side. 'See you later, mate,' one of them shouted and slammed the door. Moments later the pick-up drew away and headed back down the track. Had he just seen Graham at the wheel?

'Aren't all of you here today, then?' Nick called, puzzled.

'Nah, mate. Graham's gone to see the vineyard bloke. He'll be back in an hour or two, I expect.'

'Oh yeah?'

At least their expert carpentry didn't depend on Graham's presence, and there wasn't much skilled work left for them on site. They'd spent the previous week scarfing in sections of old beams, repairing rotten uprights in the stables and the king posts in the old roof. Reclaimed ceiling beams now spanned the building and doubled as tie beams. The old wood, where sound had been as hard as steel and Nick suspected as strong, if not stronger than a modern RSJ. He reckoned the stable block would be good for another hundred years.

'When we've got the last of the rafters attached to the ridge beam, we're done here, aren't we Dave? I mean Graham's men can do the rest.'

'Oh yeah, course they can lay the under-felt and fix the battens. We're not hanging the tiles, so–'

'We're done here, right?'

'Easy, Nick. What is it with you two? If you're taken on by Willows, you could be working with Graham from time to time in the future.'

It was alright for Dave, Nick thought later as he propped some rafters against the end of the scaffolding platform. The leering, slap-my-thigh nod-nod wink-wink innuendo wasn't directed at him, it was aimed at Nick and usually whenever Skylar was about. It was just so mind cringingly embarrassing. And if he added his innate dislike of the man – then working with him in the future might be difficult. Impossible, even.

'Dave,' a voice called from the yard, interrupting Nick's thoughts.

'He's up on the trusses,' Nick said, turning to see Vincent Core approaching. 'Can I pass up a message?'

'Ask him to have a word with me before you finish, will you. I'll be in the front turkey shed.'

It was hours later when Nick remembered Mr Core's message. He was gathering up his tools and Dave had already opened the van doors, ready to load.

'Why didn't you tell me earlier? It makes us look rude. And don't say it's because that girl showed up again after Graham got back. Your brain can't have gone that soft.'

'Sorry, Dave. But he didn't say it was urgent.'

'Oh well, you'd better come along with me in case he's forgotten that bit of the message. So where did he say he'd meet us? In his office?' Dave turned and started walking.

'No, he said he'd be in the nearest turkey shed.'

Nick slammed the van doors and hurried after Dave. They skirted around the remains of a pile of sand, sliced by spades and trampled by boots. A cheerless prefabricated office faced them, paint peeling, mould on the windows.

They headed across a corner of yard and opened a door cut into the sliding end panel of the shed-like barn. Nick had no idea what to expect as he stood in the generously-sized antechamber; certainly not the whirring of ventilation fans, nor the pungent smell of poultry droppings, nor even the grassy overtones of feeding pellets. A bench with boots and a rack of overalls had been placed next to a door with a double glazed panel. A notice warned, *Do Not Enter without Boots and Overalls.* A second notice advised, *Ring Bell for Attention.*

'I think we'll ring the bell,' Dave muttered as Nick peered through the glass and into the turkey shed beyond.

They didn't have to wait long before Vincent Core appeared on the other side of the glass panel. Warm air wafted in as he opened the door, and with it the powerful, almost sharp in-the-back-of-the-nose smell of turkey droppings. 'Ah, I'm glad I've caught you,' he said mildly.

'We were just packing up to leave....'

'Yes, and that's why I wanted to catch you, so you could measure up before you went.'

'Measure up?' Nick echoed.

'Yes it seems the stable doors are not a standard size and, well I wondered if you could work some magic with reclamation ones or even make some to fit?'

'No problem. Do you want both halves opening separately, or just the appearance of a classic stable door?' Dave asked, his shoulders visibly relaxing as he pulled a notepad from his pocket.

While Dave talked numbers, style details and quotes with Mr Core, Nick watched the turkeys through the glass in the door.

'Are you interested in the turkeys?' Mr Core asked.

'Ah sorry, it's just that I've never seen so many before. It's overwhelming. Do they ever get to go outside?'

'Oh yes, we open the panels on that side of the shed when the weather isn't so cold and it's dry. There's access to an outdoor area. We've an acre or so fenced off for them to range. These birds are quite young still, but they should be OK for Easter.'

'So what happens to them then?' It was a silly question. He realised at once. The answer was obvious.

'Ah, now you've got me onto something. I could talk about if for hours. I'm installing what they call a controlled atmosphere system to kill the turkeys.'

'What? What's that, Mr Core?'

'You see we don't supply the supermarkets. We sell to local butchers and farm shops, and direct to the public. Our customers want flavour in a bird, and that means free range and then a humane kill. It's reflected in the quality of the meat and taste.'

'But comes at a cost,' Dave murmured.

'Quite. When we first started out we used to slaughter the birds ourselves – put the head in a cone and slit the throat, kind of thing. They were our turkeys, there was no travelling to a slaughterhouse, they stayed on home ground and we minimised the stress. But we've been successful and expanded. We have a second shed, maybe a third one soon. And we've many more turkeys. So we're moving with the times and having a small chamber installed. You flush the air out of it with carbon dioxide, and the turkeys go into it, seemingly quite happy.'

'You mean they don't get distressed and fight it?'

'No, they just fall unconscious and die. They seem quite calm, and it's very fast.'

'So where are you putting this chamber? In here?' Nick asked, looking around.'

'No, we've space sectioned off in the second shed. In fact Graham is going to put in a wall for us there.'

'Right, Graham,' Nick said under his breath.

'Come on, enough about killing turkeys. Let Mr Core get back to his work, Nick. And we need to measure the stable doorways,' Dave said and led the way out of the shed.

They'd barely crossed the yard before Nick felt strong fingers grasp his shoulder. 'Ouch, what are you doing?' he yelped as he turned to face Dave.

'Don't ever down one of your co-workers to the customer, unless you've got good reason. You'll make more enemies than friends, and there'll be consequences you can't always predict. Remarks can backfire. You seem to be confusing your personal dislike of Graham with his standard of building.' Dave's kindly face was momentarily transformed by hard angry lines.

'But I didn't say anything.'

'No, but you were thinking it and sometimes your face is too expressive.'

'Sorry, Dave but he's like some grub, worming his way into everything. First the stable block, then some work over at the vineyard down the road, and now the turkey sheds.'

'Actually, knotweed comes to mind.'

'Yeah, like one of those, what did you call them? Rhizomes?' An image of *dig and dump* flashed through Nick's mind. 'I'll get the tape measure from the van,' he said, catching Dave's smile.

Thirty minutes later Nick sat in the Willows van. With each bend in the road, he rocked and swayed, but the aggressive gear changes seemed less urgent and the clutch pedal work less sudden than on the morning's journey. He glanced at Dave. For once he appeared intent on the road, unaware of the grimy knot of cobweb swinging from his hair, a vestige from the stable block.

'You should wear a woolly hat,' he murmured.

'You sound like my wife,' Dave muttered. 'Hey, do you want to have a drink after we've got the van back to

Willows? I've been thinking, maybe we should talk. I mean, what exactly is your problem with Graham? Or is it about this Skylar girl? Because I was watching this afternoon, and I'm not even sure you're her main interest anymore.'

'What? You don't think all the wilting on piles of bricks when Graham's around isn't just to make me jealous?'

'I don't know. I hadn't thought of that. I mean you'd made it pretty clear you weren't interested.' He pulled up sharply at the junction in Stowmarket and tapped the steering wheel, his beat out of time with the music on the radio, impatience written across tense muscles as he waited to turn towards Needham Market.

The uncoordinated rhythms began to grate. Nick tried to ignore them, humming a syncopated tune in his head and distancing himself with glances back at the church tower.

The tapping escalated into flamboyant finger drumming, pattering the steering wheel and drowning the melody. Nick's irritation erupted like an itch. He leaned forwards and changed the station.

'*The police have–*'

'Hey, I was enjoying that,' Dave snapped across the newsreader's voice. 'This is exactly what I mean. You're so irritable. Don't you see it?'

'*The man found ten days ago buried near the railway line in Needham Market....*'

'Listen Dave, the news,' Nick barked.

'*... has been named as Eric Haigh....*'

'That'll be our body, Dave. The knotweed one.'

'*... lived in Woodbridge but previously ran a children's home in Hemley....*'

'Hemley? Isn't that a tiny village on the Southwest banks of the Deben? It's all tidal salty mudflats,' Dave murmured. 'Only a few houses. It must've felt pretty isolated if you were a kid stuck out there. Make you want to learn to sail–'

'Or swim.'

'Yeah, just to get away.'

'... *the home was closed in two thousand and five....*'

'I'm not surprised, out of the way like that,' Nick sighed, all edginess evaporating, all thoughts of Skylar forgotten, Graham suddenly unimportant.

'Did you catch how old he was?' Dave asked as the next news item merged with the engine.

'No, you were talking and I couldn't...,' Nick let his voice drift as he imagined the man, dead and rotting in the soil. Somehow it wouldn't seem so bad if he was old and had lived some kind of a lifespan. The other one, Matt's one, had been old. He'd been sixty-three.

'Why'd they come to Needham Market? I mean, from Woodbridge? From London? What's so special about Needham Market?'

'Beats me. Mind you, we're heading for Needham Market, Dave.'

'Yeah, but it's not the centre of the bloody universe. We're locals, we work there. So, what's their reason? It's a long way to come, just to get buried. That's my point.'

'Actually, I think I read or heard somewhere that it wasn't London. The bloke was moving up to Ipswich.'

'Yeah, well that makes all the difference, Ipswich not London.' Dave slammed the gears into third and accelerated round a bend. 'Still doesn't explain why he's found dead in Needham Market though, does it Nick.'

CHAPTER 13

Matt propped the Piaggio on its parking stand and hurried into the Nags Head. Nick had sent a text a couple of hours earlier, but Matt no longer cared if he drank in company. All he knew was that he needed a pint of lager.

The ride from Bury St Edmunds had numbed his chest, the freezing wind cutting through his field jacket with the keenness of a stiletto. He blew into cupped hands, pumping and rubbing them, desperate for some feeling to return.

'Arctic,' he muttered and locked onto the barman, holding his gaze and hustling past a drinker near the dartboard. 'Lager. A pint,' he puffed, reluctant to waste warm breath on anything but his hands.

'Cold out, is it?' the barman asked mildly as he pulled a pint.

'Bloody freezin', mate.' Perhaps he should have asked for a vodka shot. He dug into his pocket, his fingers deadened and stiff. Coins erupted as he extracted his fist, loose change spinning and rolling across beer stained floorboards.

'I'll get it,' a familiar voice called, 'and I'll have another half of Land Girl.'

'Hey thanks, Nick. You're still here, mate. I thought you'd have left by now.'

'Yeah, well I was about to go home, but seeing as how you've just arrived....'

They carried their drinks over to a small table. Matt pulled back a darkly stained pine chair, gulped his lager and sank onto the seat. Gentle warmth at last flowed through his veins.

'So how was it? This debt tracing agency?'

'What? Oh yeah, Balcon & Mora. Yeah it was cool. Reckon I knocked Damon out.'

'You didn't really knock…?'

'Nah. Damon's the guy who runs the place.' Matt downed another third of his glass in a languid string of swallows, this time relishing each mouthful.

'So, the tracing? Did you track down the addresses?'

'Yeah, of course. Ferretin's dead easy when you've got the right programmes. Like I said, knocked him out with me skills.'

For a moment Matt thought back to the afternoon-into-evening session with Damon. It was the first time they'd worked together and although his head ached from uninterrupted screen work and concentration, it had been fun. He'd learnt loads, and he was going to get paid.

'Yeah, I picked up a few tricks from Damon. I'm hopin' he'll let me work on my laptop back here, but his system's real powerful. There's fibre optic broadband in Bury.'

'Closest you'll get to fibre optic round hear is if you have a colonoscopy. That's what Dave says.'

'Colon what?'

'Never mind. Something to do with looking up bums with a camera. So did you find out any more about your dead bloke, Victor Pack?'

'Not this time. I reckon Damon's watchin' me, or recording my keystrokes. Not worth the risk, mate. Not yet. But I guess with the number of keystrokes I've been makin', he won't bother checkin' after a while. Seemed impressed though.' Matt unzipped his field jacket. That's when he remembered his tee-shirt.

'Well there's the knotweed body to add to your list now, if you're interested. I can't remember his name, but they've identified him. Heard it on the radio this afternoon.'

'Yeah, he seemed impressed,' Matt muttered, his mind miles away.

The tee-shirt had been a chance find in one of Stowmarket's charity shops. Matt knew it was *the one* the moment he spotted it. Maisie of course, thought it was something to do with Nature Watch and wildlife awareness, but for IT techies it was obvious and, what could be more ideal than for Balcon & Mora? It was almost the perfect dress code for work. He let the field jacket hang open.

Nick's gaze rested on Matt's tee-shirt. He sipped his beer, his face creasing into a question. 'Hey, I've got it now. That tee - are you sure Damon wasn't stunned, kinda lost for words?'

'Nah, I could tell he was proper impressed. Anyway, Mais said she thought it matched my beard.' Matt smoothed the cotton, downwards from his chest and over his ample belly.

'Yeah, I suppose your beard looks a bit like the picture of the huge pile of twigs printed on your tee.'

'Thanks mate. And she reckoned the hedgehog was kinda cute.'

'Cute? A surfer of illegal sites, cute? You'll get arrested next.'

'Nah, it's like a double meanin'. Mais only sees a hedgehog walkin' out of a pile of sticks and twigs.'

Nick put down his glass and read out the words printed on the cotton:

THE DARK NET?
OR JUST SOMEWHERE TO
HIBERNATE?

'So have you been on the dark net, Matt?'

'Nah, but I bet Damon has. You see, mate, if you're a techie you'd realise the pile of twigs represents an interlockin' mishmash series of random IP addresses, like being untraceable on the dark net. It gives me street cred, mate. Respect.'

'So the picture of the hedgehog is code for an encrypted identity, right?'

'Yeah, reckon it could be.' Matt rested back on the pine chair feeling as if he'd placed the last piece in a jigsaw puzzle. He was, for once complete: he studied techie, he worked techie, he talked techie, and he wore techie. He caught Nick's frown.

'What? What's wrong, mate?'

'I don't know. It's work. Skylar keeps turning up there. She won't leave me alone. Graham, he's the builder doing the stable renovation, he's just so irritating. And now Dave thinks I'm difficult and grouchy and... I'm worried Willows might not offer me a job when the apprenticeship ends.'

'Frag, that's bad, mate.' Matt swigged some lager, hoping for inspiration. But what could he say. He groped for something to offer, some pearl of comfort or wisdom. Chrissie, Maisie, the girls would know what to say.

'What about the Great East Swim?' he blurted, grasping at straws and something he'd seen only hours earlier on his internet searches. 'Some reservoir near Ipswich. Alton Water, an annual swim around the reservoir.

Two miles. Yeah, and you get to wear a wetsuit. Looks pretty sexy if you ask me.'

'What?'

'Well, Mais says swimming gets rid of your tension and makes you fit.'

'Then you swim, Matt.'

'I aint the one who's tense. But no, wait. What about... I got Skylar's number when she thought she was ringing you. With my tracin' job I can find out more about her, maybe some way of getting her to leave you alone. And Graham, I don't know....'

It was only later, when Matt rammed on his helmet in the Nags Head car park that he realised Nick hadn't answered. So was he supposed to find out more about Skylar and Graham? He didn't feel comfortable with uncertainty but it was too late to ask and make sure. He'd already watched Nick ease his beat-up Ford Fiesta out of its parking space and drive away.

A blast of icy East wind caught across his chest. It focused Matt's mind as he grabbed at his flapping jacket and zipped it closed. Monday had been one hell of a long day and Skylar and Graham would have to wait till the morning. He'd think about it then.

•

Matt slept fitfully. He dreamt he was encased in a body-hugging wetsuit and submerged beneath a massive concrete slab. He fought for his life as foam neoprene squeezed his ribs. He clawed, kicked and wrestled. Sweat trickled from his hairline. Silent screams bruised his throat.

'Shit,' he muttered when his morning alarm buzzed and finally ended the torment.

'Killer app,' he murmured as the sight of familiar grimy blue walls greeted him. No wetsuit – but his duvet seemed to float like an iceberg on the floor. He guessed he must have hurled it there during the night.

The chill bit into his consciousness and sharpened the landscape as he grabbed his mobile. He snuffed the alarm and curled into a ball. His tired boxers and short sleeved tee offered little warmth; they couldn't shield him from the freezing bedroom air. There was nothing else for it. He'd have to get up.

He staggered to a pile of jumbled clothes, as cold as the air in the room. It was bad enough dragging tight fitting tees over belly rolls, and wriggling into snug jeans. How would a superhero force all those muscles into a wetsuit?

And then it dawned on him. If Nick entered the Great East Swim, then it was likely he'd also be dragged kicking and screaming to Alton Water. No way mate, he thought. It would take more than friend loyalty to get him into a wetsuit. Mais would look good in one, though.

His mind fizzed as thoughts ricocheted around his head: Nick, Skylar, Graham, the Olympic Silver App, Balcon & Mora, his course work and data structures.

By the time he closed his bedroom door he was fully awake, and as if to remind him, his stomach complained loudly. He trudged past the kitchen. He knew there'd be no comfort inside. He'd checked the fridge yesterday evening. His mum, in her faded dressing gown and shuffle slippers, was no fridge fairy. The fridge would still be barren.

'Bye, Mum' he shouted to the empty air and slammed the front door behind him.

The ride from Tumble Weed Drive took longer than the usual twelve minutes. He dawdled along, reducing the wind chill factor, preoccupied with his search tasks ahead. By the time he propped the Piaggio on its parking stand at the Academy, he had a plan and a system. Gusts pushed at his chest. He hunched against the blast and hurried around the side of the old mansion block. He followed the path, skirting the wall of the building and sheltering from the wind. He reckoned it was warmer than braving the expanse of car park for the front entrance.

'Now what?' he muttered. 'Phishing moles?' A large mound of earth had been dumped on a scruffy corner of grass where students usually took shortcuts onto the lawns. Memories of police SOC tape and people wearing all-in-one overalls flashed into his mind.

'Frag. What the phishing hell…?' He stood and stared. Was it another body?

A student, hoodie up and almost bent double in haste, knocked his shoulder as he pushed past.

'Hey!'

'Sorry mate.'

'What's all the earth about?' Matt called after him.

'The Olympic bed.'

'Olympic bed?' Matt echoed. Whichever way he twisted the words, they didn't turn into dead body. So it was all right. There'd been no more gruesome finds.

His pulse had settled down by the time he climbed the main stairs to the canteen. Minutes later he queued for a sausage beans and toast breakfast while he texted Nick for Graham's surname. Life had returned to some kind of normality when he set his loaded tray on a Formica topped table. Sounds of Radio Suffolk wafted from the kitchens, permeating the thermals with jingles, news and music, and jostling with smells of frying and the comfort of warm air.

Trays clattered, students gossiped and canteen staff shouted orders back into the kitchen. It seemed like a little slice of heaven as he cut into his sausage.

When he finally sauntered into the library, his stomach satiated, he felt more like his old self. He caught sight of Rosie sorting through a pile of books, and when she glanced up, he pulled his face into a half smile. He hoped he looked sexy.

'Hiya,' he murmured and lingered a moment.

'Have you volunteered to help plant up the Olympic flower bed, Matt?'

'What? You mean the pile of earth coverin' half the lawn?'

'They've pinned the design on the main notice board and are asking for volunteers. I thought you'd be the first to put your name down.'

Ping! Matt fumbled for his mobile. *Graham Tollington*, the text message read.

'Yeah, except,' he started to say as he turned his attention back to Rosie. He watched the way her loose ponytail moved as she raised her arm and slotted a book onto a shelf. She seemed unaware of him.

'But why would I...?'

She didn't answer. It seemed she was deaf as well forgetting he was there. He moved away, confused.

He settled at his favourite computer station, out of the way near the far wall, and pondered on what Rosie had said. So what should he research first? Was it to be Graham Tollington or something to impress Rosie? He figured he wouldn't be seeing Nick until Friday, but Rosie was in the library and now was the time if he wanted to catch her attention. It was a no-brainer. He needed something Rosie wouldn't expect him to know about. Anything to do with piles of earth, or gardening, or weeds, or... Japanese knotweed. Hadn't he heard Nick mention the exotic sounding weed? He typed Japanese knotweed into the search box.

'Frag,' he half whistled through his teeth. So that's what it looked like. And those dead hollow canes, like bamboo but easily broken? Hadn't he trampled through a thicket like that? Near the railway line, on rough ground not far from Needham Lake? He could almost hear the stems fracturing and splitting against his legs, feel them disintegrating underfoot, and sense the revulsion as the stench of death–

'Crash,' he hissed. 'Stop, stop, stop!' He held his breath and dug in his metaphorical toes.

It had to stop here. His brain was following a tree index data retrieval structure. He knew where it would end and he didn't want to go down that line, even if computing terminology helped. He couldn't abort a memory simply on the *crash* command. Revulsion lurked at the back of his mind. Stepping on a rotting hand wasn't going to be wiped so easily.

He checked the time on his computer screen. There was still another hour before his tutorial on data structures, and plenty of time to get up to speed with knotweed. He'd soon know sufficient for a casual chat with Rosie and more than enough to impress. Forcing himself to concentrate, he skimmed through several sites, and the story was always the same. Knotweed was invasive, difficult to eradicate unless you knew what you were doing, and expensive. It didn't even have natural enemies.

'See you're reading about knotweed. Why?' Rosie whispered as she passed close by, a couple of books in her hands.

'What?' The edginess cut through his voice.

'Are you OK?'

'Yeah, sure. This knotweed, I mean if there's any in that load of topsoil, you'd notice soon enough. I mean it wouldn't be very deep at first, and it'd push shoots through the flowerbed.'

'Probably through an Olympic ring.'

'Yeah, and cos it's a flowerbed, see you'd notice. Everyone'll be lookin' and admirin' the design and there'd be this dirty great green thing in the middle of it, spoilin' the show.'

'It would cause a lot of trouble. People would be upset.'

'But so long as you've spotted it, then hey, you just inject the stem with weed killer at the end of the season, or dig it out down to the rhizome. You could get it all out before it got a hold. Cool word, rhizome.'

'Try telling that to the groundsman.'

'Yeah, s'pose so, Rosie. But a couple of years down the line and you'd 've cleared the lot.'

'Hmm... I don't know. A few years ago my uncle got knotweed from some communal compost. Hell broke out amongst the raspberry canes. I think you should just stick to computing.'

He watched her cross back to the library assistant's station. Why did she always leave him wondering what he'd said to make her walk away? Maisie would have revelled in his knowledge, loved the idea of a rhizome, and more than likely had the word rhizome printed across a tee-shirt for him. He guessed that's why Maisie was his girlfriend.

'Frag!' He checked the time on his computer. If he hurried he'd just about have time to lumber down the main stairs, elbow his way through the crush of students in the main hallway and let the flow bear him along the corridor before depositing him like jetsam at a side door. From there he'd take the shortcut through the stores before braving outside in a twenty yard dash to the computer lab.

•

The tutorial on ways of organising data calmed and soothed Matt. No emotional intelligence was required to follow the concept of chaining or linear probing in dynamic hash tables. Drilling further into programming those details would be on next year's syllabus, but he wanted to know now. Damon had told Matt he needed to understand the different types of data storage and how it was retrieved if he was ever going to figure out how to crack into a database. Mr Smith had taken the tutorial and seemed happy to stay on and explain more. Matt hoped Damon would fill in the rest.

By the time Matt leaned against the library door, he'd parked his emotions in a safe backwater. The tutorial had affirmed his binary thinking. He felt rejuvenated and eager to put his knowledge to the test. He was impatient to find examples to see if he could tell how data might have been stored and then retrieved. Lunch could wait half an hour.

He let his weight push the door open. Only a smattering of students lingered in the library, and Rosie was nowhere to be seen. He headed straight to his favourite computer station, logged on and typed Companies House in the search box. The plan was simple. Would a name like

Graham Tollington be linked to a building and construction company? And if he was linked to more than one, would the information all be grouped under his name, or would the name come up in a column with a different company against each Graham Tollington? In other words, could he tell if the data was tree storage or hash tag design?

'Yeah, cool,' he muttered, and there he had it. The Stowmarket Graham Tollington, was a director of three different companies. 'Three? Frag.'

He skimmed down the list. *Graham Tollington Builder LTD* seemed obvious, but he'd never have guessed *Groundsbuild LTD* or *Build Ground LTD*. And the last one, the *Build Ground* one had been dissolved. Why? Now that could be interesting. All thoughts of data storage structures flew out the window.

A quick click and he was on the Eastern Anglia Daily Tribune site. He reckoned the local paper might have printed a story if dodgy dealings had been exposed or if the business had been in trouble.

'Frag!' He never got as far as the newspaper's search box. The day's headlines saw to that.

Needham Market Murders Linked, leapt from the screen.

'Linked?' he whispered. Linked by what? The railway line? Knotweed? He read on. It appeared both murdered men had *worked in children's homes*. Victor Pack, the first body, the one he'd trodden on, had recently retired after running *Limesgrove, a children's home in Laureldene Gardens, Southeast London*. He already knew that. The more recent find, Eric Haigh had *run a children's home in Hemley, on the southwest banks of the River Deben*. So he was Suffolk, Matt thought, not another Londoner like

Victor Pack. And the home in Hemley? It seemed it *closed in 2005*. Matt tried to picture the place, but he was pretty sure he'd never been anywhere near. He read on. *The home was demolished and apartments and a boathouse have since been built on the site.* No wonder. So couldn't it just be a coincidence that both men had worked in children's homes?

'Wouldn't make front page news, though,' Matt murmured, his mind fired with questions.

His stomach rumbled. The questions would have to wait until after lunch.

CHAPTER 14

Chrissie laid out the pieces: four tapering legs; a swollen rectangular shaped top; a square lower shelf; four curved shaped brackets; and four pierced aprons - all in solid walnut, and most with mortise or tenons. She stepped back to admire her work.

'What do you think, Mr Clegg?' She waited, hoping he'd comment on her fretsaw work. She thought she'd done pretty well on the pierced aprons and shaped brackets.

'I think you're getting quicker, Mrs Jax.'

'Really? So shall we do a dry run? Fit it together without any glue?' She imagined the finished plant stand: the wood warmly polished; all four legs perfectly balanced; and the look smart, stylish Arts & Crafts.

'Better get a wooden mallet and a block of wood then, Mrs Jax.'

She'd worked hard over the last few days, even surprising herself with the speed she'd progressed from the design drawings on paper to the table saw and thickness planer. The taper on the legs could have been her biggest challenge had it not been for Ron's cunningly simple tapering jig. She'd found it on her workbench the other morning.

'That'll make your life easier,' he'd said.

She guessed he must have dug it out of some dusty corner of the barn workshop for her. The jig allowed her to use the table saw to taper all four sides of a piece of wood in turn, and walk away with her fingers intact.

So how had she arrived so fast at this moment of plant-stand-assembly? What, she wondered had spurred her on and concentrated her efforts. Was it because she was investing now in her own future and a shared business, or was it a distraction from Clive's serial murder case? She didn't know. A mild unease had taken a hold. It skulked in the background, creeping out of the shadows just as she fell asleep. It poked a finger, saying, 'Fool. You'll never turn a profit.' If Clive was around, it prowled but didn't dare show itself. But Clive worked long hours, racking up overtime. He was trying to find a killer. He hadn't been around much recently.

'What's holding you back, Mrs Jax?'

She looked up to find Ron watching her.

'Nothing... just the responsibility of it all,' she said.

'It'll fit together, Mrs Jax. It may be a bit shorter than intended, that's if we have to lose some leg to even it up, but it'll all fit. We'll make it.'

'Has a cheque arrived from Mr Kell yet?' It was easier to ask about late payments than voice her niggling worries for the future.

'I haven't opened this morning's post yet, Mrs Jax. Let's fit the stand together and I'll have a look when we stop for tea. Now, the legs and those aprons. Let's see how well the joints fit.'

When Chrissie eventually switched the kettle on for tea, she glowed with pride and achievement. With Ron's help, they'd eased the pieces together. Admittedly, there'd been a few awkward moments and she'd had to shave a few slivers of wood from a couple of tenons, but the pieces were now a whole. It stood 110 cm high and no precious centimetres of leg had been sacrificed. They rested evenly on the concrete floor and formed the corners of an almost perfect square.

'Symmetry and style. You've a good eye.' Ron dropped a handful of letters onto his workbench.

'Really? I hope it makes a good photo for the catalogue. That's with the pot on it, I mean.'

She watched him settle on his work stool and pick up an envelope. Anxiety caught at her chest. What if Kell had no intention of sending a cheque? It could be the same with all the others she'd contacted. She knew Ron would never agree to using debt collectors, not with his rural business built on personal recommendations. An aggrieved debtor could easily spread all kinds of bad reports and drive away new clients. 'No smoke without fire,' they'd say. So what was her next move to rein in the debtors?

'Here,' she said, setting down a mug of steaming tea for him.

'Oh thank you, Mrs Jax. It looks like your efforts are paying off. Old Mr Rice has finally sent a cheque for a hundred and fifty pounds. Whatever did you say to him?'

'I was very nice. We had a chat about living in Lavenham and I asked him if he knew some of the people I knew. You can guess the kind of thing, a bit of casual name dropping till you find someone in common. That's right, I remember now. He went a bit quiet so I realised I didn't have to pretend to gossip about the church warden, the chap who does his MOT or half the parish council.'

'It was an old lectern we restored, wasn't it.'

'Exactly. So it was a toss-up between him being musical or religious.' She remembered the call. She'd done her homework and used her most charming voice. He hadn't taken long to pick up that she ostensibly moved in similar circles to him. He hadn't expected it.

'Ah! Mr Kell's cheque.' Something fell onto the bench as he unfolded a sheet of paper.

'Result.' She almost punched the air.

'And look, he's written a note.' Mr Clegg handed her the paper, the folds cutting across looping handwriting in bold dark blue ink.

Please find enclosed the cheque, as promised. And I meant it when I said you were welcome to come and look around my winery. In fact I insist! Call first and I'll make sure I'm there. Strad Kell.

'The note isn't addressed to me, so I reckon it's an open invitation. You see, Mr Clegg, we can chase down non payers and keep friendly.'

'So are you going to visit Kell's winery?'

'Clive might find it interesting. I don't know, maybe.' But she did know. Secretly she was fascinated.

Ever since she'd discovered an old copper tank built into the back of the fireplace in Ron's brick outhouse, she'd found the process of alcohol production intriguing. Admittedly the old copper tank was part of a non-operational distilling system, but the idea of modern steel fermentation tanks and all the technology used to produce a quality wine was anything but dull. And besides, Strad Kell was obviously an interesting man. Anyone who'd built up a winery and vineyard and gave second chances to troubled young people had to be interesting.

'I hope it doesn't give you ideas of making wine in the outhouse here, Mrs Jax.'

'But that would be brilliant. Thank you for suggesting it. I could raid your stock of veneers and slip some into the tanks. The hints of tannin might have a particularly unique nature.'

'Woa – stop there. Don't even think it. Whatever you do, spare my veneers.'

'I don't know, Mr Clegg. Old stock taking up space on shelves....'

She caught his smile. Of course he was taking a risk with her as well. She should keep that in mind. And then she remembered Skylar. What if she came across her again, but this time at the winery? The poor girl might start to think she was being stalked.

•

When Chrissie drove home to Woolpit that evening, she felt unusually relaxed. Success with the plant stand had given her a brief respite from self-doubt and her new found confidence was easing her anxieties about the future. It might only be short lived, she realised, but she was determined to enjoy her relative optimism while it lasted.

She flung her keys down on her narrow hall table and headed straight for the kitchen. The air felt warmer than outside, but not quite warm enough to strip off her duffle coat yet. First a mug of hot tea, she decided, and then she'd be ready to rustle up a ham, mushroom and mixed herb omelette, washed down with a glass of Chablis. It would hit the spot, as Clive might say. There was a half-empty bottle in the fridge left over from a couple of evenings ago. Clive had fallen asleep after the first glass and she hadn't felt inclined to drink the rest. He seemed permanently exhausted these days.

By the time she sank onto her comfy sofa she'd warmed through. Her TR7 Owners' Club mug permeated soothing heat as she cupped it in her hands and sipped the strong tea. Yes, it had definitely been a successful day and she felt a little tingle of excitement as she imagined Clive's voice. She'd tell him about her pot stand and successful debt collecting. He could probably do with some distraction from dental records and DNA testing. She rummaged in her bag for her mobile and pressed automatic dial.

'Come on, Clive. Answer,' she whispered, as she listened to the ring tone repeat and repeat. Finally a recorded voice cut in.

'Please leave a message after the tone. Be-e-e-p.'

'Damn,' she muttered and rang off without saying another word.

She checked her watch. Six thirty – he should be in his car and on the way home by now, but if he was driving he'd use his wireless hands free system. So why wasn't he answering? The reason was obvious, but she didn't want to think about it. He'd still be working.

While she pottered in the kitchen, beating eggs, cutting ham into rough chunks, slicing and frying mushrooms in a knob of butter with splashes of Chablis, voices from the television floated through from her living room. She wasn't really listening, but it made the cottage feel companionable and more alive. After all, she was meant to be celebrating.

'And now for the news in your region....' A signature tune sounded around her kitchen, heralding the Eastern Region's News. The music summoned up images of a logo and pictures moving around the TV screen as the camera panned in on the local news desk. She didn't need to see the screen to know the sequence.

The newscaster's tones drifted past. '... *police investigating the recent Needham Market murders, report new developments....*'

'What?'

Without thinking, she hurried to the television, the frying pan still in her hand. The bouquet of wine and mushrooms coiled up to her nose as she stood and gaped. The screen filled with a familiar head and shoulders.

'Clive?'

She nearly dropped the pan.

'*The Suffolk Police will be working closely with the Metropolitan Police.*' Clive spoke straight to camera, his voice calm, his tone matter-of-fact.

'*We will be tracing back through the records for the children's home in Laureldene Gardens, Southeast London and the children's home here in Hemley, Suffolk. We are looking for anything that might link the two homes and the two victims. We are asking anyone who has worked or been a resident in either of these children's homes to come forward if they have anything to report. There is a dedicated phone line now open. A picture of both of the murder victims will be shown on your screen and on our website. The number is....*'

She stopped listening and just gawped at the screen, hardly believing her eyes. Clive looked larger than life, and the shades were wrong. His skin was more tanned and his hair a little redder than when she'd kissed him goodbye that morning. It was definitely Clive. The voice was right but seeing him like this felt weird.

She lingered a few moments, hoping he'd appear on the screen again, but the newscaster was already onto the next item. So what was the new development in that announcement, she wondered. Everything Clive had said, the police must have known almost as soon as they'd identified the bodies. Was it a cynical manipulation of the public to maximise a response for the phone line? Or were the police just desperate because, to use their own term, there'd been no new developments?

The omelette could wait, she decided as she parked the frying pan back in the kitchen. The celebratory glass of wine was no longer optional, it was mandatory, but first she needed to try phoning him again. Buoyed with excitement she grabbed her mobile from the coffee table and pressed Clive's automatic dial number.

'Clive,' she half squealed as he answered on the second ring tone.

'Hi. Is everything all right?'

'Yes, of course. I've just seen you on TV. You were brilliant. Why didn't you tell me you'd be on?' Her words came in a rush. 'It was complete luck I saw you, and if I'd known I'd have recorded it. But hey, well done, you.'

'Thanks. And sorry. I didn't think you'd be interested. It was recorded a couple of hours ago and it's been mad here since. I've only just had time to grab a coffee. These Met guys—'

'So what are the new developments? Or are you just playing the public and managing the press?'

'Well, only what we've known for a couple of days, but we can't make a press announcement saying, "We've no records for the Hemley Home," can we? The fact it closed in 2005 and none of their records were put on the national database doesn't sound very good, does it? The press would have a field day.'

'But—'

'You see, most of their records were paper based, Chrissie. They would have dated back over fifty years. And to make things worse, it seems all the old ledgers and files are missing, probably destroyed when the home closed. And God knows what happened to the one computer they had. I don't think anyone knew where to store it or what to do with the stuff, and for all we know, Eric Haigh may have wanted everything destroyed. You know, a bit of self-interest.'

'Ah....'

'As you can imagine, the Met have been pretty scathing about it.'

'But that's nothing to do with you. It's not your fault.' She listened to office sounds as distant voices murmured and phones rang.

'At least there's something we've come up with from good old interview technique.'

'Well go on.'

'I questioned our witness again. You remember, the nervous man who works on the ferries and was visiting his mother in Needham Market? Well it seems he spent a few months in a children's home.'

'What, working?'

'No. He went in with his brothers and sisters. His mother had what sounds like a post natal depression and all the kids went in for a couple of months. Somewhere in Chelmsford. It was the nearest place that could take them at the time without having to split them up.'

'So...?'

'The Met think the poor guy must be implicated. They're desperate to find a link between him and the two victims. As you can imagine, they're trawling every database they can find.'

'And there isn't one for Hemley.'

'Exactly.'

'It's a bit of a coincidence though, isn't it? I mean, all of them connected by children's homes, don't you think, Clive?'

'Yes, but his two month stay was over fifty years ago.'

'Still a coincidence.'

'But he was only about two years old at the time, Chrissie. You're starting to sound like the Met boys.'

'Hmm....'

'But if you're right and it somehow turned him into a murderer, why come forwards as a witness? It's a bit of a risk drawing attention to yourself. People like that only seek the spotlight to get some kind of weird kick out of it. You know, being close to the investigation, fooling the police.'

'And you don't think he's the type?'

'I'm not a psychologist, but no. He's too nervy. It's usually a confident manipulative psychopath who likes to do that kind of thing. And also, he didn't strike me as physically strong enough. It must have taken a bit of muscle to kill and bury Eric Haigh like that. And another thing, the figure of the bathing boy? Our witness can't swim.'

'And fifty years is a long time to wait to take your revenge.'

'Exactly. And revenge for what?'

She listened to more crackles and voices rippling in the distance. 'Hi, are you still there? Clive?'

'Just a moment.... Look, Chrissie, I can't talk any longer.'

'I know. I'm holding you up.'

'See you later. Don't wait up. Bye.' The phone went dead.

For a moment she was carried with the buzz of the investigation and seeing Clive on TV. What a day, she thought as hunger drew her back into the kitchen. She sipped her wine and stirred the omelette mixture again, but she couldn't escape the twinge of disappointment to be alone and not part of the excitement.

It was only later as she ate her meal that she realised she would have liked to have told Clive about her pot stand, debt collecting triumphs and the invitation to a tour of Kell's winery.

CHAPTER 15

Nick stood in the van and heaved the first stable door forwards, half sliding, part lifting it down to Dave.

'OK, I've got this end. Easy now,' Dave said, grasping the bottom and stepping backwards.

Making the doors had been pretty straightforward and at least it had allowed Nick to work off site and back in the Willows workshop. He glanced across the courtyard before resting the top edge of the door on the van floor. He jumped down from the back of the van and took its weight. Together they carried it over to the stable.

This time Nick didn't bother to look around for Skylar. He guessed it was too early for her, and anyway, he was starting to feel indifferent. The couple of days spent working on the doors had restored his equilibrium and thickened his skin. Even the thought of working with Graham had lost some of its irritation.

'They've almost completed in here,' he said as he stepped onto the finishing layer of concrete, his voice resonant in the empty shell of the building.

'And they've made a good job of completing the roof,' Dave added.

'Yeah, funny how when you're here you don't see beyond the piles of rubble and chaos.'

'Hmm, it's like people. No one looks so good in socks and boxers.'

'Yeah, the plastering makes quite a difference. So we hang the stable doors at each end and the two middle doorways will be glass? Long full-length windows. Is that right Dave?' He didn't want to admit it, but Graham hadn't done such a bad job after all.

'Yes, it saves Graham knocking windows in anywhere else.'

'Yeah, and it looks kind of modern.' Nick liked innovative open plan styles, long clean lines and the feeling of space. Traditional in Suffolk usually meant beams and low ceilings, and for him, at six foot three, a graze on the head. He was about to say something about Graham's enthusiasm with a sledgehammer and reckless smashing down of walls, but Dave spoke first.

'You seem calmer, more relaxed. Did you think about what I said the other day?' he asked as they carried the second stable door from the van.

'Yeah, yeah. I've got my head round it now. And a mate said I should swim to get it out of my system. Shit, as if I had the energy after work.'

'What? The indoor pool in Stowmarket?'

'I don't know. Oh yes, I remember now. He mentioned Alton water and the Great East Swim.'

'I've heard of that,' Dave said as they set the second door down.

Tyres scrunched across the courtyard as Graham's pickup swept in.

'I'll get the trestles and workbench out of the van. You put the locks and the handles in, didn't you?' Nick asked, genuinely unruffled by Graham's arrival.

He found the rustic iron hinges, locks and the rest of the door furniture and carried the tool box and portable drill over to the workbench, ignoring Graham who stood talking to Dave. Why waste time on him?

'How's lover boy this morning?' Graham called through a leer.

'Not many more days' work and I reckon you'll be finished here,' Nick answered, refusing to rise to the jibe. He caught Dave's eye and smiled.

'Don't you worry, I'll be here a bit longer. There's some work for Mr Core in one of his turkey sheds, and then I've got some alterations to do at the winery. So I reckon I'll have time to check out your spacey girlfriend.'

'I've told you, she's not my girlfriend.'

'You have to remember, Nick's a rock god now. Crazy fans are an occupational hazard,' Dave said mildly.

'Well, then we can all bask in the spin off,' Graham sneered.

'I'd have thought she's a bit young for you, Graham.'

'You haven't seen me canoeing in a wetsuit. I'm told I look sexy.'

'Oh for God's sake, spare us.'

'You should try it Dave. Knock ten years off you,' Graham smirked.

'Which door do you want to hang first?' Nick cut in, dismissing images of middle-aged men in black neoprene.

'We might as well start with this one here. Come on, let's stand it in the door frame and check it's a good fit. Graham, haven't you and your men got some work to do?'

'Yeah, yeah. Guttering to put up this morning.'

The next few hours seemed to flash by as Nick worked with Dave, fitting rustic hinges and chiselling and drilling out recesses in the frame and door for the catches and locks. He was hardly aware of Graham up on the ladder, didn't notice any wolf whistling, and couldn't have cared less if Skylar had stood and watched, and then slipped away again.

'I think we'll take an early lunch break,' Dave said, standing back to admire their work.

The van seemed the warmest place and they sat with thermoses of hot tea and munched through doorstep sized sandwiches while watching Graham's man drill fixings for the guttering down pipe.

'There's nothing like sitting and eating while others work,' Dave murmured between mouthfuls.

'I can't see Graham.'

'He's probably round the back of the stables.'

Nick gazed beyond the stables. The ground was turkey rough and this time as he looked, he noticed the meshed fencing enclosing the area and linking to the side of the nearest turkey shed. The land sloped gently upwards following the contours of the Rattlesden valley, now washed in the cold metallic light of the short January days.

A sudden shriek shattered their peace.

'Oh God,' Dave breathed and flung open the driver's door. The drilling stopped.

'What the…?'

Nick hurried after Dave, crossing the courtyard in bounding strides. 'Is he all right? What's happened?'

'Hey, what y'all runnin' here for?' the workman shouted, his leathery skin creased in surprise.

'Someone screamed. We thought you–'

Squealing, this time muffled, seeped around the building.

'Come on, someone's been hurt.' Dave led the way.

'Sounds like… do turkeys make that kind of noise?' Nick called as he dashed after him. Images of birds with heads in cones and dripping blood flashed through his mind. He remembered Mr Core's description of old style turkey killing. That kind of death wasn't going to be silent.

'Hey, watch out,' he yelled as he smacked into Dave's back. Dazed by the collision, he tried to catch his balance.

'What the hell are you doing?' Dave bellowed.

'You stopped dead.'

'No not you. I meant Graham.'

Nick caught the flurry of heavy-weave material. For a moment he thought it was an old tarpaulin, but then he glimpsed violet coloured leggings jabbing and kicking. A girl's legs.

'Isn't that...?' He didn't need to ask. The tangles of honey blonde hair with chaotic platinum streaks told him.

'Ouch, you little bitch,' Graham wheezed.

'Hey, leave her alone, you pervert.' Surprise, shock, anger filled his head. He didn't have time to pause and think. Hot blood drove everything aside as he reacted. 'You shit-bag,' he yelled and shouldered Dave out of his way. He pounced forward, grabbed Graham and swung a punch. Smack! His fist connected with Graham's chin.

The heavy-weave material morphed into a winter poncho. The stabbing jabbing legs took flight as Graham's grip failed. He reeled backwards, swung by the force of Nick's punch, Skylar no longer a prop.

'Are you all right?' Dave called. 'You're the girl always hanging around here, aren't you? Do you need help? Did he attack you?'

'I didn't touch her. She's a crazy bitch,' Graham snarled, rubbing his chin with the back of his hand.

'That isn't how it looked from here,' Dave said quietly.

'I'm telling you. She came on to me.'

'Stop talking shit. I had to half knock you out before you let her go.' Nick spat the words.

'Do you want us to call the police or anyone for you?' Dave asked, softening his voice as he watched the girl.

'The police? Now you're crazy. Can't you see she's dangerous? You can't believe a word she says. She'll probably say we all attacked her.' Graham licked his lips.

For a moment they stood in silence, Nick wondering how the hell this was going to end, and Skylar wide eyed and pale, drawing the rough woven fabric closer.

'Not the police. Don't call the police,' she whispered.

Before Nick could think what to say, she turned and ran, her brown and black poncho flapping like wings.

'Hey stop! Wait a moment.'

She didn't look back, gaining speed as she circled the wire mesh fencing and headed in the direction of the vineyard.

'There's your proof. I couldn't have hurt her if she's running like that.'

'You bloody stupid Neanderthal, Graham. What were you thinking? Can't you control your–'

'That's enough,' Dave cut in. 'She's the same girl who took your phone, isn't she, Nick?'

'Yeah? What difference does that make?'

'None. Just getting it straight in my head.'

'Took your phone?' Graham sneered. 'See, I was right. That's what she was after. My phone. Her hands were everywhere. If I hadn't grabbed her wrists–'

'I don't believe you, you lying two-faced rat. I should have broken your jaw while I had the chance.'

'What? You'd sooner believe a crazy thieving girl like her, than me?'

'Yeah, when you put it like that. Yeah, I would.'

'Steady, Nick. The girl's gone. She ran away, remember? Mentioning the police seemed to decide it for her, so perhaps she was up to her old tricks,' Dave said quietly.

'And maybe she was just a scared kid,' Nick shouted.

He'd recognised the squealing as pure animal. She'd been terrified, all right. He was pretty sure you could fake a scream; actresses did it all the time, but that squeal was something else. It came from the soul. It was the sound of the slaughterhouse, dripping in primeval fear.

Anger smouldered, as he glared at Graham. The bloke was an insensitive, lecherous bully. Of course the pervert had tried to force his luck with her. If it hadn't been for the squeal, he wouldn't have been so sure.

'That's enough,' Dave commanded, interrupting his thoughts.

'What?'

'That's enough, Nick. You've already punched Graham once. We're not in the business of rough justice. Come on.' Dave took his arm. 'We may have to work on the same site, but we don't have to keep his company.'

'Dead right we don't.'

By the time they'd reached the van, Nick had started to cool down. The way he saw it, the sooner they finished the stable doors, the sooner they could leave. There wasn't much more to do, only a final lick of preservative sealant paint for the wood. So by unspoken agreement, they gulped their tea, wolfed their sandwiches, and a couple of hours later they were packing the van ready to go, their work for Mr Core completed.

Dave didn't seem to want to talk on the drive back to the Willows workshop. He appeared to be absorbed, miles away in his own thoughts.

'Don't speak about this to anyone,' Dave said, as he finally drew into the secure parking and switched off the engine.

'Why not? Shouldn't we tell everyone? Let the world know what a complete bastard Graham is?'

'I don't think so. You saw how quick he was to twist everything - she was stealing his phone, she came on to him, we, that'll be you and me, were attacking her. If we don't talk, I bet he won't and then he can't have the opportunity to polish and practise his lies.'

'And if she goes to the police?'

'He won't be expecting her to. So if the police suddenly appear on his doorstep and take him in for questioning, there'll be holes in his story and he won't know what we're likely to say because we'll have kept our mouths closed.'

'So what do you think really happened, Dave?'

'I don't know. The girl's got history.'

•

Nick sat in the Nags Head and massaged his knuckles. Had it really been almost seven hours ago that he'd smashed his fist into Graham's face? If his hand felt like this, then he hoped to God, Graham's chin was hurting like hell.

'Ouch,' he breathed, as he gripped the pint glass. He sipped his beer, savouring the golden, almost sweet liquid, laden with citrus notes, hops and then a dry finish.

'Let me guess. You're drinking Land Girl,' Chrissie said as she set her ginger beer down on the small table in front of him.

'Hmm,' he murmured, over the rim of his glass.

'So how's your day been?'

'Eventful. Yeah, eventful.'

'You're starting to sound like Matt. Why use several words when you can get away with only using one?' She undid her duffle coat and settled onto the pine chair.

The usual mix of early Friday drinkers mingled in the bar. Men still in work clothes hungrily gulped a pint or two while regulars, dressed for the evening ahead, sipped early chasers. Give it another half hour, Nick reckoned, and the bar would have transformed. The jukebox would be belting out an electropop number and excited voices would charge the air.

'I'm surprised Matt's not here yet,' Chrissie said, glancing around the bar.

'He said he's got something to tell me. On Monday he had some mad idea I should take up swimming–'

'Then he's probably booked you into the Great East Swim. That'll be his news.'

'What?'

'He was muttering about it last time I saw him.'

He caught her grin. 'I don't believe you. You're having me on.'

'I got you going for a moment though. Hey, talk of the devil....'

'Over here,' Nick called and waved to catch Matt's attention.

It didn't take Matt long to be served at the bar and shamble across, dripping lager from his glass. 'Hi,' he murmured, and still standing, downed half his drink.

'Frag, I needed that.' He thumped his glass onto the small table, smacked his lips and wiped his hand across his mouth and beard. 'My hands are flammin' blocks of ice.' He half collapsed onto the bench seat.

'Try wearing some decent gloves when you're on that Piaggio of yours.'

'Yeah, black neoprene ones.' Nick couldn't resist pushing the dig home further. 'I can't imagine a sexier look for you on the scooter. And if your hands are still cold indoors, the neoprene-look would complement your Dark Net tee, especially if you're tapping away on your computer at the time.'

'Really?'

'No, Matt. Don't listen to him. Time your rides to get here for Happy Hour. A vodka'd put some fire in your hands. But... a Dark Net tee? Have you gone underground kinky or something?'

'Nah, but you remembered it, Nick. An' it made you pick up your ears just now, Chrissie. I reckon I'm on to somethin' with that tee.'

'Please no,' Nick groaned. 'Not that tee again.'

'Ah, but you're smilin'. I knew I was on to somethin'.'

'So what was so eventful about your day?' Chrissie cut in.

'Graham, but I don't want to talk about it.' Instinctively he rubbed his knuckles as he spoke. Damn, he thought. Chrissie just noticed my hand. He shot a warning glance and saw the next question die on her lips.

'I did a bit of tracin' on Graham,' Matt said between sips of lager, and seemingly unaware of Nick's bruised knuckles.

'And?' Nick prompted softly.

'He's got three businesses registered on the UK Companies House website. Graham Tollington Builder LTD; Groundsbuild LTD; and Build Ground LTD.' Matt parroted the company names as if reading from a list in his head. 'The last one, the Build Ground LTD one's been dissolved.'

'So why would he have several companies, one obviously named like his brand, and the others more obtuse and without his name in the title?' Chrissie seemed to direct the question at her ginger beer.

'I don't know, Chrissie. You were the accountant. You tell us?'

'Hmm, the word obfuscation comes to mind.'

'Obfus what?' Matt muttered.

'Obfuscation. Appearing quite open and logical but actually confusing things, muddying the water.'

'You mean like money launderin'?'

'Maybe, or obscuring connections between businesses, creating a complicated money trail and tricking the taxman or the clients.'

'He doesn't strike me as clever enough for that, Chrissie.'

'He doesn't have to be, Nick. He just needs a clever accountant.'

'Phishing flamewar,' Matt murmured.

Nick stood up. 'I'm buying this round. Same again, Chrissie? Matt?'

He hardly listened to their replies. Hearing about Graham had made him restless and moving seemed to help. Another pint of Land Girl was needed. If what Chrissie said was true, Graham wasn't a clever bastard, he was just a bastard with a sense of self-preservation.

He wove his way to the bar, carelessly bumping shoulders and nudging elbows, his mind still on Graham. Dave was right, the bastard was unlikely to say anything about the incident today, and if word got back to John Willows of how he'd punched Graham on site, then any offer of a permanent job for Nick with the firm would fly out the window.

'The same again. That'll be a pint of Land Girl, Carlsberg, and a ginger beer please,' he said, catching the barman's eye and setting the empty glasses on the bar counter.

No, he thought as he watched the pints being pulled, I'm not saying a word unless the police ask. I'll give them a statement if they want one, but I'm not going looking for trouble.

The jukebox burst into life and the funky rhythm of Jessie J's *Domino* cheerfully stomped and pulsated through his head. The fast disco-like beat lifted his mood. If only everything was that simple.

'Thanks,' he shouted above the music and slopped the ginger beer as he wedged the three glasses together in his hands.

'You look happier,' Chrissie said as she rescued her glass a few moments later.

'Yeah, reckon so.'

'Hey, how's Clive's case shapin', Chrissie?'

'Ah, now that's an on-going saga. He's working on it with the Metropolitan Police. They may have a suspect, but Clive's not convinced. That's all I know. I've hardly seen him to ask more. It seems to take up all his time. I expect he'll be working this weekend as well.'

'I know what you mean. Mais don't finish till eight this evenin'. I'm collectin' her from Peakcocks.'

They sipped their drinks as the rhythmic beats boomed from the jukebox.

'Mais likes *Domino*,' Matt murmured. 'Hey, that reminds me. I aint started tracing that Skylar bird.'

'Then don't, Matt. Just leave it.'

'What?'

'I mean it, Matt. Leave it. I don't think she's going to cause me any more problems.' He caught Chrissie's quizzical look.

'Seriously, I'm cool about it now.'

He held her gaze and then slowly turned to check Matt had got the message too. He felt calm. He hoped it was written across his face. Skylar no longer had the power to trigger any attraction, and the anxiety and embarrassment he used to suffer when she was mentioned had long since faded. He was neutral about her. He wanted it to show.

'Then it's cool with me, mate,' Matt said and grinned.

'Thanks.'

The evening passed happily enough, Matt leaving to collect Maisie and then Chrissie going an hour or so later. For once Nick felt in control of his emotions. A couple of attractive girls at the bar distracted him for a short while, but in the end he preferred the beer for company.

CHAPTER 16

'So why'd someone suggest wetsuit gloves for ridin' the Piaggio?' Maisie asked. She sat huddled next to Matt on a bench, and bit into her burger bun.

'Beats me.' He sank his teeth into his king-size double slider. Two burgers, cheese and mayonnaise packed between the halves of a soft bread bun. Heaven. A string of molten cheese stretched from his beard as he lowered the warm soft parcel in its paper wrap.

'Hey, look at you,' she giggled.

'Look at what?' Flavours exploded in his mouth as he chewed.

'You've got a cheesy streamer stuck to your beard. It's like letting off one of those party-poppers.'

'What, on me chin?' He waggled his tongue across his lip and caught the wisp of cheese.

'So why's it called a slider?'

'Cos it slips an' slides when you bite it.'

'Wicked. I wish the burger van came more often.'

'Yeah.' He shifted a little closer.

They chewed in silence, their warm breath misting in the cold early evening air. If only, he thought, but he knew he couldn't afford burgers more than twice a week. Thursdays and Saturdays. That's when the mobile burger van visited Stowmarket.

'So why the wetsuit gloves?' she asked, interrupting his thoughts.

'What? Oh yeah. Told Nick he'd look sexy in a wetsuit. The Great East Swim.' He took another bite and munched. 'Relax him,' he said through his mouthful.

'How's that goin' to relax him? The bloke next door, he's as old as me dad, nearly drowned. Came over all funny in the water. If it hadn't been for a canoeist... well, it could've ended badly for him.'

Around them, market traders dismantled their stalls. Shouts and clattering resonated as boxes and bags were thrown into vans parked on pedestrianised areas. The Thursday market was closing, but the fading light gave it a festive tone.

'A canoeist? At a swimmin' event? How's that then?'

'Yeah, see what you mean. Don't know. But you aint said why wetsuit gloves for ridin' the scooter.'

'Make me look sexy.'

'That's weird.'

When he'd said it like that to Maisie, Matt wasn't sure if he'd understood it either. Weird summed it up.

'So can you work flexibly?' she asked, breaking into his train of thought.

'What, in wetsuit gloves, Mais?'

'Don't be daft. Debt tracin'. See, it would make more sense if you worked when I'm workin'. Then we'd have time to do stuff. Like today.'

'Yeah, but you never know when you'll be workin', Mais.'

'So?'

She'd lost him. He slid an arm around her, and gave her a hug.

'Oi, careful! There's mayo all over that wrapper. It'll be on me next.'

He reached across and transferred the greasy wrappings to his free hand. A cold sliver of fried onion landed on her knee. 'Sorry, Mais. Sliders don't usually come with fried onion. They're extra.'

He hadn't told Maisie, mainly because he hadn't seen her since Sunday morning, but he'd already spent an extra couple of evenings working at Balcon & Mora that week. Something made him hold back now. There'd been a flood of work at the tracing agency, and the more he did, the more Damon assigned him. In fact Damon wanted him to help out tomorrow. Under Maisie's proposal, he'd have to check with her first before saying yes.

'I don't know,' he said, nuzzling into her neck and nibbling her ear.

'Ouch! Watch out. My ear aint a slider.'

'Sorry, Mais.'

•

Early Friday afternoon, Matt rode straight to Bury St Edmunds from the Academy. His laptop lay cocooned in his backpack. A secure memory stick would have probably served his purpose just as well, but it couldn't have shielded his spine from the freezing wind. It whipped across the flatlands from the east, insinuated its way through the vents in his field jacket, and reached icy tentacles between his helmet and neck.

By the time he threaded his way into a back alley behind the Buttermarket shopping area in Bury, the two-stroke engine coughed, wheezed and complained. The frequent journeys were becoming an ordeal. He reckoned his core temperature dropped half a degree with every ten scooter-miles. Much further and he'd need more than a mug of hot chocolate laced with a vodka shot to revive him.

That's what Damon had offered him last time he'd ridden over. Strong black coffee hadn't been up to the job.

'Frag,' he muttered as he pushed the Piaggio onto its parking stand, his limbs stiff with cold. 'I can't be doing with this. It's bloody freezin'.' He looked up at the old building stacked above. 'Hot air's meant to rise aint it?'

Still wearing his helmet, he tramped up the stairs. He hoped the first floor offices would be by convection, if nothing else, half a degree warmer than the ground floor. He couldn't afford to lose any more heat.

The stark Balcon & Mora waiting room felt even bleaker than on Wednesday afternoon. He rang the office door bell.

'Hi,' Damon said, flinging the door open. 'It is you, isn't it Matt? Shit, with the helmet on, I wasn't sure for a moment.'

'Thanks mate,' he said and pulled his helmet off.

'Do you know it only turned the first of February a couple of days ago, and already it's pressure, pressure, pressure?'

'Oh yeah?'

'It's wild. All that Christmas debt? A lot of punters didn't pay again last month, so now the chasing's really started with a vengeance.'

'Poor buggers,' Matt muttered and eased his backpack from his shoulders.

'Good for us though, hey? Remember that.'

'Yeah, as long as we get paid. Aint you got any heatin' in here? It's flammin' freezin'.'

'Kettle's in the corner, drinking chocolate's in the cupboard, vodka's in my filing cabinet. And you can make me a black coffee while you're about it. When you've logged on, I'll send over a file with the first batch of names.'

The poky corner with Matt's workstation looked arctic. He eyed up Damon's trestle desk table. 'OK then,' he muttered, and squatted. A slow ungainly movement.

'What are you doing?'

'Computers generate heat, don't they?' He laid his hands on the computer stack, cosily whirring where it sat in the trestle's supporting structure. He reckoned it was a damn sight safer than clasping the kettle.

Ten minutes later he sat with his legs safely wedged under his workstation table. He leaned back against his plastic stacker chair and cupped the mug of hot chocolate in his hands. The vodka gave an extra kick as he swallowed. He imagined the fire in his belly flowing in waves and rivulets through his arms and legs. Soon he'd feel it in his fingers and toes, if he was lucky.

'Come on, Matt. You've had enough time to warm up. There's a lot to get through.'

'Yeah, OK.' He knew the format by now. The names would be organised in alphabetical order along with last known addresses and phone numbers. Usually there was a date of birth but sometimes it was missing. If he had trouble finding the current contact details, Damon had said not to waste time but to move on to the next name on the list.

'Still leave the difficult ones to you? That right Damon?'

'Yes, when we're not so busy I'll teach you some new tricks.'

They worked in silence, nothing interrupting the rhythmic patter from their keystrokes or the white noise from the computer fans in the background. Around them the light faded as the evening closed in.

'Coffee?' Damon asked when finally he stretched back in his office chair, the soft screen light making pale contours of his face.

'I could murder an 'ot chocolate, if you're makin'.'

'OK, where's your dirty mug? I'm not washing up.' He stood quickly and hurried across the room, flicking on the main light switch as he headed for the kettle.

'Damon, can I ask you somethin'?'

'What d'you want to know?'

'I've got a name, and the name's linked to three businesses. It's nothing to do with your tracin' list, by the way. How... how'd I find out more about the bloke? Or rather, how'd you go about findin' out more about the bloke?' Matt watched Damon pause for a moment before spooning coffee into a mug.

'Why are you asking?'

'I'm not planning anythin' illegal. Honest. I've a mate who's been messed about by the guy. I said if sniffing around'd help my mate, then I'd do it.'

'So what are you expecting to find?'

'I don't know, but I reckoned if my mate thought I was nosin' around, maybe it'd make him feel less stressed out. And then I figured it'd be good practice – make me a better tracer.'

'You're also a nosy bugger, Matt. Don't get me wrong. That's good in this job.'

'Thanks mate.'

'OK, then. Tell me all you know about this bloke.'

Matt told Damon what he had so far. A name, Graham Tollington, and the names of the three businesses he'd found on the Companies House registered business site, two current and one past.

'Do you have his email address, his websites? His contact details, where he lives? Anything personal on him?' Damon shot the questions.

'I-I... I aint really got goin' on him yet. P-personal stuff? Like he looks sexy in a wetsuit?' Matt stammered under the quick fire.

'So he's a surfer? Or scuba diver?' Damon handed over a mug of steaming drinking chocolate.

'Thanks. I-I... I think Nick mentioned canoes. Yeah, and he's a right pain if there's a bird around to watch.'

They sat for a moment sipping their hot drinks.

'This guy could be interesting. I think you'd need to hack into his email account, Matt.'

'What? Hack into.... Why's he sound interesting?'

'Well, he's a builder, but only the name of one of his businesses suggests land, or rather ground. Groundsbuild. The one that's defunct, Build Ground, was probably similar, judging by what it was called. I suspect he's doing land deals. Is he a builder repairer, or does he build new houses?'

'He's small scale, I guess. Alterations, renovations, extensions. That kinda thing.'

'Well, maybe he also speculates on plots of land, like a middleman, finding land and selling it on to a bigger contractor?'

'Yeah, Chrissie said somethin' on those lines. Obfuscation she called it.'

'There you are then.'

'But why an' how'd I hack into his emails?'

'Because you might find something interesting on him. Send him an email, you know, something related to canoeing. Add a link to a spoof site where he has to register his details, either to buy something or to take part in a canoeing event.'

'Cool.'

'That means creating a spoof site, of course. You could email him a couple of days later and ask him to verify his details, including his password, before sending out whatever he ordered. If he's stupid he may give you his password. Or you could implant a virus if he clicks on the link. Something like a keylogger virus.'

'Epibotics!'

'What?'

'Epic robotics. That's awesome. D'you have a keylogging programme?'

'Of course, Matt. It's installed on the computer you're using.'

'Spammin' hell.'

'Don't tell me you hadn't guessed.'

'Yeah, I s'pose I'd figured it out.'

He'd suspected, but he hadn't been sure. He nudged his backpack with his foot and felt the solid shape of his laptop through the canvas. Damon would know if he downloaded any files, apps or programme onto his own system. It was a big risk to take without asking. He needed to impress Damon first.

'But this Graham bloke, see I'd root around more before takin' the trouble of plantin' a keylogger or makin' a spoof website. I'd try and find out which clubs provide canoeists to marshal swimmers in the Great East Swim. I reckon his canoeing club site would be easy to hack for information.'

'No doubt. But I bet you'd get his address and phone number, just by visiting his Graham Tollington Builder LTD website, and with no effort required. It'd be part of his marketing contact details.'

'Yeah, but that don't give me any info about past convictions or why he closed down one of his registered businesses.'

'No, but once you've got his password you can check through his old mail. You'll find emails from his accountant, solicitor, customers - all sorts of things.'

'But I could look up on local newspaper sites—'

'You haven't built a website before. That's what this is about. Right, Matt?'

'No it aint.' But it was.

It felt as if Damon had burst his balloon.

He downed the dregs of hot chocolate; the sweet, comforting flavours filling his mouth. Memories of a teasing older brother surged through his mind. Never expose a weakness, he reminded himself. Tom had always known how to humiliate. He'd twist the mocking knife and draw the last drop of blood with a final thrusting taunt. It was his signature. Matt didn't want to visit that place. The past was the past and Tom had long since left home. The position of bully might be vacant, but Matt wasn't looking for a candidate to fill it.

He killed further discussion by turning to his computer screen.

'I'm sending you another batch of names. Now,' Damon said.

The next couple of hours passed without any chat. Matt worked through his list of names, hardly noticing the time pass as he concentrated on his task.

'Are you done?' Damon asked, breaking the silence.

'Yeah.'

'You're getting faster. Look, I'm not sure how much you've done with websites, but next session, when we have our coffee–'

'Chocolate an' vodka.'

'Yes, I'll start taking you through how I like to build a website. OK?'

'OK then. Cool.' A pro teaching him to build a website? Awesome. He bit back his excitement. If he wasn't careful he'd expose too much of himself. Maisie had taught him street cred mattered. Then he remembered.

'Mais! I said I'd meet her after work. Stowmarket. Frag.'

'Better split, then.'

'I aint told her I was workin' tonight. She'll kill me.'

He grabbed his backpack, knocked over his empty mug and rammed on his helmet.

'Frag,' he muttered as he loped out of the office and thundered down the stairs. He'd told himself Maisie didn't need to know his every move. He reckoned that could have been a mistake.

CHAPTER 17

'Wow,' Chrissie murmured, her mind still filled with the greens, reds and gold of the renovated auditorium.

'That was amazing,' she called back to Clive, who was following somewhere close behind in the slow mass exodus.

They threaded their way through the crush in the foyer, and out into the street. The early evening air shocked after the warmth of the theatre. She turned, almost bumping into him as he jostled alongside.

'There you are. Thanks for getting, the tickets,' she said, linking her arm in his.

'Well as I said, they were freebies. I saw it was called Top Girls and–'

'Thought of me?'

'Something like that, although I wouldn't describe you as a girl from the eighties. Shame it was a matinee, though. Evening performances are more–'

'Atmospheric?'

'It makes a difference if it's dark when you come out of the theatre. Mind you it's bloody cold and dark now.' He drew her closer as they walked.

'I swear we've just stepped back into the last ice age.' She paused, almost pulling him sideways to gaze at the Theatre Royal, its Regency arches gracing the old front.

'That's a bit harsh, Chrissie. I'd have said it was more like an experience of theatre-going in pre-Victorian Britain.'

'Oh shut up. I bet you got that line straight from the programme.'

She knew he was trying to make up for the last ten days. She'd hardly seen him, and when they'd spoken, he'd been distracted and irritable. If they'd gone to the evening performance she suspected he'd have fallen asleep the moment the house lights dimmed. At least this way they could enjoy a meal. No need to bolt it down, one eye on the clock so as to be sure they'd make it to their seats on time.

'So where do you fancy eating?' she asked.

Around them Bury St Edmunds cranked up its rhythm from cold February market day to a Saturday night tempo. They strode on, enjoying the freedom to move and work their legs, and headed for an Indian restaurant tucked off Westgate Street.

While Chrissie studied the menu, Clive ordered poppadoms and a couple of lagers.

'I'm going to choose something fiery. That'll warm me up. I reckon plenty of rice and a cucumber raita, washed down with a lager, should protect me. What about you?' she said, watching Clive run his finger down the closely printed pages.

'God, I've had it up to here with looking through lists,' he muttered, and lightly taped his forehead in a loose salute.

She guessed he was looking for lamb rogan josh.

'It's more or less all we've done for the last couple of weeks, hoping a name crops up more than once somewhere,' he murmured.

'I thought you used computers for that sort of thing.'

'Police constables, you mean. Bloody computers – half the databases are incomplete, haven't been loaded onto the system, or are incompatible with our search programmes. It's a shambles. Remember, we're looking back over more than twenty to thirty years, and in different counties.'

'But you must have made some progress. It can't all be hopeless.'

'You might not call it progress, but the Met can't find any record of the kids from the Limesgrove Children's Home ever having swimming lessons in Thamesmead. No swimming galas, diving competitions, or lifesaving training. Certainly no trophies presented. Nothing, remotely water related.'

'But there must've been a swimming pool nearby. Or one attached to schools they attended?'

'Apparently not around Laureldene Gardens.'

'But Thamesmead suggests the Thames. What about sailing, or canoeing?'

'Not that section of Thames. Much too busy and dangerous.'

Chrissie thought for a moment. 'The bathing boy figure was found with Eric Haigh's body, wasn't it? He ran the children's home on the Deben. That'll be the home with the swimming connection.'

'Yes, and that's the one that's been demolished.'

'But it's the one on your patch, or would have been if it was still standing. At least you can nose around without the Met guys interfering.'

'Well there's that I suppose. Ah, the waiter's coming over.'

While the waiter took their order, Chrissie sipped her lager. It felt cold in her mouth, slicing down through her chest as she swallowed. Great with fiery chilli, she thought, but hardly the best choice to thaw a glacial evening. It'll sharpen my mind, she decided. There wouldn't be enough warmth to waste on frivolous thoughts.

'Do people actually swim for pleasure in the Deben?' she asked as the waiter disappeared into the kitchens.

'Oh yes. It's called wild swimming. A kind of endurance swim up or down the river with the tide. And as long as you don't get caught in the currents at the river mouth, you live to tell the tale.'

'But would kids, or rather kids in a children's home with no wet suits, do wild swimming? I'd guess sailing and canoeing, but wild swimming?'

'I don't know, but you can't assume they didn't have wetsuits. We've been looking back through old newspaper records to see if there's anything from before 2005 when the home closed. Local community newsletters, millennium celebration reports - anything which might have run a story, reported winners in a competition, accidents, drownings… anything.'

'There must be something.'

'I'm afraid not. No bloody records. It's as if Eric Haigh wiped all traces off the face of the Earth.'

'So what he knew died with him.'

'Most of it.' He sounded weary. 'But this evening isn't about my case. Have you heard back from Snape Maltings yet?'

'The Antiques & Fine Arts Fair? I phoned to check they'd got my entry form. It seems the photo of our French pot on the wooden stand I made, is causing quite a stir.'

'Really? Good for you.'

The smell of onions, peppers, turmeric and cumin overwhelmed her senses as the waiter arrived pushing a trolley laden with plate warmers, bubbling curries, saffron rice and naans. Mouth-watering hints of coriander and mint distracted her. The pot and entry form were elbowed into oblivion as pangs of hunger took over.

'I've missed hearing about your case,' she said as she spooned rice onto her plate. 'And I've missed you as well, of course,' she added as an afterthought.

'Hmm... this usually means you're about to come up with something deep and meaningful.'

'Not really. I just wondered what you'd found on their emails, phone calls, and the stuff on their computers.'

'Eric Haigh was seventy-two when he died. Emails and online banking had passed him by. It seems he'd recently bought a laptop and discovered how to download images from a paedo site.'

'What? Are you serious?'

'Afraid so. The broken bathing boy figure was a clear message, and taken in the context of those computer images....'

'Oh no, was he a chat room cruiser?'

'I don't think he had the computer skills, even if he had the inclination.'

They ate in silence for a few minutes, Chrissie reeling from Clive's revelation.

'Did he buy wine on line?' she finally asked.

'Nothing to suggest it. It was the other victim, Victor Pack who'd been seen in a wine delivery van. And before you ask, he was sixty-three and a completely different kettle of fish. His computer held a programme to get onto the dark net. Whatever images he was into must've been stored somewhere on a cloud, not on his hard drive. And he'll have paid with bitcoins.'

'That's sick. Those poor kids. It puts a completely different slant on the killings. It sounds as if those two had it coming to them.'

'That doesn't make kangaroo courts and rough justice right though, does it Chrissie? How's your jalfrezi?'

'Hot.' She sipped her lager. 'Are abuse victims being put off from coming forwards to give evidence, in case they become murder suspects? I mean, it might make you think twice. Take your poor witness. Didn't he become a suspect simply because he'd spent a couple of weeks in a children's home?'

'That's the Met for you. But every call is being followed up, and to be honest, they're all related to Victor. Nothing linked to Eric, so far.

'So what was this Eric chap like? I mean, his home in Woodbridge? There must've been something.'

'Apart from several months' post on his mat? He was a loner. We know far more about Victor. For instance, we know he took the train from London and got off at Stowmarket. There's CCTV footage showing him getting off the train.'

'Was he wearing the tartan anorak?' Chrissie asked, imagining how he'd have cut quite a dash just before Christmas.

'No, not on the footage. But he had a carrier bag with him. Why?'

'But....' An idea crystallised. 'If he wasn't seen wearing it on the CCTV, was it like the bathing boy figure? You know, a message. Something only significant to both Victor and the killer.'

Clive didn't answer. She watched him tear off a piece of naan and mop it through the rogan josh. She knew he was miles away, hardly aware of the rich spicy flavours hitting his palate. He'd be thinking about what she'd just said.

'The Met boys reckon he must've been carrying it in the bag,' he murmured, but she sensed the eureka moment.

Conversation died. They concentrated on eating; Chrissie deep in her own thoughts as she digested what Clive had told her. Lowlife came in degrees, she decided, but this was like dredging a sewer.

'Well that was delicious. I'll burst if I eat another mouthful,' Clive said, laying his fork on his plate and leaning back in his chair.

She read his face. It was obvious he didn't want to talk about work anymore, and if she was honest, she'd heard enough disturbing revelations for one evening.

They skipped coffee, settled the bill and made their way out into the freezing night. She was glad Clive would be driving. It meant her thoughts could go off on tangents, no need to rein them in and focus on the road.

•

'Mrs Jax, this call's for you,' Ron said, thrusting the handset towards her.

'For me?' she was surprised. She couldn't remember anyone ringing the workshop number and specifically asking for her before.

'Don't look so worried. It's the Antiques & Fine Arts Fair people. Your name was the contact on the booking form. Best if you deal with it.'

She put down the rebate plane, wiped her hands on her jeans and took the handset.

'Hello. Chrissie Jax speaking. How can I help you?'

'Good morning, Mrs Jax. You sent a photo with your entry for the summer Antiques & Fine Arts Fair at Snape Maltings. It was of a rustic ceramic pot sitting on an Arts & Craft styled plant stand, wasn't it?' The voice sounded business-like, confident.

'Yes.'

'Well it's caught our attention and we think it'll generate lots of interest in the fair.'

'Well thank you.' She tried to keep the breathiness out of her voice. Sound professional, she told herself. In a few months she'd be a partner in Ron's business.

'We don't usually do this, but the organisers like the photo so much they want to see how it'd look on the front cover of the catalogue.'

'Really?' She glowed.

'Well, the idea of it. The quality needed for the catalogue cover means they'll use their own photographer. They also want to try some slightly different angles on the shot. And with more focus on the pot.'

'More focus on the pot?'

'Yes, so would it be alright for the photographer to call your workshop and arrange a time to do that?'

'Of course, but you keep mentioning the pot. Is it the pot or the stand, or the whole composition that's catching people's interest?'

'The pot, of course.'

'Oh.' She swallowed her disappointment. 'Well I must say I love it as well. We found it in a Paris flea market. Are you sure–'

'It is yours? You will be bringing it to the fair, won't you?'

'Yes of course, but why all the fuss about the pot?'

'You must know.'

'Know what?'

'Well,' the voice dropped to a conspiratorial whisper, 'don't take it as gospel, but I heard the name Bernard Palissy being bandied around.'

'Bernard Palissy,' Chrissie echoed, no idea where this was leading.

'It has been authenticated, hasn't it?'

'Authenticated?' She was sinking in quicksand, each move sucking her in deeper.

'Good. That's all sorted then. The photographer is called Tina Wibble and she'll phone you on this number by the end of the week.'

'Right.'

'Goodbye, Mrs Jax, and thank you for agreeing to the photograph.'

It was still only Monday morning and already she felt any restorative effects of her weekend were stretched.

'What did they want?' Ron asked, as she handed the phone back. He wore a faded brushed cotton shirt, the checks the colour of autumn leaves.

'They want to take a photo of my pot on the plant stand, Mr Clegg.'

She knew she ought to be excited, but it was the pot, not her carpentry which was generating the interest. Without really thinking, she ran her fingers along the rebate she'd been cutting with the rebate plane. She was preparing a section of wood to repair the top of a Pembroke table. A country piece. The rebate would show when the table leaf was folded down. It needed to look hand tooled, not the work of a modern power router.

'You seem a bit lukewarm about the idea, Mrs Jax. Time for a mug of tea, do you think?'

'Hmm,' she sighed. Perhaps she could persuade Tina Wibble to take some publicity shots on the side. They might be good on some business cards, but Ron would need a bit of a dust down first.

'The photo'll be good for us, Mr Clegg. Good publicity and all that, but now it seems the pot may be more special than I thought. I'll need to get it valued and insured. If I'm not selling it, it's just an expense I hadn't expected.'

'And Bernard Palissy?'

'I don't know who he is.' She gazed up into the height of the barn for inspiration. Wooden beams straddled the span where structure and design joined hands to support the roof. She'd read something about architecture and early pottery, but she couldn't quite place the details.

'You're right. A mug of tea might help,' she said.

While Chrissie busied with the tea bags and kettle, Ron eased off his work stool, skirted past the thickness planer, and headed for the far corner of the workshop. He brushed his hand over an old clock casing balanced on a stack of Edwardian chairs and picked up the pot-like chalice where it sat on Chrissie's plant stand.

'You're causing a stir,' he said. 'Where did you come from? Whoever made you? I reckon they must have known how to work with silver or pewter.' He ran his finger over the coloured glazes. 'It's like inlay, or enamel on metal. I can feel the age,' he murmured, weighing it in his hands.

'Sounds like I need to find something out about Bernard Palissy. I'll Google him. I've already done a bit of research on the net, but that was after we got back from Paris. To be honest, at the time I didn't know whether to look up earthenware, stoneware or porcelain. I still don't really know.'

'Sounds like you need an expert.'

'Yes, I can see that now. But if it is valuable, do you reckon it's OK just to keep it in the workshop, and over there on the stand like that? Do you think it'll be safe?'

'It's up to you, Mrs Jax, but it's tucked away with the furniture waiting to be repaired. We can wrap it up in something, if you like.' He made his way back, carrying the pot as if it was eggshell.

'Do you know an expert, Mr Clegg?' She put his mug of tea on his workbench.

'Well there's Abe. He used to restore damaged china but I haven't seen him for a while. People used to bring him all sorts of pieces to identify and value. He's a mine of information. I suppose you'd call him an expert. He lives out at Felixstowe. I used to see him from time to time at the auctions houses, though not for a while. Yes, Abraham Pawcett. I've got his address somewhere.'

'Brilliant. Thank you. I knew you'd have a contact. I hope he's still around.'

She gazed at the pot and sipped her tea. Clive would be excited. And to think, he'd carried it in his backpack all the way from Paris, probably with less care than a bottle of wine. She hoped he'd have time to visit the expert with her, but she was doubtful. He still couldn't say when he'd be free to take a tour of Kell's winery. She was going to have to bite the bullet and accept he wouldn't be available, at least not while the killings in Needham Market were taking all his time. But it didn't mean she had to put everything on hold.

'If this is going to generate so much attention, we'd better get on and prepare many more pieces for the fair, Mrs Jax.'

'I know. The table I'm working on was probably made in Suffolk, or possibly Norfolk. There's nothing like a bit of local interest to get the punters in.'

'Exactly, but let's see how it looks when you've finished.'

By the time Chrissie swigged down the dregs of her tea, she felt more positive. After all, her plant stand would appear on the programme cover, and even if the focus was primarily the ceramic legend, her work would be right underneath it.

'You realise we're going to need a website and internet access for the business, Mr Clegg?'

'Hmm.' He slid from his stool. 'I'll go and look for Abe's address.'

Ping! Chrissie reached for her mobile.

'More about the celebrity pot?' Ron asked mildly.

'No. Just Nick texting to say he's off to Kell's place in Rattlesden.' She looked up from her mobile and hoped she hadn't shown her surprise. It would mean explaining to Ron about the crazy girl and the phone. The message merely said something about Graham breaking the contract and Willows taking it on instead. But why text me, she wondered.

She made a decision. Kell's name kept cropping up. It was a kind of destiny.

CHAPTER 18

Nick slipped his mobile back into his pocket. He knew Chrissie would get the irony of his text message. It wasn't that he was worried about going back to Rattlesden, it was more a case of being surprised. Unless the police wanted a witness statement, he'd assumed he'd never see or hear of Skylar again. The crazy fan should have been past history. But this altered things.

What was the betting he'd come across her at the vineyard? She'd pop up out of nowhere, like one of those hydraulic anti-parking bollards, but more troublesome. It was inevitable. After all, she worked for Strad Kell.

'So why do you suppose Graham isn't doing the work for Mr Kell?' Nick had asked when Alfred Walsh, the Willows foreman broke the news to them at the workshop, first thing that morning.

'All I know is Mr Kell rang the boss at the weekend. It seems Graham's left.'

'What do you mean he's left?'

'I was told he'd gone to do a job back at the turkey farm.'

'That'll be the atmosphere killing thing they're installing. Easter in a couple of months.' Nick shivered at the memory.

'But we're not builders. We can't complete building work for him,' Dave had reasoned.

'That's exactly what I said to the boss. He told me it was mostly joinery and Mr Kell had paid up front for the timber. It's already on site. He's got a plasterer, electrician and plumber lined up.'

'But what was the boss thinking, Alfred? Why'd he say yes?'

'I reckon Mr Kell's paying well. He also said Mr Kell knew you'd been working recently on a job at the turkey farm with Graham. Nothing but good reports. Reckoned you were used to how Graham worked, so you'd be able to pick up where he'd left off, so to speak. Apparently Mr Kell asked for you two by name.'

'What?'

'I expect Graham will've given him our names, Nick. But what about the job? Can you tell us more?'

'It's a wine tasting room. Mr Kell has faxed over the plans. I'm sorry, but you know what the boss is like – a bit of flattery, someone in trouble.... For all I know he could've recommended Graham in the first place.'

'Well unless it's a wooden construction, calling us in is a crazy idea, Mr Walsh.'

'Steady, Nick. I understand he's also asking us to kit out the inside. Bespoke wall racks for bottles, boxes and that kind of thing. The boss made him agree to it first.'

'Well I suppose it softens the blow a bit. But it's hardly what I'd expected to be told first thing Monday morning. Let's have a look at the plans, Alfred.' And that's how Dave had left it.

When Nick got his chance to scrutinise the plans he'd realised the wine tasting room had simple stud walls - wood frame and plasterboard finish. There would be a sink and drainage, space for a tasting and mixing table, and a large glass panel cut into one wall to give a view into the rest of the winery. It looked nice on paper.

'Maybe not so bad,' he'd thought as they loaded the van. He was curious; it was an unexpected turn of events. A sudden thought displaced any misgivings.

'Do you reckon it's anything like a brewery, Dave? I've done the Greene King tour in Bury St Edmunds. All those beery smells, it makes you desperate for a pint. Do you think we'll get to sample the wine?'

'I hadn't put you down as a wine drinker.'

'I'm not but....' That's when he'd decided to text Chrissie. She'd get the whole irony thing.

By the time he slipped his phone back into his pocket, Dave had started the van.

The journey out to Rattlesden was a whirlwind of hedgerows. Nick swayed and steadied himself, gripping the seat as Dave threw the van into corners and accelerated along straights. He couldn't help imagining the fermentation tanks in a winery, and then had to keep his mouth closed in case bile started to rise. When Dave swung the van off the road and finally lurched onto the rough tarmac and gravel track, Nick swallowed hard, determined to quell his motion sickness. He focused on a sighting of the vines streaking the gentle hillside ahead.

'We turn left here, I guess,' Dave said, and slowed slightly. They'd only ever followed the arrow pointing right to the turkey farm before.

'Awesome,' Nick murmured. 'So we're not working anywhere near Kell's converted barn down in Rattlesden.' He was relieved. That's where Chrissie had seen Skylar and also where he'd originally met her.

They drove along the border of the vineyard. He felt as if they'd driven past acres and acres of vines, but it was probably only a couple of hundred yards before a large notice stylishly announced the entrance to Kell's vineyard.

'Stupid bugger,' Dave hissed. 'Graham's left the wood outside. Not even under any sort of cover.'

'Maybe he left in a hurry?'

'Or he was pissed off with Mr Kell.'

They drew up and parked outside the front of a metal-clad industrial unit, the height and size of a warehouse. No windows and painted green. An arrow directed deliveries and collections to somewhere around the back of the unit. Smaller, older barns and storehouses clustered towards the rear of the site.

'Come on. Front entrance for us,' Dave said, getting out of the van.

'So it's going to be in here. I couldn't quite work out where,' Nick said under his breath as he trailed behind Dave. A faint scent of grapes pervaded the air. It was sharp, like stale wine spilled on a carpet, left to dry, and then layered with yeasty tones.

'I could get partial to this,' Nick murmured. He glanced up towards the roof and noticed the CCTV cameras. They were discrete, but watching.

Dave's finger barely touched the entrance bell before the door opened. A bald-headed man stood in the doorway and smiled a greeting.

'Hello, good morning.' The voice was warm, vibrant, welcoming.

'Mr Kell? We're from Willows. I'm Dave and this is Nick.'

'Yes, I guessed. You've got Willows written on the side of your van.' The man shot a glance at each of them in turn, and then looked more searchingly at Nick.

'I'm so grateful you were able to come at such short notice. But don't stand outside, follow me, please.' He turned and led the way.

Nick couldn't believe his eyes. He'd stepped into an echoing warehouse filled with shiny stainless steel. Along one wall three circular tanks stood like tall bloated pillars. He'd seen something similar on his tour of the brewery, but the tanks there had been on a much larger scale. At the far end, where he guessed the grapes were delivered, he saw stainless steel tables and bulky units with pipes.

'That's where we sort the grapes and remove the stalks before they go into the press,' Mr Kell said, pointing into the distance.

'And that thing with all those tubes and pipes?' Nick asked.

'Our wine filtration unit, or did you mean our bottling equipment over there?'

'And this must be the wine tasting room, or rather it's going to be, when it's finished,' Dave said, gazing at a partially built structure. The wood framework jutted towards them from the warehouse wall, and stretched upwards from the concrete floor. It was one storey high. Nick imagined it would look like a large neat box sitting inside an empty storeroom, when finished.

'And you're running a spur from the water supply over there?' Dave continued.

While Dave talked drainage and plug sockets with Mr Kell, Nick looked more closely at Graham's work. Large sheets of plasterboard had been nailed to the inside face of most of the framework, creating cavity walls when hardboard was nailed to the external surfaces. The side nearest the steel tanks was still unclad and had a large aperture in the framework. That'll be for the viewing window and door, he guessed. But something struck Nick as wrong. The construction area didn't look as if there'd been a downing of tools mid-job. He'd spent long enough on the same site as Graham to know how he left his handiwork mid-construction. This was too neat.

'Hardboard sheets on the outer surface of the ceiling, plasterboard on the inside?' Dave's voice resonated somewhere behind, blending with Mr Kell's richly sensuous tones. To Nick's ear, it sounded almost musical.

He turned and watched Dave and Mr Kell, one with thinning hair, the other with a scalp so smooth it reflected the light. It looked as if it had been burnished, like the stainless steel around them. Involuntarily he touched his own short-cropped hair for reassurance.

'Right, so first we get the ceiling and that wall clad, then it's ready for the plasterer,' Dave said, indicating the wall with the window aperture. 'We'll sketch out a design for the wine racks, counter and sink, and when the plaster is dry, we can get on with some real carpentry. We need to get the wood outside under cover, Mr Kell,' Dave added.

The next few hours flew. They cut sheets of plasterboard and hardboard to size with the circular saw they'd brought, and nailed them to the ceiling and wall framework.

'I must say it's looking better than I'd expected,' Dave murmured, when they stopped for a tea break.

'You're fast workers,' Mr Kell said in his rich voice, as he wandered over to check on their progress.

'Just the door and window frame to make and I reckon the plasterer can get on with it tomorrow,' Dave said by way of reply.

'I hope you don't mind me asking, Mr Kell, but why did Graham walk out?' Nick heard Dave catch his breath. He guessed he'd get a ticking off later for being nosy and embarrassing a customer. But why shouldn't he ask?

'We didn't see eye to eye over certain things.'

Nick nodded, as if he understood, but really it was the perfect brushoff. No information at all.

'There is one thing I wanted to ask you two. It's about a completely different matter, but mentioning Graham reminded me.'

'Oh yes?'

'You may not be aware of this, but I employ troubled young people. It's a scheme linked with the local authority to try and get sixteen to eighteen year-olds back into society. You know – able to hold down a job, get an employment record, that kind of thing.'

'Very commendable,' Dave murmured.

'Very,' Nick echoed and sipped his tea. He had a bad feeling he knew where this might be leading. He decided to leave the talking to Dave.

'I think you've both met Skylar.'

'Do you mean the girl who kept turning up at the turkey farm while we were working on the stable?' Dave asked without missing a beat.

'Yes, she probably kept visiting the place. She said Graham attacked her,' he let his voice drift, 'and you both saved her.'

'Something like that. I'm guessing you've asked Graham about it?'

'Yes. He said she'd stolen his phone and he was trying to get it back. You were there. So who do I believe? Skylar or Graham?'

'Skylar,' Nick murmured under his breath.

'We ran to where we heard screaming. We interrupted something. I don't know about any phone. All we saw was that Graham had grabbed hold of her. He was being very rough.'

'I punched him,' Nick added.

'You see,' Mr Kell spoke softly, 'she has a history, but not of lying.'

'I suppose most of your troubled young people have some kind of a–'

'A history, yes. They're vulnerable. They need to be nurtured and supported, not taken advantage of.'

'Of course.'

They fell into an awkward silence. Nick stared into his tea and felt uncomfortable. So had Mr Kell fired Graham because of the Skylar incident? Was he testing them all? He seemed like a really good bloke, but was he gunning for Dave and him now?

'Come on, best be getting on with the window and door frame,' Dave said, breaking into Nick's thoughts and bringing him back to the moment.

Later, when the door and window frame were in place and they were packing up to leave, Mr Kell drew Nick to one side.

'I know Skylar took your phone, Nick. When Graham told me she'd tried to steal his, I naturally asked her about it. And she denied it, but she told me about your phone. As I said earlier, she doesn't lie. It seems she's been up to her old tricks.'

'Oh?'

'What I don't understand is why you didn't say when we were talking about it earlier. Most people would've, so why didn't you?'

'I... because,' Nick groped for the right words, 'because I got it back, or rather she swopped it for a bottle with my signature.' Oh God, he thought. That sounds really bad.

'I sing in a band. It's fans, followers of the band kind of stuff. They collect autographs, mementos,' he tried to explain. 'No one got cross. No one got nasty. Chrissie and Sarah would never.... Look, if I'd said, it would've only made it sound as if she must've taken Graham's phone as well.'

'But you don't think she did?'

'The scream. You don't scream like that unless you're really scared.'

Mr Kell held Nick's gaze for a moment, seemed to make a decision and nodded.

'Are you, I mean, does Skylar want to do anything about Graham?' Nick asked.

'Like reporting him to the police? She doesn't think anyone would believe her. He'd give his version of the story very convincingly and poor Skylar would be traumatised by another brush with the system. No, there's nothing I can do, but at least I don't have to have him working here for me anymore.'

'Right,' Nick murmured. 'Only we haven't said anything to anyone about the thing with Graham before. You're the first person we've told. But if you think it would help Skylar—'

'No, don't say anything to anyone. It'll only cause trouble for her. It might even set her back.'

'OK, Mr Kell. If that's what you think.'

'Nick, where are you?' Dave called from outside.

'Sorry, I'm holding you up. Off you go, Nick, and thank you.' His tone was warm, he looked relaxed.

Outside again, Nick inhaled deeply. The air was cold, the light already fading from dusk into a wintery evening. The winery towered over him, a jolly green giant who'd been on a bender and smelled of wine. He liked this place and he liked Mr Kell.

A few moments later Nick slammed the van door and slipped his seatbelt across his shoulder. Dave revved the engine.

'Mr Kell seems a thoroughly nice kind of bloke. I can see how the boss agreed to help him out,' Dave said, throwing the van into gear and accelerating hard.

'I was a bit worried when he asked us about Skylar, though. Do you think he'll give us a tour of the winery?'

'What?' Dave asked as he swung the van onto the track.

'Nothing.'

Nick let his thoughts drift. Mr Kell didn't seem the kind of bloke who'd mind him asking for a tour.

'His voice, it's kind of.... Do you think he'll have a good singing voice, Dave?'

'What? How'd I know? A nice speaking voice doesn't mean you can sing. You've only got to go to a karaoke evening to know that. Can be diabolical.'

'Strange, you'd think it'd follow.'

'People aren't predictable, Nick.'

'I don't know, Graham is. Give him a choice and he'll always behave like a bastard.'

CHAPTER 19

Matt found his thoughts drifting. Grey, metallic light filtered through the window. It bathed him from behind in cold February hues, while above, the library striplights beamed harsh and white. This time last week, he'd been preoccupied with Maisie and, if he was honest, the burger van. He remembered the king-size double slider, and brooded. Perhaps they could meet at the Nags Head late on Friday. But there was a problem. He couldn't tell if she was still annoyed about his extra sessions at Balcon & Mora, or if as a pair, they were simply out of sync. One was working when the other wasn't.

It really was time he sent her a message. He texted, *Nags Heads after work tomorrow?* He didn't bother to add an emoticon; there was a distinct chance he'd choose one with an eyebrow down when it should be up. It was a risk he didn't want to take. He pressed send.

Across the library, he spotted Rosie talking to Martine, the two library assistants apparently sharing a joke. He watched them laugh. If he got the chance, he resolved to try and impress Rosie with something. It had been Japanese knotweed last time, this time he supposed he'd have to come up with something new.

He turned his attention back to his course work, and completed the algorithm he'd been constructing. A few clicks later and he'd saved it to a file and emailed the file to his tutor. Now he was free to pursue his own agenda. Tomorrow, Friday was another Balcon & Mora half day in Bury St Edmunds and he didn't want to appear a complete numpty. Damon had as good as set him a challenge to see how much he could find out about Graham without hacking into his email account. So he needed to spend the next few hours chasing and tracing, and then start mugging up on Java, the programming language for websites.

Graham Tollington, he typed into the Google search box, and waited.

'What? These weren't here last time,' he muttered, as the search engine threw up a smattering of links to the regional news sites.

He selected the BBC Radio Suffolk News link. *Stowmarket Man Found Dead at Turkey Farm*, the headline screamed. His eyes flew across the screen. *Graham Tollington, a 41 year old local builder was found collapsed early today at a turkey breeder on Gipsy Lane, Rattlesden. Mr Core, the owner, appeared visibly shocked when he described finding Mr Tollington inside one of the turkey sheds. 'We called an ambulance, but it was obvious he was already dead,' Mr Core said.*

'But he can't be,' Matt breathed. 'Why the hell...?' He read on, clicking the links, desperate to get more information.

Thought to have had a heart attack, Matt read. Did people still have heart attacks these days, he wondered, and skimmed further. It seemed they were *unable to say what was the cause of death*, but then Matt reckoned they never said, even when a body was found with a knife sticking out of it. At least not at first, not in the initial stages of breaking news. He scanned through the tired phrases about *a post mortem telling more*, and ruling out any *unnatural causes*.

He tried another link and stumbled onto a few lines and a photo, something between a life sketch and an obituary.

'So 'e was a canoe lifeguard.' It fitted in with what Nick had said and it showed a picture of him in a kayak on Alton Water at the Great East Swim. One end of his paddle broke the surface water while the other end swept through the air, mid-stroke. It was posed like an action shot: live, vibrant, sexy, a bear of a man. It didn't look like someone about to be plucked from this world by a heart attack.

'It don't make sense,' he muttered, blanking out Rosie, Martine and the other students in the library. He focused on Graham's smiling face and made a decision.

In algorithmic terms, he'd trodden on a dead Victor Pack, but before the fateful step he'd never heard of him. There was only an imprint of his trainer to link them. Recent appeals for people who knew Victor to come forward, didn't connect or apply to Matt. He was curious, to the point of nosiness, but he didn't know Victor.

On the other hand, Graham Tollington was different. Matt had been trying over the past few weeks to find out about him and therefore the connection predated his death. In Matt's book it made him a virtual acquaintance. There was already a bond. He felt as if he knew him.

Driven by fresh resolve, he located Graham Tollington on the Stowmarket trades site listed under builders. A few keystrokes later and he'd found a telephone number, an address and his website email. Armed with these details, he linked to the Crown Court websites for Norwich, Ipswich, Colchester and Chelmsford and searched each site in turn for past judgements and cases heard. Nothing.

'What about the Land Registry website?' he muttered. If Graham had been acting as a middleman selling land for building, maybe the plots of land were registered as belonging to one of his companies.

'Hi.'

'What? Oh hi, Rosie,' he said looking up.

'I've been standing here for ages. You usually notice me straight away. So what's so interesting? You've been glued to that screen.' She moved closer and peered at the columns of print. A hint of fresh flowers permeated the air.

'The Land Registry?' she continued. 'Last time it was knotweed. You're becoming agricultural, Matt. Next, you'll be signing up to help with the Olympic flowerbed.'

'Yeah, no, I mean, I was lookin' up stuff about this bloke who's been found dead out at Rattlesden this morning.'

'What? There's been another body? You're like one of those ambulance chasers. Last I'd heard, you'd found–'

'Yeah, a body. Victor Pack. That was nearly five weeks ago.'

'Did you see the appeal for information about him on TV? Seems he may have been, you know, a bit of a....'

'Telly aint my thing, Rosie,' he said, trying to appear indifferent. He'd already guessed from his own searches there'd be something related to kids behind the murder, but he hadn't wanted to find words to express it, even to himself. He'd read the insinuating newspaper articles. Nothing had been stated directly, but there'd been enough hints to make Victor retire early. Matt was forced to face the obvious. The man was, to use prison terminology, more than likely a nonce, a Not On Normal Courtyard Exercise kind of pervert.

'Yeah, well maybe he got what was comin' to him,' he muttered. No wonder his algorithm didn't connect with Victor. He didn't want it to.

'You're turning into a right ghoul, Matt. Really you are. So who's this latest one? And why are you glued to the Land Registry site?'

'It's Graham Tollington, an' he's a local builder. A mate of mine knows him. I was lookin' for land registered in 'is name.'

'Why? So now he's dead you'll snap up his plots? You're like a vulture picking over the bones.'

'No I aint. I was lookin' for dodgy deals he might've done, that's all. Anythin' shady about him.'

'Dodgy deals? There's plenty of dodgy land out there.'

'Oh yeah?'

'You know, ground polluted with asbestos, or that floods. And at the back of my uncle's garden there's a building plot not been sold for ages. He was the one I told you about. He had the knotweed, remember?' She swept back her hair with a flick of her wrist.

'So where's he live then?'

'My uncle? In Elmswell. And there's me thinking you'd want to know my address, Matt.'

'What?' he said, already only listening with half an ear, as he keyed Elmswell into the search box along with Groundsbuild LTD. 'Spammin' hell,' he muttered.

'Now what, Matt?'

'Awesome. Seems Graham Tollington, or rather Groundsbuild, own several plots of land round Elmswell.'

'So, what are you saying, Matt? Are we going to find more bodies buried... dotted around Elmswell?' She seemed to rock back on her feet.

'Nah, don't be daft, Rosie. How'd I know?' He turned and studied her face. Colour flamed her cheeks. 'D'you fancy a coffee?' he asked, avoiding her eyes and focusing on her auburn hair. Nice, he thought, the way she'd drawn it into a ponytail, more strands escaping and loose than caught in the tie.

'Thanks, but no thanks, Matt. I'm working.'

She drifted away, seemingly deaf to his, 'Maybe another time, then Rosie?'

So, had he told her enough to impress, or too much? At least he was dressed OK. He knew he looked sharp because Maisie had said, 'It's... alright, I suppose,' as she'd run her eye over the tee-shirt. They'd been in a charity shop in Stowmarket at the time.

'Moon Walk? Aint it a bit Michael Jackson? It's faded,' she'd added.

'It's retro. Shows it's authentic, Mais,' he'd explained.

And now he smoothed the tired cotton across his chest. He squinted down at the words, bold lettering on greying textile.

1969
APOLLO 11 & FIRST MOON WALK
40 YEARS ON
STILL A GIANT LEAP FOR MANKIND

The year *2009* was printed in massive numerals across the back. He felt pleased, at least the fortieth anniversary tee had been a winner with Rosie, otherwise she wouldn't have stopped to talk for so long.

He clicked back onto the Google Maps site and typed Elmswell in the search box, all the while imagining Neil Armstrong and Buzz Aldrin gazing at the Earth from Space. Would it have appeared like the Google Earth map he stared at now, but more distant and wrapped in wisps of cloud? And migrating birds – how did it look to them?

He closed his eyes. Rosie had called him a vulture. For a moment he was transported to his comic-strip world – a vulture with an image problem; a bird with a scavenging habit and a sticky beak, a preference to be known as a buzzard, and a penchant to be called Buzz. He pictured Graham's plots of land around Elmswell, and swooped from the sky like a buzzard, raking his talons across the ground. What, he wondered had Graham been up to. Whatever it was he was going to find out.

He made a decision. On the way to Balcon & Mora tomorrow, he'd scooter via Elmswell and take a look. Maisie might want to come. If he threw in a rum and coke, he reckoned it'd count as a date. He sent her another text.

Feeling pleased with how things were shaping out, Matt logged off the computer and got to his feet. He figured a canteen break was needed before he made a start on learning Java. He pushed back his chair, the legs scraping and squealing across the old floorboards.

Rosie must have heard the noise, because she looked across from the library assistant's station. It seemed like a sign to Matt, an invitation to pause as he walked past.

'Sure you don't want a coffee, Rosie?'

'No thanks, Matt. And watch your feet. No leaping for mankind. You'll only break something.'

•

'We're going through Elmswell, right?' Maisie said as he revved the two-stroke engine.

'Yeah, Mais. I told you.'

It was Friday lunchtime. They'd agreed they'd take the back route to Elmswell, check out land belonging to

Groundsbuild and then ride on to Bury St Edmunds in time for Matt's session with Balcon & Mora.

'If we see somewhere nice, can we stop an' eat?'

'Sure, Mais.'

The wind pulled, worrying Matt's jacket. Maisie held onto to him, wrapping her arms around his chest and leaning into his back. It felt nice, as if he'd added an extra layer.

'Which plot we startin' with?' she yelled from behind his shoulder.

He pictured the Google Earth map and headed past the old church and almshouses. He'd already marked out the plots on his visual cortex. They seemed to cluster near the railway line and beyond the industrial site, but first there was somewhere he wanted to check. He slowed and pulled into the side of the road. Fields sloped away gently from the verge, not a house in sight, the road seemingly a natural boundary. On the other side, behind him, there was a narrow field and then housing. It seemed to buffer the spreading Elmswell from the road.

'Why we stoppin', Matt?'

'Well, that field there. It kinda looks out of place, ripe for building.' He pointed to a strip of ground planted with winter barley.

'Looks like a field to me.'

'Yeah, but don't you reckon this road'd make a better edge to Elmswell? That field'd make a good building plot, don't you reckon?'

'So?'

'Groundsbuild didn't buy it. I can see it'd be pricey.'

'Was it for sale?' she shouted, but her words were taken by the wind.

'Come on,' he said and eased the scooter forwards. He knew where he wanted to go next. The scooter wheels jolted and jarred over the railway crossing as they headed for a plot near the industrial area.

'Here,' he shouted as he stopped.

A rough fence separated some ground from the road. Matt peered over the wooden slats. It had been left to go to waste. Scrubby overgrown weeds covered the soil, dry thistle heads bobbed above wild grasses, Timothy vied with Cocksfoot their stems browned and dying back, broken by winter. Grey cane-like stems, nudged through a pile of rubble. No foliage, just stems. He looked again.

'I've seen somethin' like them before,' he said, staring at the grey canes. He leaned against the fencing and strained to get a closer look. Something cracked. Wood splintered.

'Watch out, Matt. What you doin'?' Maisie squealed.

'I reckon…. Can you get through here, Mais?'

'Yeah. Why?'

'Those dead canes, can you get me one?'

He watched her squeeze between the broken slats, a final wiggle of her bottom clearing a shard of wood. She stooped over the canes, and pushed at the loose rubble with her Huggi boot, legs like sticks in her maroon jeggings.

'There's a plastic bag under this lot. Like a grow bag,' she said.

'What d'you mean? Like that cane thing's been planted in it?'

She didn't answer, but bent and kicked at the stones and fragments of brick and concrete. The canes split and fractured under her feet as she worked.

'Are they hollow. Mais?'

'Yeah. They're just dead stems and they break ever so easily. How'd you know they were hollow?'

'Just a hunch, that's all.'

'This grow bag's funny. Aint seen my uncle plantin' tomatoes in anythin' like this.'

'Take a photo, Mais. With your phone, yeah? And bring back some of that cane stuff, so I can see.'

When she pushed back through the fencing, her face was flushed.

'It's kinda exciting. What we lookin' for, Matt?' She handed him a piece of the dead stem.

Matt turned it over, scrutinising its hollow structure, running his finger along its surface and feeling the nodes where branches or leaves had formed. It weighed almost nothing, a stalk that had died along with its leaves for the winter.

'It's like the bare bones of a plant,' he murmured. The memories came flooding back. He swallowed. 'There was stuff like this where I found that bloke, Victor Pack.'

'So it aint asbestos?'

'No, Mais. I did some readin' a few weeks ago an' it looks like pictures of knotweed. Let's see your photo.'

They hunched over Maisie's phone as she flicked through her shots. 'Weird,' he murmured, his brain working overtime. 'Come on, there're more plots to see.'

She leapt back onto the scooter. 'Yea!' she squawked and flicked her visor back down.

They rode around Elmswell, stopping near ground partitioned from houses with large gardens, rough driveways leading to banks of garaging, and land bordering the railway line. Always it was the same story. They'd find the identical grey cane-like stalks protruding in clumps from a small mound of rubble. If they disturbed the rubble, an inch or two down their fingers would scrape along the surface of a reinforced plastic grow bag. Except Maisie said they weren't like normal grow bags because there was no writing on them, no instructions of where to break into the bags, and no pictures of tomatoes. He'd kicked at one of them. The heavy-duty material refused to split or puncture.

While Maisie took photos with her mobile, Matt became increasingly convinced he was seeing cuttings bedded-out for a specific reason. He was looking at a plant with its roots contained by a special plastic material designed to be strong and seemingly impenetrable, like Kevlar. Realisation slowly dawned. This was intended to control something moving slowly and with less force than a bullet. But what? He racked his brains. He'd read about rhizomes. Could the bags have been planted with knotweed rhizomes? But why?

He checked the time. 'Frag, Mais. We've been ages on this. I've got to get goin' or I'll be late for Damon.'

'Awe... already? I was enjoying this. How about I ride up to Bury with you. We can come back together when you've finished your work. That way I get a rum an' coke afterwards at the Nags Head.'

'But I won't be done till after seven.'

'That's all right. I want to check out the shops and I can meet my friend Kerry. I aint seen her for a while.'

They didn't talk as they headed along small country roads through Tostock, Thurston and on into Bury. By the time Matt parked the Piaggio outside Balcon & Mora he'd developed a grudging respect for Graham. The bloke must have been involved in one hell of a scam.

He reckoned a building plot appearing to be infested with knotweed would be difficult to sell. Once cleared, an easy job if the roots and rhizomes were contained in special grow bags, the land could be sold on for building and with a tidy profit.

The question was, had Graham been the one who concealed the infested grow bags on someone else's land, and then had he, behind the mask of Groundsbuild, bought each plot for a knock-down price? His theory hinged on the timing of when the special grow bags were concealed on the plots of land.

He trudged up the stairs, his mind working the scam. He hardly noticed the stark waiting room, the lights already switched on despite it still being early in the afternoon. He rang the bell for the office and waited, thoughts racing.

'Hi, come on in,' Damon said as he opened the door and disappeared back into his office.

Matt pulled off his helmet and followed Damon. This time he didn't need to bang his hands together or swing his arms to generate heat. Simply having Maisie clinging to him as she'd ridden pillion on the scooter had stopped him from freezing.

'So how's the Graham Tollingotn challenge going?' Damon asked, as he flicked the kettle on.

'How'd you know I was thinkin' about him?' Matt countered, surprised.

'I didn't. Hot chocolate with the usual shot?'

'Yeah thanks.'

'And Graham Tollington? What did you find out about him?'

'Well yeah, I've found loads.' He unzipped his field jacket and grinned.

'Go on, tell.'

'Right, well....' Matt reeled off Graham's address, telephone number, website email address, canoe lifeguard status, and then the Land Registry search followed by the Elmswell tour and his discoveries.

'Awesome. You're good. Here, drink your hot chocolate. And have an extra shot of vodka.'

'Thanks mate. So how would hacking into his emails tell you more?'

'Ah, I'll tell you.'

'What, you mean you've–'

'Yeah, sure I have. Had to prove a point, didn't I?'

'Frag. That wasn't what tipped him over the edge, was it? You do know don't you? He's dead.'

'Dead? Why didn't you tell me?'

'You didn't ask. An' anyway, it was only yesterday. Didn't your hacking tell you?'

'How could it? Dead men don't send emails.'

They sat in silence for a few minutes, Matt sipping his chocolate and vodka, Damon staring at his computer screen.

'Who knows about this knotweed scam, Matt? If it gets out and the police become involved, they might do a forensic on his computer. I'm going to have to delete the keylogger bug from his system before anyone starts looking. I can't have the police tracing anything back to me.'

'Yeah, but what did your hackin' discover?'

'I've got it all on a USB flash drive. Top tip for today - never risk saving stuff like that straight to your computer. You never know what shit it's going to be, and by the time you find out, then it's too late. You don't want Forensics discovering it on your hard drive. Deleting may not be enough. Now keep your nose clean. Here.' He handed Matt the USB flash drive stick.

'Wicked! Thanks mate,' Matt said, his head buzzing with excitement.

'No, don't look at it now. We've wasted enough time. There's work to be getting on with.'

Matt slipped it into his jeans pocket. 'Thanks mate.'

CHAPTER 20

'Sounds like you could be developing a taste for wine,' Chrissie said and tipped back her glass to get the last few drops of ginger beer. She glanced around the bar. A busy Friday evening crush. A group caught her attention, or rather their hair-dos stood out from the crowd – beehives, bouffants, pixies and bobs. Had the Nags Head been transported back in time, she wondered.

'Just because I've been making wine racks doesn't mean I like wine,' Nick said, and then as if to illustrate his point, he gulped down some beer.

'It's all you've talked about for the last half hour. The winery, Kell, the wine tasting room....' The rest of her words were lost as the Shangri-Las' *Leader of the Pack* boomed out, as if from nowhere.

'Sixties Girls Night meets Vinyl Night,' Nick mouthed to her.

'Meets Friday Night,' she shouted.

While the music thundered, Chrissie watched him. He seemed to hardly look, but she knew he'd have taken in the miniskirts, turtlenecks and box dresses. One of the group, a girl in knee high go-go boots gazed across at him.

'You haven't mentioned Skylar. I take it she's no longer a problem.'

'Skylar? No, but then I've been at Willows most of the week making–'

'Wine racks. Yes, you said.'

The motorbike sound effect roared from the speakers. Chrissie waited for the *Leader of the Pack* vocals to fade before continuing, 'If they play that track later when Matt gets here, he'll be wanting to upgrade his scooter to a motorbike.'

'Don't even think it. Time for another drink? Ginger beer OK for you?'

She caught his grin. She knew his purpose. He'd make a beeline for the girl with the heavy eyeliner and the box dress who'd been casting come-hither looks. It wouldn't appear like that, of course – just a light brush past the Sixties group near the bar, but he'd have her number by the time he returned with their drinks.

She settled back in the old pine chair and waited. She didn't mind. It had been a good week. Tina Wibble, true to promise, had phoned before driving over from her photographic studio in Ipswich. The flea market pot had received the full star treatment: lighting, composition, close-ups, everything short of airbrushing. It had been like a professional makeover. Even Ron was pleased and smiled for the camera. And now Nick had waxed lyrical about Kell and his winery. She was intrigued.

Around her the Sixties theme notched up a gear, as The Supremes burst into *Stop! In the Name of Love*. Where do they get these old tracks, she wondered and unthinkingly tapped her foot to the beat.

'How's Clive's case shaping up? Is he getting close to cracking it?' Nick asked, making her jump as he appeared with dripping overfilled glasses. He put them down on the small table in front of her. 'I see the music's got you going,' he said, addressing her foot.

'I was just thinking it makes a change from the jukebox.'

'So you don't want to talk about Clive or the railway bodies, right?'

'What? No. I was miles away thinking about Sixties music, that's all.'

'So? Any breakthrough yet?'

'No. At least I don't think so. It's been endless checking of names on lists, cross-referencing and then trying to trace and interview people. Very tedious, and of course all the time the press are on his back. Victor Pack, that's the one Matt found, is turning into a high profile case.'

'I sort of heard, but to be honest, I hadn't been following the details. So he's working late again?'

'Yes, but then so is Matt.' She didn't bother to add it wasn't the long hours that bothered her. Clive's frustration with the case was the problem. It didn't always make for good company. He just needed a breakthrough, one small piece of luck, he kept telling her. She dragged her mind back to the moment. 'So have I won my bet?'

'What bet, Chrissie?'

'The girl in the black and white dress. I'm betting she gave you her phone number, at the bar just now.' She watched his face redden. 'I knew it.'

The Supremes faded out.

'You see,' she said, speaking her thoughts, 'it's ironic, but it's struck me that another dead body, another railway line killing would be... well, it would be tragic but it would give more clues. Like the Yorkshire Ripper, or the Ipswich prostitute killer, remember? They got careless, over confident, and slipped up. Obviously it would add to the pressure on Clive, but at the moment there seems to be nothing to go on.' She felt defeated. If only there was something she could do, beyond being positive and supportive for Clive.

'Seems a bit extreme, Chrissie.'

'Yes, I know. Careful what you wish for, and all that.'

'Yeah. You heard Graham died yesterday?'

'What? I don't believe it. He was the bloke winding you up when you were working on the stables over at the turkey farm, wasn't he?'

'Hmm....'

She tried to catch his expression, gauge his feelings, but he avoided her eyes and sipped his beer.

'I didn't hear the news yesterday. What happened?' she said, keeping her tone even.

'I only know because Matt texted me a link to the Radio Suffolk news site. He was found dead in a turkey hut. It isn't big in regional news terms, so there hasn't been much about it since. Seems he just... died.'

'What like a heart attack, or something?'

'Yeah, I suppose something like that.'

'Poor bloke,' she said automatically, but she couldn't help wondering if Nick's relaxed mood was because of Graham's death.

'Hey, Matt's arrived,' he said, interrupting her thoughts.

She looked towards the door as the Vinyl Night selection swung into West Coast medley. 'Hi,' she called as The Beach Boys belted out *Good Vibrations*.

The throng near the bar seemed to have grown as more drinkers gathered near the girls sporting the Sixties look. Matt waved and pushed through with Maisie close on his heels. His face looked flushed by the time he made his way over with a couple of drinks.

'Hiya, everyone,' Maisie squealed. 'Isn't it great? Hey Matt, I've just realised your tee's got 1969 on it! I would've dressed Sixties if I'd known.' She took the tumbler from his hand and drank.

'I promised Mais a rum an' coke,' he muttered by way of a greeting. His face told Chrissie he was bursting to share some news.

'I know that look, Matt. You've got something to tell us, haven't you?'

He rummaged in his jeans pocket, pulled out a USB memory stick and slapped it down on the table.

'It's about Graham Tollington,' he said.

The next half hour was spent listening to Matt, while Stevie Wonder competed in the background with Marianne Faithfull for Sixties feel.

'Shit!' Nick said when Matt finally paused to drink his lager.

'So what's on the memory stick?' she asked.

'Dunno yet. Aint had a chance to look.'

'So the bloke died of a heart attack, you said?'

'Yeah, apparently. Must've made one hell of a lot of enemies over the knotweed, though.'

Chrissie bit back her next question. It felt as if she'd swallowed a huge unchewed mouthful and it was stretching its way down her throat. It needed digesting. Time to go home, she decided. Clive would be back soon.

Twenty minutes later she'd left her friends to the rest of the Sixties night and was hum-singing *Suspicious Minds* as she drove back to Woolpit. 'Eat your heart out, Elvis,' she muttered, and crooned the chorus riff again.

By the time Clive opened her front door, she'd been home for long enough to slip yesterday's half eaten macaroni cheese into the oven and fill the cafetiere.

'I don't know if you've eaten yet, but there's supper if you want it,' she called, her thoughts racing, on fire with all Matt had discovered about Graham Tollington.

Clive seemed preoccupied as he wandered into the kitchen, kissed her and then helped himself to a beer from the fridge. She wanted to tell him, but forced herself to hold back. It wasn't the moment to just blurt it all out.

'How's your day been?' she asked as he opened the bottle.

'Challenging, but we've made a bit of a step forward. The Met boys have found something to back up a report from someone who came forward after the appeal.'

'Really? That's fantastic.'

'It's not a lot, but an old secretary who used to work a couple of days a week at Limesgrove, that's Victor Pack's children's home, contacted us. She retired years ago. It seems she remembers him talking about spending time in Suffolk, possibly a holiday. She's sure he said Hemley because it sounded so like Henley. She even recalls him saying, "Not Henley on Thames. It's Hemley, and it's on the Deben."'

'And you believe her?'

'She's quite certain. And the Met have finally finished combing through everything in Victor Pack's London house. Interestingly there's an old photo which we're pretty sure is of the Hemley children's home.'

'Right. So he must've visited it. That connects both men with Hemley. The killer must be something to do with the Suffolk end, not the London end. It stands to reason, after all they were both killed in Suffolk; one was living in Suffolk, the other was moving to Suffolk.'

'Wow, slow down. You're jumping to conclusions.'

'Do we know when he visited? Was anyone in the photo?'

'Slow down, Chrissie. We can't date the photo precisely, but our octogenarian secretary thinks her chat with Victor was in 1990. She moved job soon after. That's how she can date the conversation.'

'So, twenty-two years ago. And the people in the photo?' Her thoughts rushed on.

'No there weren't any, just the house. Victor was careful not to keep photos of people or faces. They'll be stored on a dark cloud on the dark net somewhere.'

'What about the others who came forward after the appeal? Any of them see Eric in London or Victor in Hemley?' She opened the oven door to check on the macaroni cheese and a blast of hot air and cheesy fumes caught her face.

'I think that's probably warmed through, Chrissie.'

It was obvious she'd set the oven too high. The flavour trail rocketed through her small kitchen filling it with the smell of burnt crispy macaroni. She needed to calm down.

'Come on,' he said. 'Let's give my case a rest for a moment.'

They ate, plates resting on their laps as they sat on the sofa in the living room.

But her mind wouldn't let go. 'What about GP records? There must've been a GP's surgery looking after the children's home in Hemley? Wouldn't the GPs have a list of names, or something?'

'We thought of that. Seems the kids were registered at the Woodbridge GP's surgery but were mostly seen at the children's home. The names never even got onto the appointments system. When the kids eventually moved on, their paper records were sent back to the GP Primary Care Trust and then on to wherever they registered next with a doctor. There isn't a national computerised patient notes system. It's a paper trail and it's like looking for a needle in a haystack.'

'What about the national census? Have you thought of that? It's every ten years. Children are supposed to be on it as well as adults.'

'But no one has to be added if they're considered to be transient on the night of the census. We made a special request to the National Census Office for the names. It seems Eric considered the kids a transient population for the purposes of the census, and didn't include them.'

'Could he do that? I mean how could he get away with it?'

'Because the census is read by a national census computer, not the local authority. I don't think anyone realised what he'd done, or rather in this case, not done. I'm afraid most of the names we've got are from people who came forward following the appeal. But it's by no means complete, and I was surprised how many have changed their names.'

'A case of shedding your memories with your old name, kind of thing? Have you had any hoax callers?' she asked as her mind sped from the two dead men to the kids.

'Hey, slow down. What's got into you? You're not usually like this.'

'I know. It's just....' She gathered the dirty plates from the coffee table and carried them through to the kitchen. 'Coffee?' she called over her shoulder as she scrapped charred macaroni from the sides of the oven dish.

'Not if it's going to hype you up more. And why don't you leave that to soak?'

'OK.' She made a decision. 'I wasn't going to say but,' she walked back into the living room, 'I can see I'm going to have tell you. Matt found something out today. Actually he found loads out today and... well it might have a bearing on someone's death.'

'What? Oh no, what've you been up to, Chrissie?'

'Nothing. But what do you know about Graham Tollington? He's a builder and he was found dead yesterday at the turkey farm where Nick was working on a job last week.'

•

Chrissie listened to the ringtone. She felt a momentary flutter of anxiety as she waited for Mr Kell to answer. Was she doing the right thing, she wondered. He had, after all invited her to visit his winery. He'd even insisted she phone him first so as to be sure of the full tour. Hearing Nick describe the huge stainless steel tanks and the pervading scents of wine, grapes and yeast had been fascinating, but she'd also been intrigued by Strad Kell. He obviously had an interest in giving employment to troubled young people and she wondered if he'd have an angle on why they became troubled in the first place. All this talk of children's homes had set her thinking, but she doubted she'd feel free to ask about everything she wanted to know if Clive was with her.

'Hello. Stad Kell speaking. Is that Chrissie Jax?'

'Hi.'

She hesitated as she bit back the *how did you know?* He must've put her number in his phone's directory for the caller ID to show on his phone. Why would he do that?

'Hi,' she repeated, regaining her momentum. 'Yes, it's Chrissie Jax from Clegg's Furniture Restorers.'

'There hasn't been any trouble with my cheque going through, has there?'

'No, no. Nothing like that, Mr Kell. I was phoning because... I was hoping to visit your winery. I don't know if you remember, but you said I should ring first. We have an old disused still in one of the outhouses at our furniture repair site and... well I've always found the whole process fascinating. Would... would sometime today be OK?'

'Yes, of course I remember saying you should ring me. An old still?' His tones were almost as rich over the phone as in real life. 'You never know, you might be inspired to get the old still working again, but we'll have to arrange another day. Saturdays can be difficult.'

They settled on Monday. No one would miss her if she slipped away early from the apprentice release day. Before she rang off she felt compelled to ask, 'So how did you know my mobile number? I've only ever rung you on the workshop phone before.'

'I seem to remember you booked a table at my bistro. It'll be the number alongside your booking contact details. Why?'

'Of course. I'd forgotten.' She felt stupid, but did he really put all the diners' booking contact numbers into his phone's directory?

Not knowing quite what to think or believe, she turned her mind to her French flea market pot. It was time she organised an appointment with Abraham Pawcett, the china restorer living in Felixstowe.

'Clive,' she called up the stairs. 'Did you say you wanted to come to the china expert with me?'

She listened to him padding barefoot from the shower and along the landing. He paused at the top of the stairs.

'Why didn't you wake me? You knew I was working today? It's already nine thirty.'

'Clive, it is Saturday morning. You've been working overtime all week and you slept through the alarm. No one's called asking for you. I reckoned you'd be better off getting a couple of hours extra sleep. If some Chief Detective Inspector wants to get shirty about it, put them through to me.'

'But Chrissie–'

'Then say my macaroni cheese did for you.'

'Chrissie–'

'A couple of hours lost from thousands of police hours already spent on this case aren't going to make any difference. I take it you won't have time to come to the china expert with me.'

'Sorry, Chrissie. Just arrange a time and if I can make it I will, otherwise you'll have to go without me. Is that OK?'

'I kind of thought you'd say something like that. Have you got time for a mug of tea and toast?'

CHAPTER 21

Nick felt his impatience growing. Why the delay, he wondered. He looked around. Students huddled in twos and threes. Some had sunk to the floor and sat cross-legged or leaned against the locked canteen doors. Most were busy texting and messaging with android phones and tablets.

'What's the hold up?' someone asked.

'It should be open by now,' another voice bellyached.

The queue was loose. No one shoved, jostled or edged closer. There was no point; nothing was moving. Nick breathed in slowly. The usual cheesy smells, frying oil, and hints of bacon and toast weren't floating in the air. Instead all he picked up were the faint citrus and waxy traces of cleaning materials.

'Wasn't there a notice about maintenance work over the weekend and into Monday? I'm sure I read something on the website,' a student said loudly, as if making an announcement.

'More than likely,' Nick muttered. Ever since the explosion in the kitchens almost two years earlier, the Academy had taken the well-being of its ovens very seriously. It was understandable but bloody annoying when you were hungry. 'Shit,' he cursed. The canteen cooked breakfast was like a rite of passage.

'Hiya,' Matt puffed as he trudged up to him.

'Have you heard? The canteen's closed. Come on, let's go and find some breakfast.'

'What? I've only just got here. Where you goin'? Hey slow down.'

Matt's feet pounded behind as Nick took the stairs two at a time down to the main entrance hall. Movement was a safety valve. He knew he didn't need to walk so fast but irritation and frustration were threatening to bubble over.

'Hey stop, mate,' Matt whinged.

'Yeah, OK.' He stopped dead and Matt collided with his shoulder.

'Where're we goin'?' Matt, flushed and unfit, wheezed as he caught his breath.

'I don't know. Somewhere. Anywhere. I don't suppose there's any bacon in your fridge?' He watched Matt's pained expression.

'What? What you talkin' about, Nick?'

'Canteen's closed. Hey, I've got it. We could go into Stowmarket. Fancy a breakfast Sub?'

Matt drove the Piaggio while Nick perched on the back. He reckoned it would be easier to park a scooter than his Fiesta in the centre of Stowmarket. The wind ruffled his anorak, but with Matt in front, only his legs caught the worst of the icy blast. And with each degree of wind chill, his edginess settled.

'So what's bitten you?' Matt asked as they waited for their order.

'I don't know.' It was a reasonable question, but Nick hadn't thought to confront or analyse his irritation. He'd reacted. Now, as he waited in line with the smell of cooked bacon flirting with his senses, he honestly didn't know what, as Matt put it, had bitten him.

'It can't be this Tollington bloke that's gettin' to you. He's dead, Nick.'

'I know, but it still feels kind of wrong. And after what you found out about the knotweed, I can't help wondering if–'

'Two breakfast Subs, two coffees... anything else, guys?'

They carried their bread rolls, the shape of submarines and packed with crispy bacon, over to a table bar near the window and sat on tall stools.

'You're better when you're doing stuff, Nick. You know, like exercise.'

'Hmm....'

'You're an active bloke, mate. I said before about swimmin'. You'd look great in a wetsuit. And well, at least now you won't be lookin' over your shoulder all the time in case Tollington appears all kitted out like a canoe lifeguard.'

'Hmm, I think I'd rather be on the water than in it. Canoeing not swimming.'

'Either way, you still get to wear a wetsuit. There's loads of canoein' clubs around. Sea, river, reservoir, you name it, mate. I've looked most of 'em up.'

'Why? I can't see you in a canoe.'

'Nah, I was tryin' to find stuff out. I needed somethin' the Tollington bloke was bound to open if I sent it in an email. Reckoned canoein' gear would work OK.'

'And did it?'

'Don't know. Damon sent him a keylogger bug before I got a chance to send my email. But the research aint wasted. I'll text you the canoein' clubs and the contact numbers. It's all up here.' He tapped his head.

'Thanks.'

Nick watched Matt chew the breakfast Sub, a kind of slow grinding movement. How, he wondered, did he retain information like websites and phone numbers. It was incomprehensible. And how could he recommend exercise when he was as good as allergic to it himself? Extraordinary. Nick sipped his coffee. Mind you, Matt might have a point. Nick had always enjoyed the physical side of his job. It gave him a feeling of wellbeing. He made up his mind. Perhaps he would make enquiries about canoeing after all.

'So what's on the memory stick?' he asked.

'Still workin' on it, mate. But there's some weird things. I reckon it's chat room stuff.'

'How do you mean? Like jargon and anagrams? Sounds like you could be getting into a can of worms.'

'Nah, it's from live internet stuff. It's like a footprint. I only got keystrokes from one side of conversations over about a week. Then, well the bloke died. I can read all his emails though. They're stored on his email website, not on his computer. All I needed was the password. The keylogger gave it.'

'What'll you do when you've read it all?'

'Don't know. Depends what I find. Why?'

'Just be careful, Matt.' There wasn't much else he could think to say. Matt was probably already breaking the law by snooping into Graham's internet account.

They swallowed the last tasty scraps of crispy bacon and swilled down their coffee. At least this time, as Nick perched on the back of the scooter, he felt the satisfying inner warmth unique to a bacon butty, not so unlike the glow depicted on commercials for porridge.

The rest of Nick's apprentice release day went pretty much like all the other apprentice release days before, except this time he spent most of his lunch hour phoning canoeing clubs, and Chrissie slipped away early.

CHAPTER 22

Chrissie drove out of the Academy car park and headed for Rattlesden. Nick had told her to watch out for a track on the right, about a mile before she reached the village. 'If you get into Rattlesden, you've gone too far,' he'd said. 'Follow the track and take the left fork to the vineyard. If you find yourself in a turkey farm, you'll know you've gone wrong.'

She was relieved he hadn't asked too many questions. He'd seemed more interested in something Matt had texted. He'd barely grunted when she told him she was taking a tour of Kell's winery. 'Lucky you,' he'd said.

The light was beginning to fade by the time she eased the TR7 off the road and followed the roughly gravelled and thinly tarmacked track. An arrow-like notice pointed off to the right. 'TURKEYS,' she murmured. 'I don't go that way.'

A small knot tightened in her stomach. She was about to cross the lines between curious visitor, investigative journalist, and detective. Yes, of course she was interested in how the wine was produced, but she was also fascinated by Strad Kell himself. He had an undeniably sexy voice, and he ran a successful business. She guessed both would be subjects close to his heart and she hoped he'd talk freely about them. But how, she wondered was she going to make her interest in the youths he employed sound casual. How to ask about the kind of person who'd kill and leave two men dead near a railway line because of... because of what? Something those two men might have done to kids in their care? And how to ask questions without hinting she had privileged access to police information, or giving herself away? Strad Kell thought Clive was her husband. As far as she knew, he had no idea Clive was Detective Inspector Merry.

She drove past the vines, ghost-like in the failing light. On and on they stretched, merging with the darkness of the gentle slope to the side of her. In the distance she spotted the large Kell's vineyard notice standing out like a beacon.

'What the...?' she said as she turned in through the entrance. Why was a Willows van parked in front of the huge green metal-clad warehouse? Surprise scattered her qualms. She drew up alongside it.

'But why would Nick–'

Her words died as a door opened in the front expanse of the building. Strad Kell stepped out into the deepening gloom. A security light burst into life above him, both illuminating and reflecting off the top of his smooth head.

'My God, he's a bloody saint,' she breathed.

'Hello, Mrs Jax. Spot on time.' He smiled a welcome.

She glanced at her watch. Four o'clock, but as always, the time on the dashboard was something completely different. Few instruments could boast the inaccuracy of an original 1981 TR7 clock she thought, and beamed back a smile. She tried to look elegant as she climbed out of her car.

'Come on in,' he said and led the way back into the winery.

She already had an inkling of what to expect from Nick's description, but when she stepped over the threshold, it was as mind-blowingly amazing as any industrial architecture she'd ever seen. She guessed he must have read her face.

'It's a surprise, isn't it? People don't expect to find something like this inside. More used to seeing bales of hay or stacked crates. I suppose it's all the stainless steel that does it.' He turned and continued, 'Finished for today?' He addressed a man who'd appeared from a single storey room dwarfed by the huge scale of the warehouse space.

'Yes, I'm off now, Mr Kell. Nick should be with me tomorrow.'

'Dave?' she murmured, and then felt stupid. She should have guessed he'd be here. Of course work went on as normal while trainees like her were on the apprentice release days. Her face flamed.

Dave acknowledged her with a nod, but dropped his gaze and looked embarrassed as he headed out through the door.

Oh God he thinks I'm.... Her cheeks burned more.

'That's going to be our wine tasting room. Somewhere to do our blending and mixing as well as for our visitors,' he said. His voice soothed, like massaging oil.

'Hmm, I see you've got Willows & Son working on it.'

'Yes, it's going to be a real asset when it's finished. Now let me take you on the tour.'

He guided her towards the stainless steel fermentation tanks, all the while talking in his relaxed easy manner. 'Of course fermentation produces alcohol, but people often forget about the by-products. Carbon dioxide and heat. And the temperature is key to some of the qualities of the wine.'

'You mean like drinking reds at room temperature and whites–'

'No, no. I mean the temperature of the fermentation process. If you want brash flavours, as in some reds, then a warmer temperature helps to agitate the must–'

'The must?'

'Sorry, the pressed grape juice. It may contain skins and fragments of seeds, or even stems.'

'And white wine?'

'That needs a cooler fermenting temperature so as to keep the aromas and flavours delicate and subtle. I mean that's what you'd expect from a white table wine. It's easier to control the temperature in a taller tank with a narrower diameter.'

'So that's why they look like snub-nosed rockets.'

'Well, kind of, but to my mind they're more complex.'

Chrissie only half listened as he explained how coolant jackets worked and how air had to be kept away from the fermentation process to prevent oxidation as carbon dioxide escaped through fermentation traps. He gesticulated and pointed, illustrating and describing the processes in ever more complex wine-making jargon. He indicated taps, hoses and gauges. Terms like *yeast autolysis*, *lactic-acid bacteria* and *malolactic fermentation* rolled from his tongue. She thought she had a handle on the meaning of *clarification* and *filtration*. But *fining*?

'What's that for?' she asked, brushing her fingers against a stainless steel hatchway near the bottom of a fermentation tank. It reminded her of a submarine door.

'Oh that's a racking port.'

She didn't ask him to elucidate. He'd already moved on to the next subject of aging and bottling. Several things struck her as she watched him. His phrases, the language - it was lyrical; almost hypnotic. Really, he could have been speaking about anything and it would still have mesmerised her.

'You mention carbon dioxide a lot. That's the same gas you get from fermentation, isn't it?'

'Yes, and we also use it in the bottling process.'

'Well that's convenient. Do you collect it, you know, to use it in your bottling machine?'

'Recycle it? I suppose we could, but really it's more reliable and easier to buy one of these cylinders.' He tapped something the size and shape of a long torpedo, standing up-ended, and with pressure valves and gauges instead of a warhead. It leaned against its own metal rack which had wheels, she guessed for ease of moving.

'You see,' he continued, 'the bottling machine has two tubes which come right down low into the bottle. First carbon dioxide is blown in and flushes out the air, then using the second tube, the bottle is filled with wine. If air gets trapped with the wine in the bottle, there's a risk of oxidation.'

'And the wine is ruined. Ingenious. Is carbon dioxide heavier than air, then?' she asked, trying to work out how carbon dioxide drove the air out of the bottle.

'Yes. Clever you.' He held her glance for a moment.

She felt awkward. 'So, aging? How do you age the wine?'

'Good question. Some of my whites only need about 6 months, so they can do that in the bottle. I see you're looking around. We store them in one of the outbuildings. It's a smaller unit, and easier to keep at a cool steady temperature. It's difficult in a great big warehouse like this.'

'Yes of course, the outbuildings.'

'Well I've talked and talked, no doubt in too much detail. I think it's time to taste a selection of my wines and hear about your still at the Clegg workshop.'

'Well it's hardly an operational project. It's really only a shaped copper tank in the back of a fireplace. Nothing on the scale of all this. There are a few bits of old pipe left, so you can tell it was used for distilling. Probably nothing more exciting than lavender oil.'

'It sounds fascinating. I tell you what, if you're interested in the history of wine making and distilling, I've a small collection of wine-related antiques and curios. If we walk over to my cottage, you can take a look while you try the wine. What do you say?'

Chrissie kept her face neutral, but in her head she metaphorically punched the air. This was playing right into her hands.

'Excellent idea,' she said, taking care not to sound too keen, 'but you're forgetting we repaired your wine tray. That's how I came to ring you in the first place. Remember? I kind of guessed you had an interest in all things wine related.'

She watched him smile before guiding her past a grape sorting table near the delivery bay, and then out through a door at the rear of the winery. She sensed he was trying to decide if she was a wine enthusiast, a potential distiller, or someone angling for a flirtatious affair.

The cottage was a surprise. It was hidden behind the winery and various outbuildings, as if the track or lane originally running past its front door had moved away, leaving it stranded. It was typical *old Suffolk*, dominated by its roof and chimneys, and appeared ill at ease with its towering twenty-first century neighbour, the metal-clad winery. Tiles replaced what almost certainly had once been thatch, and the upstairs dormer windows blinked out of the low roofline. It was too dark to be sure, but she guessed it was painted in Suffolk pink.

He seemed pleased by her surprise. 'I like being close to work. When the wine's fermenting, I can check on it anytime. And if I look out of my front windows, I can see what I've achieved. If I look out of the back windows, I see countryside and vines. What more could I wish for?'

'The old juxtaposed with the new,' she murmured.

He showed her into a cosy living room. It had low beams and an open fireplace with a wood burner.

'I won't be a moment. I'll just get some glasses and a selection of the wines.'

It was her chance to scan the room quickly before he reappeared. What was she looking for? Something to give her a lead into talking about troubled youngsters? Photos were usually a good starting point, she decided, and turned her attention to a large framed collage hanging on one wall. At least ten shots of Strad Kell crowded together in the frame. They showed a younger Strad with a thinner body and in various poses: holding a bottle of wine, another drinking from a glass, picking a bunch of grapes, standing next to a young vine, dressed in football kit, holding a wooden spade, crouching by a bicycle, and proud next to a first car. It told a story in snapshot timeframes, his hairless head always unmistakable as the years stretched back.

'I see those photos caught your interest.'

She jumped. 'I didn't realise… I didn't hear you come back. I hope you don't mind me looking.'

'Not at all. Friends and thirtieth birthdays. Someone thought it'd be fun. The record of a decade. But of course the years keep rolling on and I've just about clocked up another half decade since then.'

'You'll need more wall space. Hey, I'm pleased to see you're enjoying the wine tray,' she said, as he set it down on a low table. She walked over to take a closer look. The beautifully turned and shaped spindles, about four inches high, were topped with a delicate wooden rail and fenced in the bottles like a balustrade. She remembered Ron's reference to its melon feet and tried not to smile.

'The labels on the bottles aren't the commercial ones. As you can see: year of pressing, length of time aging in bottle, mix of grapes or years.' The list flowed from his tongue as he pointed to the plain labels covered in roughly pencilled numbers and hieroglyphics.

'A work in progress.'

'Yes, it's the part I really enjoy. It's a matter of palate. The art of aging and mixing. Damn, I forgot to bring the glasses.'

This time she made sure she didn't have her back to the door while he was out of the room. When he returned with a handful of glasses, she was ready for him.

'Is that you receiving an award?' she asked, indicating a small photo frame she'd spotted on a square-leg server under the window.

'Yes, for employing troubled young people. It was a couple of years ago.'

Now was her chance. 'Rattlesden can't be the only place with troubled youngsters. Surely some must come from elsewhere in Suffolk?'

He held her gaze before answering, 'It varies from year to year, but yes, they come from as far afield as Ipswich and Sudbury. And yes, it means finding accommodation for them. But that can be a good experience too. It provides an escape from institutions or dysfunctional families, and lodging with the locals in Rattlesden and the villages around, can provide... well the closest they've ever got to a normal home life.'

'So Skylar–'

'Yes, you met Skylar, didn't you?'

'Hmm.'

'She's not from around these parts. Suffolk, but not local.' He handed her a glass with a small volume of white wine, saying, 'This is from 2010, and this,' he passed her a second glass, 'is from our most recent grape harvest, summer 2011.'

'The first one tastes a little sweeter. Am I right?'

'Yes, more sun later in the season.'

'Hmm... but, to get back to what you were telling me earlier, what turns a normal child into a troubled young person?'

'Ah, that's a difficult one. Of course there's the old question, nurture or nature? There are so many points where it can go wrong: so called friends, school, and adults in positions of authority, even the lollypop lady holding up the traffic for the school crossing. And then there are the temptations of drugs, alcohol and the internet. Remember, a lot of adults are pretty screwed up themselves. It's not surprising they mess up when they bring up their kids.'

'So I should be asking, how come anyone turns out normal?'

'Yes, that's the mystery. I'm not a psychologist, but I believe you need areas of structure in your life if you're going to have any chance of a normal life. You need a routine, a job that pays money, people behaving normally around you, and a feeling of self-worth and self-respect. Only then can you start to mend what's broken in you.'

'And that's what you try to provide?'

'Yes.'

'But why, what makes you want to help?'

'I'm a business man. I want a brand that's known for giving back to the community and as a by-product, free publicity. And let's face it, this way half my workforce is handpicked for me, and subsidised by the authorities. If I have problems with any of them, I can bounce them back. The revolving door into and out of social services.'

'And into and out of prison,' she murmured.

She sipped her wine while she sized him up. Did he really mean what he'd just said? Did she buy into the hardnosed businessman angle? To be where he was today at the age of, she reckoned thirty-five, meant he was a man with focus, driven by his vision and ambition.

'And there was me thinking you were the patron saint of troubled youngsters, Mr Kell.'

He laughed, a rich mellow sound. 'Me, a saint? But you've given me an idea. I could call one of my wines, St Stradivarius. What do you think? And please, call me Strad.'

It was her turn to laugh. 'OK, I'll call you plain old Strad and save the saint category for your wine. Now let me see the wine memorabilia you wanted to show me.'

•

By the time she drove her TR7 out of the vineyard entrance it was dark but not yet pitch black. She'd agreed to make him a display cabinet for his collection of corkscrews and wine bottle openers. Not a bad result, she thought. Normally she didn't like to talk about herself, but she'd dropped the French flea market pot into the banter and described the stand she'd made. Somehow it seemed to change the direction of conversation and within minutes she had a deal on her hands, the display cabinet. Definitely a successful wine tasting.

So how did she rate herself as a detective? She wasn't sure. Certainly this detecting business was more difficult than it looked, particularly if you didn't want to appear as if you were asking questions. And what had she learnt about Strad and troubled youngsters she wondered, her tyres spitting gravel on the roughly tarmacked route alongside the vineyard as she headed towards the fork.

'Oh my God,' she screeched as she shot onto the main track to the road.

Brakes squealed. Black bodywork streaked past her headlights, then off towards the turkey farm. She looked in her rear view mirror. The dark car stopped. Oh God, she thought. What now?

The number plate looked familiar. The driver's door opened and a figure got out.

'Chrissie?'

'My God, Clive.' She wound down her window, her pulse still hurdling. 'You frightened the life out of me.'

'Well this is a surprise. I didn't expect to see you here.'

'And I didn't expect to see a car coming towards me.'

'That's obvious. You nearly smashed into me.'

'Yes, I know. I'm sorry. But what are you doing here?'

'I've come to look at one of the sheds on the turkey farm. After what you told me the other evening, I made a few enquiries about Graham Tollington. The post mortem doesn't really tell us why he died, at least nothing obvious yet, so I thought I'd just take a look on the way home. You know, before too much time passes and the scene's completely buggered up. I can always secure it or send the SOCO team in if something strikes me as odd. How about you?'

'I thought I'd follow up on the invite to see Kell's winery. Nick's been working on the wine tasting room and it's given me an idea to repair the still at Clegg's.' She relaxed as she caught her breath. 'You'll never guess. I got a commission to make a display cabinet for Kell's collection of antique corkscrews and bottle openers. I'll tell you about it when you get home.'

'OK, see you soon. And for God's sake drive carefully. I'll give you a call if I get delayed at the turkey farm.' He leaned through the window and kissed her cheek.

She smiled and waved as she eased the car forwards, but not before she caught the frown as he turned to walk back to his Ford Mondeo.

She checked the time on the dashboard. A quarter to midnight. She flicked on the car radio.

'*And now for the five thirty traffic update....*'

'Bloody factory original clock,' she muttered.

CHAPTER 23

'Say again? I don't really follow.' Matt scratched his beard and tried to stay awake. This wasn't at all what was supposed to happen. He knew Damon hadn't wanted to get involved. He'd said something to that effect when he'd given him the memory stick, and now it was all spiralling out of control.

He shifted the mobile. It felt hot against his ear.

'Matt? Matt are you still there?' Chrissie's voice sounded tinny, distant.

'Yeah, yeah.' He stared up at his bedroom ceiling. He knew if he screwed up his eyes just the right amount, the grubby white emulsion with its flaky stained patches would transform into a smudgy face, an image or a superhero.

'Where are you?' he asked.

'What's that got to do with anything? Honestly Matt, have you even been listening to a word I've said?'

'Yeah, I've been listenin'. Just not been followin'. It's kind of easier if I know where you are. Sort of makes this real, like it aint a dream. What's the time?'

'Time for you to wake up and take this in.'

He stifled a yawn. 'So you're sayin' you told Clive about the memory stick an' now he wants it?'

'Yes.'

'And you're sayin' he mustn't know who gave him the memory stick, right?'

'Right. If you drop it off at Stowmarket police station in an envelope addressed to DI Merry, and with an anonymous note explaining about the knotweed, then it's a tip-off. He'll be able to request permission to access Tollington's phone records and emails, and seize his computer. Are you listening, Matt?'

'Hmm....'

'If it's to be admissible in court, he can't use evidence from an unauthorized phone or email tap. Tollington may be dead, but he won't have been working alone. Clive needs to find out who his accomplices were and so it's got to be done by the book.'

'Yeah, but–'

'Oh for God's sake, Matt. I'm at home and about to leave for work. Clive left about twenty minutes ago. He said this is important and... between you and me, well there's a question mark over how or why Tollington died. Now wake up and please get this done.'

'Yeah,' he mumbled, as the flaking paint morphed into a yellowy wedge-shaped bonnet, a bit like the nose of Chrissie's car.

'So is that a yes you'll write an anonymous note and leave the memory stick for him?'

'Yeah,' he sighed.

'Thanks, Matt. Look, I'll phone later to see how you got on. And I'll buy you a drink after work.' The phone cut out.

So what time was it, he wondered. Maybe she'd said and he'd missed that bit. He glared at his mobile. 07:20 blurred and fuzzed as he strained to focus. 'Frag,' he groaned and rolled onto his side. The mobile slipped to the floor as he drifted back into dreamy sleep.

'Flamin' robotics,' he yelped when he woke with a start thirty minutes later. What did he have to do? Where was he supposed to go? It all came back like a kick in the guts. Or was the raw twisting, just hunger? It was time to get up. He needed a plan. Envelope. Paper. Memory stick. Police station.

He found a pair of clean but tired boxers, dragged on a sweatshirt, grabbed the last sock in the drawer and paired it with a fairly rank one. Old jeans and the field jacket, his rig was complete.

'Cool,' he murmured as he combed his hair with his fingers. He reckoned he looked pretty anonymous.

There was no point searching for paper or envelopes; the bungalow would be barren. His best bet was the Utterly Academy library. He patted his pocket. Yes, the memory stick was still safe. He stumbled from his bedroom, past the sounds of his mum in the bathroom and through the drab hallway, where a blend of sickly air freshener and stale cooking oil fought to escape.

'Bye, Mum,' he tossed over his shoulder and slammed the door.

His mind moved faster than his fingers as he pulled on his helmet.

Maisie's knotweed photos were already attached to an email. He'd need to load them onto the memory stick. And once the police were involved he wouldn't be able to use Graham's passwords to access stuff. If he wanted to copy anything from the stick, now was his last chance. The plan was forming.

'Fingerprints,' he muttered. He'd need to wear gloves and wipe his dabs from the stick. The Alpine Monsters, a spent pair of motorbike gauntlets and his latest find in a charity shop, would have to do. He fired up the Piaggio.

Half an hour later he let the Academy library door swing closed behind him. 'Where can I get an envelope?' he asked, but no one seemed to hear.

He scanned the space, as if he'd entered a western saloon bar. He imagined a honky tonk piano playing in the background, as he swaggered past some students and headed for the library assistant's station. He waited his turn.

'Is Rosie in today?' he asked.

'No, but can I help?'

'Oh yeah, hi Martine. I need an envelope. You know, one of those big ones. It's kind of important.'

She stared at him for a moment. 'I'm afraid we don't really keep any. We're almost paperless now. I'll go and see if there's a used one lying around somewhere, if that'll help.'

'Almost paperless?' he echoed, gazing at the racks of journals close by. She disappeared into Mrs Wesley's office and moments later returned with a brown A4-sized envelope.

'Here, you can have this. And take off your helmet and gloves, if you're staying. It's kind of unsettling. You're not a courier are you?'

'Nah, but....' He turned the envelope over. It was addressed to Mrs Wesley, Librarian, Utterly Academy, Stowmarket. It was hardly anonymous. 'This all you got?'

'Yes. Just cross that out and write the new address. OK?' She blinked his dismissal and turned to the student behind him. He reckoned he'd become invisible amongst all the paper.

'Flamin' dongle,' he muttered and headed for his favourite computer station. It was time to rethink the plan. Still wrestling with the conundrum, while the honky tonk piano played in his head, he opened his email account and transferred Maisie's attached photos to the memory stick. Next he opened Word and started to type.

For the attention of DI Merry.

This is a tip off. Graham Tollington secretly planted sacks of Japanese knotweed on land he wanted to buy. Contaminated land is bought cheap. It's all on the stick. Check out Elmswell. Check out Groundsbuild LTD. Now he's dead.

And just to make sure there was no confusion, Matt ended it with the word, *Anonymous.*

He pressed *print*, *close*, *don't save*, left his helmet on his chair, and wearing the Alpine Monsters lumbered over to retrieve the letter from the print tray near the library assistant's station.

Back again at his computer, he phoned Maisie.

'Hi Mais. Any chance you can help out with an anonymous drop?'

'What?'

'You'd need to wear your woolly gloves and you'd need a plain envelope without your dabs and with nothin' written on it.'

'I aint a mule. I don't do drugs, Matt.'

'Course not, Mais. But we don't want it traced back to us, yeah? Look....' He told her about Chrissie's call.

'So she's buyin' drinks this evening?'

'Yeah, but you're not to say anythin' about any of this. Not to anyone. We don't want to get Damon into trouble. Right?'

She didn't need much persuading. In fact he thought she seemed quite excited by the idea when he said to wear a woolly hat and her hair tucked in.

'Undercover. Wicked,' she squealed.

•

Matt let the scooter pretty much freewheel to a halt, then cut the engine. The light over the Nags Head door looked eerie in the six o'clock murkiness.

'Why d'you always park next to the bins?' Maisie asked, leaning closer as she swung her leg off the scooter.

'Reckon no one'll notice it here. Don't want it nicked or keyed.'

'What, like go faster stripes? Come on, let's get a drink.'

He followed her into the bar. Apart from the late morning drop with Maisie, he'd spent the rest of the day trying to master Java syntax. He was starting to get somewhere with it, and that feat, along with the sight of Maisie in her skinny jeans and the prospect of a drink, made him feel pretty damn good. He even swaggered a little as he imagined saloon doors swinging behind. If he'd been wearing spurs, he'd have had them clinking and spinning as well.

'Howdy,' he called when he spotted Chrissie sitting on an old bench seat in the snug area of the bar. She stared into her glass as if an earwig had dropped into it, seemingly unaware he'd arrived.

'Hi, Chrissie,' he called again.

'What? Oh hi.' Her face livened up.

'Chrissie, are you OK?' Maisie asked.

'Yes of course. I was miles away. Hey, well done you two. I hear you were a real star today, Maisie. Now, I'm buying the drinks.' Chrissie stood up and thumped his shoulder lightly.

'Do you think the police will look after me, you know, now I'm a source?' Maisie asked while Chrissie went to get the round.

'What you mean, Mais? How'd they know who you are? We wrote *Anonymous*, remember?' He cuddled up closer.

'Yeah, suppose so. You better take off them Alien Mobsters when we're drinkin'. It aint cool.'

'Alpine Monsters,' he murmured.

'Yeah well, whatever they're called.'

He let his mind drift. He hadn't told Maisie everything. She thought most of the things on the memory stick were her photos and emails, courtesy of Damon's keylogging bug. She knew he'd read some of the material, but not about the chat room stuff. In fact he couldn't really work it out himself. Half-conversations were almost meaningless. It was a bit like faces. An obvious smile or frown was straightforward, but how to make sense of half expressions? Take Chrissie just now.

He reached for the glass she'd left behind on the table, and peered through her ginger beer. No earwig. He sniffed and it smelled OK. So why had she looked–

'Hey, getting desperate for your drinks? I don't think you'll like my ginger beer,' Chrissie said as she returned. She handed him a glass dripping lager, and a rum and coke to Maisie.

'Why were you lookin',' he groped for the right word, 'glum when we arrived?'

'I wasn't glum, Matt. I was thinking.'

So that was thinking. 'About what?'

'I had a look round Strad Kell's winery yesterday. He's asked me to make him a display cabinet for his collection of corkscrews and bottle openers. I was thinking I don't know anything about them.'

'Corkscrews? Aint that mean he's… yeah, I've seen it written somewhere… yeah, a helixophile? That's what he'll be if he collects 'em.'

'Aw… if you're goin' to talk helix stuff, I'm goin' to put some music on.'

'OK, Mais.' He watched her as she set her glass on the table and headed over to the jukebox. 'Yeah,' he continued, 'didn't they use somethin' like that to get unspent charges out of musket barrels? A gun worm?' He spoke the words as he saw them in his visual memory, as clear as the day he'd first read them on a computer screen. 'Yeah, 1630s.' And then he added for good measure, 'I reckon.'

The sound of electropop burst from the jukebox. For a moment he was distracted as he watched Maisie jig around to *Moves like Jagger*. A few chin thrusts and shoulder moves, and then she started to make her way back, neat footwork keeping time with the beat, her face a bit like Chrissie's earlier *thinking* look. Concentrating on Jagger moves, Matt reckoned.

'Absorbed, that's the word,' he muttered.

'Yes, he's very committed to the winery, and quite an interesting bloke.' Chrissie's voice broke through the music. 'But you know, I spent over an hour with him, and apart from learning about wine making and discovering he collects corkscrews, I know nothing about him.'

'But why'd you want to know more than that? You're only makin' a display cabinet.'

'Oh Matt, aren't you sometimes, I don't know, just a bit curious about people? Interested in what makes them tick? Imagine establishing a business like his by the time you're thirty-five.'

'But I don't want to start a winery, Chrissie. I s'pose I could trace him, find out stuff, if you like. What you want to know?'

'I don't know. Anything I suppose. He's thirty-five. The name Strad is short for Stradivarius, he collects corkscrews, and I know his address and postcode. That's something to go on, isn't it? I mean, you've often got less info for your debt tracing.'

'Yeah, and if I'd known you were interested I could've done some work on him yesterday. Monday afternoon was my day workin' at Damon's this week.' He felt important. It was nice.

'I don't suppose,' she sipped her ginger beer, 'you could find out about Skylar, while you're about it?'

He glanced up as Maisie re-joined them. When he looked back at Chrissie, he caught a different expression on her face. What was going on behind her grey blue eyes, he wondered. Was it Skylar she'd really been angling to find out about all along?

'Skylar aint easy,' he said slowly. 'I tried ages ago when she nicked the phone. Mind you, that was before I started workin' for Damon. I know more tricks now.'

'So why aint she easy? There can't be many Skylars out there,' Maisie said, her face slightly flushed as she sat down next to Matt again.

'Cos I aint got a last name, an age, or an address. I already checked Facebook and Googled her.'

'Do you reckon it's really her name? Could be made up.' Maisie reached for her drink.

'She won't have changed her face, though,' Chrissie said.

'Damon's got a facial recognition app he sometimes uses for tracin'. I'll ask him about it, but I think I'll need a photo of Skylar first.'

'You're talkin' to the official photographer here,' Maisie squealed.

'So the app makes a search for pictures of the same face you load in?'

'Yeah, Chrissie. There's bound to be a few of her out there on the net.' He didn't mention the dark net. He didn't want to broach that subject.

'I suppose there'll be photos on sites like Missing Persons.'

'You think she's a missin' person, Chrissie?'

'No, I just... well, I suppose she could be. I hadn't thought about it. I was just trying to come up with websites with photos of faces.'

'If she's run away from somewhere, then Skylar definitely won't be her real name. Damon says when people want to disappear they nearly always change their names. Happens a lot in Damon's business.'

He leaned back and listened to the pounding rhythm from the jukebox. For the first time in his life he felt like an expert. He knew if there wasn't a photo tagged with her real name, then he hadn't a cat in hell's chance of finding her real identity. Damon had given him a quick tutorial on tracing name changers, as they called them. He reckoned if you relocated and didn't want to be linked to your old name, and there were no photos, then it was flaming difficult to trace you when you left your old life behind.

But Strad had a last name, and Matt reckoned he'd be easier. Would Chrissie mind if he concentrated on him first?

He felt Maisie pulling at his arm. 'What, Mais?'

'Do you want me to take a shot of Skylar?'

He caught Chrissie's frown. 'Stay away from her, she's trouble,' he said.

'Yes, have another rum and coke and forget about her,' Chrissie added.

'OK, just thought you wanted a photo of her, that's all. Can you put *Moves like Jagger* on again while you're up at the bar, Chrissie?'

CHAPTER 24

Nick turned off the A12 and headed down the hill into Woodbridge on the River Deben side of the town. Jake sat next to him. Behind them, the rear seat was down flat and the old Ford Fiesta groaned with microphone stands, amplifiers, massive speakers, and Jake's guitar.

'You're sure you don't mind taking a look at the canoeing club with me?' Nick asked, checking the time on the dashboard. It didn't seem very busy for a Saturday.

'Yeah, cool. We've plenty of time before the gig. Makes a change to have a look around before we set up. I don't really know Woodbridge.'

They drove past Woodbridge Station and along Quay Side. Glimpses of water reflected like steel in the fading February afternoon. Nick read out the names as they passed, 'Lime Quay, Old Maltings, Deben Mill, Dock Lane.' They evoked a former time, overtaken and forgotten by modern life.

'So where's this canoeing place?' Jake asked.

'When I rang, I was told to take the Wilford Bridge Road and then turn off towards the river, just before we get to Melton Station and the unmanned railway crossing. It can't be far now.'

Jake nodded in a rhythmic way, chanting, '*Lime Quay, Old Maltings, Dock Lane.*' He repeated it a few times before adding, 'It could be the riff to a song. Hey, this is great. I'm on a roll.'

By the time they spotted canoes dragged up onto the shoreline, and kayaks stacked five or six high on racks, they were well into vocal harmonies, taping out beats, jamming without instruments.

They parked next to some cars near a concrete slipway. The tide was out and muddy silt bridged the metre from the end of the slipway to the water. A man in a wetsuit, with a splash cover hanging around his waist like a skirt, glanced at them. Nick slammed the car door.

'Hi,' the man called as he dragged his kayak off the mud and carried it up the slipway.

'Are you Roy? We spoke on the phone. I'm Nick and I'm interested in learning to canoe.'

'Yes. That's great. Why don't you wait in the clubhouse. I'll join you in a moment. Just need to hose off this mud.'

While Jake lingered in the car, scribbling down words to his riff, Nick headed to the clubhouse, a hut covered in darkly stained weatherboard. Inside was a surprise. Lockers flanked one wall. A small sink, drainer and unit with a kettle and mugs stood in a corner. It was a hut of two halves. One end felt like a clubhouse with framed photos and certificates hanging on the wall and plastic chairs arranged around a table; the other had the feel of a locker room. Paddles, lifejackets and helmets were propped against the walls or hung from racks.

The smell of the estuary pervaded the air, a kind of salty, muddy signature with faint undertones of sewage. Plastics and oilskins added their own unique contribution. Nick took a deep breath and let the hustle and pressures of the week melt away.

The winery seemed a world apart. He'd almost ceased to notice its own particular scent as he'd worked with Dave in Kell's tasting room. His mind had been filled with measurements as they cut lengths of wood, fixed their bespoke wine racks to the walls, fitted the large tasting unit, and finally the door to the room itself. And every time he'd driven down the rough roadway to the winery, police cars, SOCO vans and unmarked cars had shared the common track from the main road until branching off to the turkey farm.

He hadn't asked and he didn't want to know what was going on, but he had his suspicions. Matt's revelations about the knotweed deals were a clue. Graham Tollington was dead and it was enough for Nick to know he wouldn't have to work with the bloke again. But keeping a mental distance from it all and concentrating on Kell's tasting room had taken its toll. He felt exhausted, both in mind and body.

He took a longer breath, filling his lungs with the estuary-laden clubhouse air, and relaxed.

'So what's the difference between kayaking and canoeing?' Jake's voice broke into the peace of the clubhouse as the door swung open and he followed Roy inside.

'Haven't you put the kettle on and made yourself at home yet?' Roy said to Nick, before turning to Jake and continuing, 'Perhaps the confusion arose because of the Canadian canoe. You knelt in it and paddled with a single ended paddle. For kayaks, you use a double ended paddle, and you sit in it.'

'But I'm sure I've seen people sitting in canoes and using single ended paddles.'

'Yeah well, kneeling's pretty much gone out of fashion these days.'

Nick made mugs of hot black coffee while Roy talked about the club and the river. 'I can't find any milk, but there's sugar,' he said.

They toured the hut, Roy talking equipment, and pointing out a wall mounted chart of the River Deben and aerial views of the estuary.

'The club must have been here a while. Some of these photos go back a bit, don't they?'

'Yes, we brought them with us from the old clubhouse. In fact the club's moved several times over the years. Originally it used to be out at Waldringfield, but that was way before my time.'

'Where's Waldringfield?' Jake asked.

'Oh, just out towards the coast from here, maybe three miles downriver. A tiny place. Most of the members came from Woodbridge, so I expect that's why it eventually moved.' Roy tapped the chart. 'Here.'

They both peered at the sun-bleached paper. Nick traced the Deben as it snaked out to the sea. A place name leapt from the chart. 'Hemley?' he murmured. It sounded familiar, but for the life of him he couldn't think why.

He turned his attention to the framed photos on the wall. They seemed to be arranged by year, dating back to the 1980s. Youths dressed in shorts and tee-shirts and posing with paddles looked out at him, their faces recorded for all time. Names had been written in spider fine letters at the bottom of the photos, just about still legible. 'Were they competition winners?' he asked.

'Yes. We get the best of all worlds here. Sea, estuary and river, but if you want white water and rapids, this isn't the place for you.'

Something about the wall of framed photos conjured up a feeling of nostalgia. With a bit of tweaking and fuzzing, it'd make a great cover or poster for a music track, he thought, remembering Jake's riff. 'Do you mind if I take a shot of it on my phone?'

'I think they'll be too old and faded to–'

'That's exactly the effect I'm after.' He stood back and sized up the image.

'Do we really need to wear wetsuits? None of this lot seem to have them,' Jake said, indicating the photos.

'Competitions run in the summer months. That's when those photos would've been taken. If you want to be in the water in February....'

'Yeah, of course.'

They talked a little longer and finally left, armed with phone numbers and instructions to contact Roy in late March or April. It would be a more sensible time for beginners to take to the water and start some lessons.

'Well that took longer than I expected. It feels kind of spooky now it's dark. You know, down by the water like this,' Jake said, as Nick eased the Fiesta over the gravelly concrete and threaded his way back to the main road.

'It's atmospheric. Think of it as the second verse before the riff repeat.'

'Wicked. Hey how long've we got before setting up? You said The Oak & Oyster wasn't far from here, yeah? I'm dying for a drink.'

The journey back along Quay Side and up towards Broom Hill wasn't far, and Nick drove slowly. It fitted his relaxed mood.

'It's just after six now. We're virtually there. It's a bit early, I know, but we can park and unload easily. And you can get a pint. It'll give us plenty of time before the punters start arriving.'

'Hey, isn't that Jason's car? He must be here already.' Jake pointed to a hatchback full of drum cases. It was parked close to The Oak & Oyster's side entrance door. They drew up nearby.

It didn't take long before they were unloading the equipment and setting it up on some minimal staging in the Oak & Oyster's events room. Nick always felt like an outsider when they were getting ready for a gig. Apart from his carrying powers, this was about musicians and their instruments, or rather the electronic aspect of producing their sound. They were tuning guitars, balancing treble and bass, fussing over amplifiers and speakers, setting microphones on symbols, snares and drums – and now the keyboard player and bass guitarist were adding to the mix.

Nick left them to it and headed to the bar for some bottled water and a glass of traditional lemonade. His instrument was his voice and he knew he was supposed to drink plenty of fluid to protect it.

He returned to the events room with his drinks and sat on a stool at the back watching his band mates. He reckoned by now they'd probably forgotten he even existed. They'd remember soon enough when he was needed for the final sound checks, but until then it was a time to chill.

Feeling mellow, he sipped his water and thought back over the afternoon. It seemed like a good moment to look at the shots of the kayaks and clubhouse. He fished his mobile from his pocket and looked at the image of the photo wall. It was a nice effect. Who were these people? Some adults, some youngsters? He expanded the picture and moved it around with the touchscreen, trying to see the faces more clearly and decipher the spider writing. It was difficult because the definition was poor, but he skated around, picking up a blurry face here, a clearer one there. He guessed he needed to look at it on a larger screen.

It was hours later after the gig, when he was driving home to Barking Tye in the early hours of the morning that he remembered.

'Hemley!'

'What?' Jake asked, stirring from his soporific state in the passage seat.

'Hemley. I've just remembered why it sounded familiar. The bloke they found buried behind Willows was supposed to have run a children's home in Hemley. And on that chart you can see it was damn close to Waldringfield. You know, where the canoeing club was originally.'

'What are you on about?' Jake murmured, his head lolling back.

'Chrissie was talking about Hemley and endurance swimming and maybe even canoeing. She might be interested in my photo. Apparently they're trying to trace the kids from the home, but there aren't any records. She might think it's worth showing to Clive.'

Jake snored softly.

'Sorry. Am I keeping you awake?'

Perhaps Jake was right. Not the best time for a conversation. Just concentrate on the road ahead.

CHAPTER 25

'Come on, Clive,' Chrissie called over her shoulder. It was early Sunday afternoon and Clive had the day off. He'd spent most of it sleeping, but she'd finally dragged him out of bed and persuaded him that a walk might restore his spirits.

'You're usually the one who likes to walk. It'll do you good. Clear your head.' She didn't bother to listen to his reply.

'Anyway, it's time you got some fresh air,' she continued, the fresh air in question hitting the back of her throat. It felt cold, a little damp, definitely February.

'Bracing,' she added.

The footpath stretched ahead, the grass stunted and worn, unable to cover muddy earth where water collected in slicks. The fields wore their seasonal coats of winter wheat and barley.

'It's not far. We come out in Drinkstone by the church. We can walk further if you like, or circuit back to Woolpit. How do you feel now? Go on, admit it. Walking's already blowing the cobwebs away.' She stopped and turned, watching him as he strode towards her. She knew from his gait and the easy smile, he was virtually back to his normal self.

'What are you talking about? I didn't catch a word of any of that.'

'I said–'

'Shush... look, just over there.' He pointed to something beyond her shoulder.

She twisted slowly. 'What am I looking at?'

Something rushed at her from behind. 'Agh–'

'Got you!' He grabbed her about the waist, swung her around and kissed her.

'Right,' he said. 'How far is it to Drinkstone?'

He set the pace, striding ahead. She caught up with him as they approached the church from the fields. They circled around it and gazed at the ancient walls, constructed from random flint rubble and with stone dressings. The bell tower was built of old weathered bricks, the red colour blending uneasily with the greys of the flint walls and slate roof. It felt old, a survivor marked by its history, scarred, comfortable and safe.

'Let's sit down for a moment, shall we,' she said, spotting a wooden bench. A mild chill caught at her. She crossed her arms and hugged her anorak close, pleased she'd only suggested a short walk. Clive sat down beside her.

'It's so peaceful here. I'm only aware of...,' he let his voice drift.

'The calm? The stillness?'

'Yes. You can feel it, just like sometimes you can sense evil. Strange how one picks up different vibes. Take the turkey farm. As soon as I stepped inside the shed where Graham Tollington died, I felt... no, I knew something was wrong.'

'Really?'

'Maybe just seeing the atmosphere killing chamber affected me. I mean it's only really a metal tank. The birds walk into a crate and the crate is lowered into it.'

'It doesn't sound very nice.'

'Well, apparently it's meant to be kinder than other methods being used. It's prefilled with carbon dioxide, so the birds have no oxygen to breathe, and just get sleepy, fall unconscious and die within seconds.'

'So where did they find Tollington?' It was the obvious question to ask.

'On the staging around the tank. I think when he collapsed, he'd fallen so that his head was down in the tank.'

'You mean he smashed his head or broke his neck, or something?'

'No. No marks on his head at all.'

'So had someone filled the chamber with carbon dioxide?'

'I don't think so. Mr Core, the turkey breeder assures me he hadn't ordered any cylinders yet, and we didn't find any on site. And we checked with the suppliers.'

'So what happened?'

'The post mortem examination doesn't show anything other than natural causes. His heart just stopped beating. And blood toxicology hasn't come up with anything yet. The pathologist says it's impossible to say accurately from the blood what the levels of oxygen and carbon dioxide were before death, if you get my meaning.'

'Not really. Why can't they say what the levels were?'

'Because Graham Tollington died when his heart stopped beating. But until he was put in the mortuary cold storage, his cells went on dying and breaking down, leaching chemicals into his blood. It confuses the blood gas tests. At least, that's how the pathologist explained it to me.'

'So he just died? No one killed him?'

'If he died quickly from lack of oxygen, then the pathologist can't tell us anything more without some very sophisticated tests. He'd have needed to take specimens at the time.'

'But when you were there you sensed something was wrong?'

'Yes. I searched around, and I found an empty gas cylinder. The type used as a shielding gas in welding. An argon / carbon dioxide mixture. I assumed it was left by the people who'd installed the atmosphere killing chamber. I didn't think too much about it initially.'

'You're starting to lose me, Clive.'

'The point is when I asked the pathologist, he said the shielding gas would work as well as carbon dioxide.'

'Would work as well doing what, Clive?'

'Killing. It would be lethal in the chamber because there'd be no oxygen in the mixture, and dangerously high carbon dioxide.'

'But what about the argon? Wouldn't it be obvious in the tests?'

'It's inert. Really difficult to test for. He said something about... he called it GC – MS, that's gas chromatography – mass spectrometry. You have to collect the samples in a special way, to seal the air in the container so any argon leaching back into the trapped air from the specimen is captured and can go through the... GC – MS.'

'Difficult sounds like code for expensive. So did the shielding gas belong to the installation guys?'

'No. We checked.'

'Shit. So where did it come from?'

'That's what we're trying to find out.'

'Wow.'

Chrissie let the information sink in. The old gravestones around the church reminded her of the brevity of existence and the natural cycle of life and death, but what Clive had just told her was evil. It seemed horribly at odds with the peaceful surroundings. She uncrossed her arms and gave him a hug.

'You've been incredibly clever. Well done you.'

'The memory stick's been useful too. There's nothing like having one's sources.'

They stood up, muscles stiffening from too long sitting in the cold.

'Come on, time to walk home. I could murder a mug of tea.'

They took their time as they ambled back from Drinkstone. The village was little more than a mile from Woolpit and Chrissie was happier to enjoy the nip in the air now she knew a mug of steaming tea was on the horizon.

'So,' she said, linking her arm through Clive's, 'you think Tollington's murder has something to do with his land acquisition deals? He possibly upset one person too many?'

'That's the most likely reason, but it's an extraordinary way to kill someone. The obvious suspect has to be Core, the turkey breeder.'

'Because he had access and knew about atmosphere killing?'

'Precisely. But he doesn't seem to have a motive. At least we haven't found one yet.'

'Sounds like there's a lot of tedious police work to do.'

'It's what catches people, Chrissie. At least we've more to go on with this one than Pack and Haigh. The trail had gone pretty cold by the time we discovered their bodies, remember.'

She shivered. 'So are we looking for a welder?'

Clive didn't answer for a moment. 'We're looking for someone with knowhow and motive. That should narrow the field.'

The rest of the walk passed in silence, Chrissie deep in her own thoughts and Clive, judging by his face, back to mulling things over.

•

Chrissie was in a hurry. She'd slept fitfully, her mind darting between Clive's murder investigations and the list of things she needed to do in the week ahead. Usually she liked to spend half an hour or so on a Sunday evening checking through her emails and organising her schedule. This Sunday had been different. She'd been distracted by talking to Clive, too busy cooking coq au vin, and then overly full of the loud inky Beaujolais left over from the meal. She hadn't given Monday a thought.

Realisation struck like a thunderbolt during the night as she'd tossed and turned, somewhere between dream sleep and wakefulness. She needed to get her drawings of the display cabinet to Strad Kell as soon as possible. It was almost a week since she'd accepted the project. If she wanted to appear professional and efficient, then it meant sending them as a file attached to an email. Had she allowed herself enough time?

She'd woken with a start and a muzzy-head, the sort that comes from falling asleep just before the alarm shrieks its second wake up call. Clive had already left early. She had the house and the bathroom to herself, but if she didn't get a move on she was going to be late. There were no excuses. She hit the ground running.

'Thank God there's a scanner in the Academy library,' she said as she stood under the shower, hot water stair rodding down. If her modest home printer had a scanning mode, the plans could have been scanned, attached to an email and winging their way to Kell by now.

'Why can't Ron connect the business to the internet?' she moaned, as she threw on her clothes. But of course that would mean he'd have to join the twenty-first century. It was definitely one of the first things she was going to do when she became a partner.

'Come on, come on,' she yelled at her TR7, as the cold engine turned and finally spluttered into life. She threw the car into gear and accelerated away. It was only a short detour via the Academy and the library scanner, but it meant she'd get caught in all the Stowmarket traffic on the way to work.

She drew in at an angle, straddling two parking places. There was no point in straightening up; she wasn't intending to stay long. She leapt from her car and dashed into the Academy's main entrance hallway. Inside, the cold elegance and pale marble flooring calmed her agitation a little. She glanced at the large clock with roman numerals. Eight o'clock.

She took the main staircase two steps at a time, nipping past dawdling students. The library was still quiet and the printer/scanner near the library assistant's station seemed to be in sleep mode. She placed her drawings under its scanning unit and headed for a computer.

While she waited for the printer to respond to her scan document command, she thought back over her plans. It was a plain design, nothing too fancy, almost verging on minimalist and with sliding glass doors.

'I think Mr Kell likes to contrast the old with the new,' she'd said to Ron. 'He wants slanted display shelves and I suggested making sliding dividers.' She liked the idea of accommodating just about any shape or sized corkscrew.

'It sounds like a fixed louvered ventilation panel for a roof.' He must have caught the surprise on her face. 'No, no, I mean how to construct it. You'll need to set up a jig for the router to cut the slanting grooves in the side sections.'

She smiled at the memory. They'd been drinking mugs of tea at lunchtime in the old barn workshop. He'd gone on to ask how she was going to make the sliding dividers. She'd guessed from what he hadn't said, it was going to be the real challenge.

The screen flashed *scanning complete*. Great, she thought and opened her email account. Should she adopt a chatty tone, she wondered. *Hello*, *Hi*, plain *Strad*, or just forget the niceties and get straight into the message? This was taking too long. She typed *Good morning* and got on with it. She attached the file with the scanned plans and an explanatory message, and clicked send.

'Hey,' she murmured as she cast an eye over her inbox. What had Nick sent her with an attachment? 'Too bad,' she muttered, 'I haven't got time, now. It'll have to wait.'

She logged out and hurried past the library assistant's table, fishing the plans from the scanning unit as she flew by.

When she finally parked outside the Clegg's old barn workshop just before a quarter to nine, she felt as if she'd already done a day's work.

'Sorry I'm late, Mr Clegg,' she called, breathless as she dropped her bag onto a workbench, 'but if we had a computer and printer/scanner, I'd have been here ages ago. I stopped off and used the one in the Utterly Academy library.'

'Good morning, Mrs Jax. From what I've heard, the internet speeds around here are so slow, there's no point in being connected.'

'It was the fastest way to get those plans to Mr Kell. You know, for his display cabinet? I wanted them there when he checked his emails this morning?'

'Hmm, I was thinking about the sliding glass panels. They might be easier to slide if there were three of them. They wouldn't be so heavy.'

'But it wouldn't look so designer, if you get my meaning.'

She watched him nod slowly, her irritation with his internet aversion threatening to bubble over. She guessed his preference would be for a more traditional hinged door with wooden surround and central glass panel. 'I've sketched some alternative door designs for the front of the cabinet, but when I initially discussed it with Mr Kell, he said all glass.'

'If that's what he wants, but it'll have to be tempered or thickened. Have you heard from my pottery expert Abe, in Felixstowe, Mrs Jax?'

'Ah, that reminds me. I was going to ring him again. He was meant to get back to me, but he hasn't yet.'

She rubbed her forehead. She was usually so organised, but everything seemed to have got away from her this morning. Images flashed through her mind as she remembered the French flea market pot zooming in and out of her broken sleep, spinning and breaking, reforming, then shattering again. She'd woken in a sweat, only to fall asleep as she reminded herself to scan her drawings. Moments later, steel worms escaped from the cabinet because there was no glass where there should have been doors, only to die on the floor where an odourless colourless gas crept.

'Are you feeling all right, Mrs Jax?'

'Yes, yes, Mr Clegg. I'll put the kettle on.'

She needed to get her head straight and concentrate on the day ahead, she told herself.

CHAPTER 26

Matt sat at his computer station, the plastic stacker chair pulled in tight and his legs squeezed under the table. Despite his cramped position, he would have been hard pressed to find anywhere he'd rather have been on a Monday afternoon. The tired office, along with all its computing paraphernalia made Balcon & Mora feel like a second home.

'You've finished that chocolate and vodka already? I'll have to start taking it out of your wages soon.'

Matt twisted awkwardly to look at him. 'What? Really?'

Damon leaned back in his office chair, stretched his arms and then clasped his hands behind his head. 'No, but when the bottle's died, I'm not replacing it. You can buy the next one. So what did you do with the memory stick I gave you?'

'I-I....' Matt swallowed. The home from home morphed into a suffocating attic filled with flying bats.

'You gave it to the police, didn't you? It's OK. I knew you would. It was the smart thing to do. The guy died. Unexpectedly. I assume you found his passwords for the dark net?'

Matt gulped more air.

'The sequence was hidden in the code identifiers for a photo in his picture files. The keylogger showed he kept going to a particular one and copying and pasting the sequence.'

'But how'd you know where to look?'

'The keylogger gave him away. I'd say he was a frequent surfer, or should I say, diver.'

'Frag. That's wicked. I aint got you into trouble though? I mean I did what I could. I wiped all our dabs off, wrote an anonymous note an' got someone else deliverin' it with the shots of knotweed.'

'It's all cool. Quite the little snoop aren't you?'

'So you aint cross? And you got his dark net passwords?'

'Not exactly. I'd need to look at his hard drive and his picture files. Best leave that to the police. Their computer forensics will find them. Clever to copy and paste though. Got the better of my keylogger bug. Neat.'

'Beats tracin' debtors, right?'

'Cases like Graham Tollington don't pay the rent, not unless you're into blackmail, which for the record we're not. But finding information, handing it in, and acting squeaky clean, well it builds a kind of reputation.'

'Yeah, s'pose. Can I ask somethin'?'

If Damon wasn't cross, Matt reckoned it was the moment to push his luck. 'What about facial recognition programmes? Do we have one?'

'Woa. Where's this going? You really are into tracing, aren't you, Matt?' Damon's tone had an edge to it.

'A good mate of mine, her bloke's a detective in the police. This mate sometimes asks me to find stuff out, but I wouldn't call it tracin', it's more exploratory. And yeah, I enjoy it.'

'Well that helps explain why you handed in the memory stick.'

'It don't matter to me I don't get paid or anythin'. It's kind of a challenge. Cat an' mouse stuff, except no one knows there's a cat out there.'

'Of course, your interview. You traced all that stuff about the bloke found dead near the railway line. Yeah, I really think you are into all this. You definitely have a nose for it. But don't think you're swanning in here, learning all our tricks and then setting up on your own.'

'What you talkin' about, Damon? I aint got business skills. I wouldn't know how to. I can't do that stuff. I just want to use my brain.'

They held each other's gaze until Matt felt his cheeks burn.

'Do you know, I believe you. I really think you're stupid enough to mean it.'

'Hey thanks, Damon.' Matt turned back to his computer and clicked on the next name to trace. The attic switched into a nest and the bats evaporated. He was back in his home from home. He'd worked through his batch of ten before Damon's voice broke his concentration.

'Next set of names coming, Matt.'

'Yeah, thanks,' he murmured. It felt as if Damon was inside his head.

By six thirty Matt's brain was almost in shutdown mode. He'd traced fifty names, double checked them, and for the tricky ones, verified contact details from more than one source. He didn't do phone calls, but Damon had rung a couple of gyms and fitness centres for him, pretending to be a prospective member and friend, and somehow managed to coax out a confirmation of an address or contact number.

'Right, final coffee. Switch the kettle on will you. Let's do that face recognition. I'll take you through it.'

'Really? Wicked.' Matt scraped back his chair and stood up. This was about to turn into an awesome day. A surge of enthusiasm rebooted his brain, swiftly followed by an uncomfortable thought.

'I aint... faces don't....' How to say it? His visual memory didn't run to automatic recognition of facial biometrics, at least not for subtle expressions. He hadn't told Damon, and now it was about to be aired in the open like his grubby washing. Sweat broke out on the palms of his hands.

'Give me a name,' Damon said.

'Strad Kell.' It was a flash decision. A toss between Skylar and Strad. He reckoned he'd never seen Strad before, so his problems matching images would be masked, understandable. His street cred preserved.

'OK, is he likely to be on Facebook or Linkedin?'

'Yeah. Runs a winery in Rattlesden. An' he's thirty-five.'

Matt heaped coffee granules into Damon's mug, and drinking chocolate into his own and waited for the kettle to boil.

'Right, once we've got an image of him on Facebook, then we use a reverse image search. First Facebook and then Google's reverse image search site. See if he comes up anywhere with a different name or profile.'

'And where he comes up, yeah?' Matt poured boiling water into the mugs and set the coffee down by Damon.

'Hey, this is interesting. If this one's your bloke, he's bald. Not even a shaved hairline.'

Matt peered over Damon's shoulder at the screen. Frag, he thought, there isn't any hair on him. 'No flamin' eyebrows. Weird.' But worse than that, it was a parameter Matt couldn't use to help interpret facial expressions.

'I don't think I've had one like this to chase before. It'll reduce the measure points, mess up the algorithms the computer programme uses. Could be a problem. Another first you've come up with for me.'

Matt caught Damon's smile. Yeah, he got that. He wasn't in trouble.

It didn't take Damon long. The reverse search engine came up with images of Strad, despite his hairlessness. There were shots of him planting vines, opening his bistro restaurant, restoring the old barn, on holiday in France in a vineyard – but never in a group with others, always wine related and only going back about eight years.

'Does that mean somethin'? Nothin' from years ago?'

'It's not unusual. It's only in the last few years there's been such an explosion of people posting pictures on social media sites. You can see the algorithm doesn't bring up profiles, so we're getting full face only. I'd already put *similar* in the search to widen it a bit.'

'OK, how about tryin' Skylar?'

'Is that a first or second name? Male or female?'

'I dunno. She's a bird.'

Matt explained.

Damon went through the same type of search he'd used for Strad, and just like Matt some weeks before, he found nothing on Facebook. 'I think you need a picture of her. If she's changed her name, or only using half her name, I reckon your best bet will be to use a picture and reverse search.'

'Right.' Matt sipped his chocolate.

'So what's so interesting about this Stad Kell guy? What's your mate expecting to find?'

It was a fair question. He thought he'd understood when Chrissie had explained, but now, almost a week later, it seemed a bit fuzzy. Matt scratched his beard.

'I dunno. Maybe she fancies him,' he blurted.

•

Matt took his time as he scootered the back route from Bury to Stowmarket. At least with his Alpine Monsters cocooning his hands, he wasn't distracted by freezing fingers. One more week and February would have moved into March. But where was the flaming better weather? He'd read somewhere about a milder spell being on its way.

'Bloomin' arctic,' he moaned, as his headlight cut through the dark and cold.

He would have felt happier if he'd had something to report back to Chrissie. The euphoria of Damon showing him the reverse image searching techniques was starting to wear thin. The wind chill and drop in night temperature were seeing to that. In the past he'd have taken refuge in his comic-strip heroes, Dirt Track Jack and Corporal Blaze, dispatch riders on the Western Front. In his mind he'd have spun his wheels, spat gravel and dirt, leapt through the air and burnt rubber as he raced to Stowmarket. But now somehow, being Matt wasn't so bad after all. Matt and his Alpine Monsters, alone on the road to....

'Woolpit!' He almost steamed up his visor. Of course, it wasn't far out of his way. Chrissie was bound to be at home by now. Why not drop in? It'd be easier to explain in person about the searches for Skylar and Strad Kell. And if he was really in luck, she might be cooking some nosh.

He followed the sign to Drinkstone and then onto Woolpit. He drew up outside No. 3 Albert Cottages, and driven by the hope of edibles, hurried to her door.

'Hi, Matt,' she said moments later. 'Come in, come in. Leave your helmet there. Is everything OK?' She pointed to the hall table as she led the way through to the living room.

'Yeah, just passin'. Reckoned you'd be in.'

'So...?'

He sniffed the air. Mouth-watering aromas of something cooking in herbs, onions and wine, filled his nostrils. 'Is your laptop in the kitchen?'

'You rode all the way out here to ask if my laptop was in the kitchen?'

'No.' He hoped he sounded indignant.

'But you can smell the coq au vin, right?'

'What's cock oven?'

'Au vin. It's French. Basically chicken casseroled in wine with scraps of ham and....' She seemed to watch his face as she continued, 'onions, garlic, carrots, mushrooms and herbs. We had it yesterday. What's left over is in the oven for this evening.'

'Don't know anythin' 'bout that, but it don't half smell good.'

'OK, I've got it. You're starving. Yes, you can eat here, but there's a trade-off. Peel the potatoes for some mash. And don't go and cut yourself and get blood over everything.'

'Thanks, Chrissie.' He followed her into the small kitchen. Her laptop was open on the narrow pine table, the writing frozen on the screen. One glance from a distance was enough to tell him she'd been looking at her emails.

'Any news from your searches?' she asked as she pulled a bag of potatoes out of a cupboard, before sitting at her table.

'Yeah, well that's really why I called in. I've been at Bury doin' me tracing work all afternoon. Before we packed up, Damon took me through reverse image searchin'. We got absolutely zilch on Skylar cos there aint any images of her out there, and nothin' you didn't already know on Strad Kell. I've been fishin' around on him, but nothin' goes back further than eight, maybe ten years, max.'

'And Skylar?' she asked, her eyes back on the screen.

'As I said, zilch, zippo, nothin', and Damon reckons it won't be her real name. Without a picture it's a waste of time.' He ambled over, automatically drawn to have a closer look at her computer. 'What you reading?' He saw at once. 'Frag, what you up to, Chrissie?'

'It's an email from Strad Kell.' She looked up at him and laughed. 'I can see exactly what you're thinking, and it's nothing like that. You can see for yourself.'

'How'd you know what I'm thinking?'

'It's written all over your face.'

Phishing hell, he thought. Damon and Chrissie were as good as inside his head.

'He likes your glass sliding doors?' Matt mumbled, as he read the email.

'For the display cabinet. He needs to decide if he wants tempered or thickened glass, and if he wants oak or beech. I need to give him a quote for both.'

'Yeah, an',' he read out, '*Can you drop round with some samples*? Do you fancy him, then?'

'I've already told you once. No I don't, but he's got a sexy voice.'

Matt tried to digest her answer and gave up. 'Hey, there's an email with an attachment from Nick. What's he sending?'

'Shit! I forgot about that. I saw it earlier but didn't have time to....' She clicked on his email, and then on the attachment.

'Wow,' Matt breathed. 'A wall covered in pictures of faces!'

'From the canoeing club. Nick's email says it was once a stone's throw from Hemley. And, if we magnify... look, names in tiny writing and dates.'

'I don't know if I get it, Chrissie. Why'd you want that?'

'It's not for me, it's for Clive. I guess a bit of, what did you call it? Reverse–'

'Reverse image searchin'.'

'Well, whatever. But Nick reckons it might come up with people who could have lived in the children's home in Hemley.'

'Here, let me have a play with it.' He eased onto a chair at the narrow table and turned the laptop, to get a better view. He saved the image to a file and in different formats before zooming, and skating around.

Chrissie's voice cut into his consciousness. 'Potatoes! You haven't peeled any. Come on, Matt. Clive will be home soon.'

'OK, OK.' He forwarded Nick's email and attachment to himself, and memorised Strad Kell's email address.

'Right, I'm all yours. Potatoes?'

'God spare us,' Chrissie murmured.

Later, after Clive had arrived and Chrissie served plates heaped with Matt's lumpy mashed potato and coq au vin, they sat in the living room and ate, for the most part too busy enjoying the flavours to talk.

'That was delicious,' Clive said, laying down his knife and fork.

'Hmm,' Matt grunted.

'I've been thinking. Those photos... what a brilliant find. Probably the most sensible thing is if I send one of my sergeants over to Woodbridge to have a look around the clubhouse. Then we can either copy or borrow them. Having the originals, or the nearest damn thing to the originals, will give us the best chance of identifying anyone or linking them to the home.'

It was only afterwards, as Matt sat on his Piaggio outside No 3 and started the two-stroke engine, that something struck him as strange. Clive had seemed to assume, when he'd walked through the front door, that Matt was there because of the photos. Clive knew they came from Nick, but somehow his presence and the open laptop must have suggested his input. Chrissie hadn't said anything to dissuade Clive, and what's more, hadn't mentioned anything about the searches she'd requested on Skylar and Kell. It was odd. What game was she playing?

He made a decision. He'd magnify the emailed image and cull the names. He felt happier searching names than faces. It was what he did every Monday afternoon, and maybe, if he asked, Damon might give him more tips.

CHAPTER 27

Nick sat in the Willows restroom office and bit into his doorstep-sized sandwich filled with lashings of plum chutney and his favourite cheese, Suffolk Gold. He was taking an early lunch break with Dave, prior to setting off to Coddenham, a village a few miles to the east of the A14 and only a short drive from Needham Market.

'Coddenham's got a really narrow High Street, and it's on a hill. As if you'd expect to find a hill round here? I mean, have you ever tried parking there? And we've got the van.'

Nick was about to mumble something through his mouthful of half chewed bready-cheese mix, when his mobile burst into life.

'Don't you ever turn that damn thing off?' Dave's usually genial voice rasped with irritation.

'OK, OK, Dave,' he spluttered, coughing and choking on the fruity pickle as he fumbled in his pocket for the phone.

'Hi!' Chrissie's voice cut through the restroom air.

'Chrissie–'

'I just wanted to... are you OK? You sound as if you're suffocating.'

'No, I'm fine. Something went down the wrong way, that's all.'

'Oh. Well, I just wanted to say thanks for the photo of the inside of the canoeing hut. Clive agrees with you. It could be useful, and he's sending someone down there to have a look.'

'Great. I was amazed, it's a fascinating place.'

'I didn't open your email till yesterday evening. Sorry, but it's been crazy this end.'

'Yeah? Look I can't really talk right now.' He glanced at Dave.

'No problem. I'll give you a call this evening, OK? Bye.'

He caught Dave watching him, as he slipped his mobile back into his pocket. He knew the look. Dave was itching to ask about the call, it was obvious.

'Canoeing,' Nick said, hoping it would be enough. He didn't want to say more if Dave was going to be grouchy.

Half an hour later, the lunch break over, they walked to the secure parking at the back of the Willows workshop. A metallic crash, then a thud reverberated from the waste ground beyond the fencing. Diesel engines revved. It felt seismic.

'Sounds like they're digging again,' Nick said anxiously.

'Yes, but it's the knotweed diggers. The police've been over every inch of it with metal detectors and their geophysics. Some kind of ground penetrating radio waves. I read all about it somewhere.'

'Yeah?'

'If they're after the knotweed again it'll mean the contractors've got the all clear. Probably safe to assume there won't be any more bodies out there.'

'Let's hope you're right.'

'I'm always right. OK, have we got everything we need to take with us?'

'Tape measures, laser measure, notepad… it's only a carport we're measuring up for, right?'

Nick sat in the passenger seat as Dave eased the van through the gates enclosing the secure parking, and past the Willows workshop. Why was Dave so tetchy, he wondered. He had the face of a man who'd put salt in his tea by mistake. Usually at this stage of a journey he was full of chat, one hand on the wheel, the other gesticulating wildly as they accelerated onto the main road. Best to say nothing and wait for his mood to lift, he decided.

The van slowed to a halt. Dave slipped the gear into first, gave the throttle some weight, let the clutch in with a bang and gunned into the main road.

'Shit! You'll get us killed.'

'So what's all this about canoeing? Are you thinking of taking it up then?' Dave didn't seem to notice the horn still blaring behind them.

'I thought I might give it a try, check it out. I was gigging with the band over at Woodbridge on Saturday, so I dropped in at the canoeing club earlier in the day.'

'Yeah, I've heard of the Woodbridge club. I think Graham may have been a member once. But I could be wrong.'

'Ipswich, wasn't he?'

'Yes, but that's been more recent.'

'Funny how his name keeps cropping up,' Nick said under his breath.

'I heard they think there was something suspicious about the way he died.'

'I heard he had his fingers in a lot of pies. Too many to survive his middle age, it seems. But you know what I think about him.' Nick closed his eyes as Dave swung the van off the roundabout and onto the Norwich road. Two lanes of dual carriageway stretched ahead. Dave floored the accelerator.

The tension in the van seemed to lessen as the speed shot up, the uneasy atmosphere evaporating. Nick had no idea why, but he was sure of it, as two minutes later Dave braked, throwing him forwards against his seatbelt. They turned across the on-coming carriageway, and sped onto the road to Coddenham. Harmony had been restored.

There was nothing but open sloping fields, straight road and the occasional farm building for a couple of miles. Soon Dave hit the bends as the road twisted past the church and into the heart of the village. It was ancient, pretty and reassuring. The Suffolk plastered and beamy-style houses looked down on the van as they climbed the narrow High Street in low gear. It helped distract Nick from the rising plum chutney flavoured bile.

'Up here,' Dave said as they turned onto a smaller lane and tracked north above the village. 'Cooper's Sky. Keep your eyes skinned.'

'Is that the name of a house or a warning about tomorrow's weather?' Nick asked, looking to either side.

'Hey, less lip.' But Dave was smiling. 'Ah, this must be it.'

A cold wind caught at Nick's anorak as he jumped down from the van. The house was probably a post war, nineteen-fifties build, he reckoned as he stepped sideways to get a better view.

'Aggh! he shrieked as he trod heavily into the surprise pothole. Over he went sidelong, cracking his elbow on the stony drive as he went down. 'Y-o-uch,' he yelled.

Intense sickening pain shot from his elbow, engulfed his arm and filled his head. He rolled over and sat up, conscious both Dave and the customer must be watching. He felt stupid, and tried to make light of it, desperate for the agony to ease.

'Are you OK?'

'Yeah, yeah.' But he winced as he tried to straighten his arm. It could have been on fire.

•

Nick groped for his phone. He knew it was Chrissie from the caller ID. He half sat, half lay with his legs outstretched on his parents' three-seater sofa. The temporary cast and sling smelled of hospital, the open plan room, of air freshener. Both were unpleasant, suffocating him with antiseptic or sickly spring flowers. The painkillers had taken hold, but they couldn't help his mood.

'Shit,' he hissed, as he tried to perfect his one handed tap and slide technique to answer the call.

'Hi,' the familiar voice seemed to convey so much as it travelled over the airwaves. 'OK to talk now?'

'Hiya, Chrissie.'

He listened to the pause before she asked, 'So what's up?'

'I had a slight accident and... my arm's in a sling.' He recounted the almost, but not yet comic sideways fall from a four inch pothole.

'What?'

'I cracked my olecranon.'

'What's that?'

'I've got a hairline break through the pointy bit of my elbow. Stupid really.'

'Shit, that sounds really sore. So what happens? It just heals?'

'Basically, yes. Ipswich A & E said I was lucky. My elbow joint's OK, but it hurts when I straighten my arm. And it will for a bit.' He attempted a laugh, wanted to make light of it. He needed to banish the memory of excruciating pain.

'So you're off work for a while?'

'Yes. I'll know more once I've been to the fracture clinic.'

'So it's only your elbow. A hairline? You know you're going to get bored after a few days. Do you fancy a trip to Felixstowe with me to visit the pot expert?'

'I don't know what a pot expert is, but it's got to be better than sitting here.' Anything, he thought, to get away from the cloying concern, air freshener and frequent offers of another cup of tea.

CHAPTER 28

Chrissie changed down a gear and turned in through the entrance to Kell's vineyard and winery. Two pieces of four inch board rested on the carpet in the footwell and lay propped against the passenger seat. After Strad's email reply to her on Monday, she'd spent part of the day looking through catalogues and phoning wood yards. She'd held back until she'd got estimates and costs for both the oak and beech and now, early Tuesday evening, she'd arranged to drop them in for him on her way home.

A moment of excited anticipation caught her breath as the TR7's headlights illuminated a patch of metal-clad industrial unit. It felt theatrical as almost immediately the security lights burst onto the scene, casting shadows inside her car. She drove past the front entrance door and followed the side of the building. Outhouses, small barns and storage units dotted her route on one side and clustered towards the delivery and collection area. She headed past the rear of the winery and stopped outside Strad's cottage. She knew he'd be expecting her, but she was surprised he was outside, his front door thrown open and a welcoming smile on his face.

'Must have security cameras,' she muttered.

'Hello, Chrissie,' he said, his rich tones warming the evening air for her.

She got out of the car and walked around to the passenger door, acutely aware of him.

'I've a couple of samples of wood for you, and I've prepared separate quotes for the oak and beech.' She opened the car door and lifted out the wood, before slipping her bag over her shoulder.

'Excellent. Bring them inside. The temperature's dropping. Can't you just feel it?'

'Hmm,' she said and followed him into the cottage.

This time he led her through the hallway and into the kitchen at the back of the house. It felt warm. A pine refectory table stretched the length of the room, an assortment of kitchen chairs pushed in tight against it.

'Do you entertain a lot?' The question slipped out.

What was she thinking? He ran a restaurant. She felt embarrassed and turned away, hiding her flaming cheeks as she put the sample boards on the table.

'I don't know if I'd elevate it to the category of entertaining, but when we're harvesting the grapes, we all eat in here in the evening. They're long days and it helps keep up morale. I find people perform better if you treat them well.'

'Yes of course, the grape harvest.'

'Now let me have a look. This is the oak and... oh I like the beech.'

'You need to look at the samples against the wood in the tasting room. If you're putting the display cabinet in there, you might want to match the oak. Or if you want it to stand out, maybe go for the beech?' She hoped she sounded professional, in control.

'And here are the quotes,' she said, whipping an envelope out her bag.

'Coffee? Or can I tempt you with a glass of wine?'

'Coffee would be nice,' she said, sensing he wanted to get away from the subject of cost. Of course that was how she'd met him in the first place, over the small matter of his account.

She glanced around the kitchen looking for clues of family, partners or friends. Anything to pad him out, give him some background beyond the vineyard. While he fussed over the coffee maker, she cruised about, looking at framed collages of wine labels, catching her foot on a cat's bowl and gazing at a dresser stacked with old cups and plates. She tried to look casual, bored even.

'You seem restless. Just say if you've got to rush off.'

The aroma of fresh coffee began to fill the air, disseminating hints of bitter roast, deep rich earthy flavours overlaid with sweeter, almost chocolaty tones. Chrissie's nose was in heaven.

'No, no. The coffee smells delicious. I was interested in your china. I… don't want to bore you but I'm finally taking my pot to be looked at by an expert.'

'Yes, I remember, your French flea market find. That's good. You told me about it last time.'

'Yes, it's been on my mind. Anyway, I'm off to see someone in Felixstowe. Abraham Pawcett. I don't know if you've heard of him.'

'I don't think so. At least I think I'd remember if we'd delivered wine to him.'

They pulled a couple of the old chairs back from the table and sat down with their coffee and the sample boards. Chrissie relaxed and the conversation flowed. He mentioned a beach hut near Felixstowe Ferry.

'Is it near the container port?'

'No, it's along the coast a bit. Beyond old Felixstowe. If you're over there visiting your pot expert, take a look. It's only a mile further on.'

'It seems a long way from here to go for a beach hut.'

'Not really. What are the alternatives? Aldeburgh? And Woodbridge and Ipswich are muddy estuary shorelines. Not really for gazing out to sea and enjoying a mug of tea with your feet in the sand and a hankie on your head. You'll understand if you pay it a visit.'

She caught his humour. 'Hmm, more likely to stub your toe on the pebbles. Do you use it much?'

'I let some of my employees use it in the summer. And I go down when I have time, which isn't often these days.'

'You could….' She bit back the words. She'd already asked Nick to come with her when she went to visit Mr Pawcett in Felixstowe. For a moment she'd almost asked Strad instead. She felt stupid. What exactly was the nature of their friendship? A useful client connection? Someone to help her restore Clegg's old still? Something deeper and beyond that? She didn't even know if he lived in the cottage alone.

'I could… what?' he asked.

'Nothing. It was a silly thought. Now I must be getting home. Let me know as soon as you've made up your mind about the wood. And please look at the quotes.' She gulped down the last of her coffee and reached for her bag.

'Are you sure you've got to rush away? Another coffee? Wine? You could tell me about your silly thought. Maybe it isn't so silly?'

She groped for an answer. 'It… just struck me, you had room in here for a second display cabinet. It'd kind of fit with the wine harvest theme. As I said, it was silly. Now I really must be going.'

He smiled and led the way to the front door. Outside, inky darkness veiled the large industrial unit, and for a moment it seemed as if the vineyard and winery were just an illusion. Knowing it loomed somewhere in the blackness felt oppressive, menacing. Seconds passed, and then the motion-sensing security system exploded into action and drenched the rear of the unit in light. Thank God, she thought and climbed into her TR7.

She put the headlights on full beam as she slipped the car into gear. It felt reassuring: the bright yellow bodywork, the pop-up headlights on the wedge shaped bonnet, the sound of the two litre engine. She'd be able to spotlight the vines. It would stop them morphing into grizzled stooping figures in the shadows.

'Bye.' She waved to Strad as she pulled away.

She swept around the rear of the unit, her lights flooding a wider radius. For a moment they shone into one of the store buildings, the doors still open. They caught the outline of vehicles, she recognised the shape, saw the wheels. She guessed they'd be dark green, knew there'd be writing or a design on the side, but there was something about the way the images caught her headlights. Her foot touched the brakes for a longer look, but she was moving on the arc of a circle, she didn't want to skid… and then she was past and heading alongside the metal-clad winery.

She checked her rear view mirror. Had she glimpsed Strad before she turned the corner? It looked as if he'd been walking towards the store building. Probably going to close the door on the wine delivery vans, she decided, and without further thought drove out through the entrance gates.

It didn't take Chrissie long to drive home along the narrow lanes from the vineyard. She felt unsettled as she asked herself, why she was so captivated by Strad Kell?

To her mind, he was an entrepreneur. Someone, who at thirty-five had established a vineyard, a winery and a restaurant, even had his picture in the papers for good works. She, by comparison, at forty-three and a half was a soon-to-be partner in a cabinet maker and restorers, a tiny business without even a website or computer on the premises. Was she emotionally rich but asset poor, while he was asset rich and emotionally poor? This was the whole point. She didn't know anything about his private life. Did achievement on one front preclude success on the other?

It was a knotty issue. She threw her keys onto the hall table and made for the kitchen. How was she going to preserve the essence of the Clegg business and drag it into the twenty-first century? Should they take on a new apprentice and expand the manpower? She opened her laptop and checked her emails.

•

It was Thursday lunchtime and Chrissie slid the gearstick into fifth, and cruised along the A14. Nick sat beside her in the TR7, his left arm in a temporary cast. A spongy foam strip, secured in a pink figure-of-eight, hung from his neck as a sling. Chrissie thought the seat belt looked awkward and uncomfortable, but his face suggested he was relaxed.

'Are you OK? Not being thrown around?' Chrissie asked.

'I'm fine. It's just wonderful to get out of the house. It's the fracture clinic tomorrow so that'll get me out again.'

'You've only been off for a day and a half and you're moaning already. I'd like to point out I'm driving smoothly because of my pot, not your arm. Pottery doesn't heal.' The chalice-like vessel was cocooned in bubble wrap, and secure in a cardboard box in the boot.

It felt strange taking what was effectively a half day off. She suspected Ron had only agreed because, if she was joining the firm, then she needed to establish a range of contacts. As such, she was determined to appear a worthy connection in her own right, and had spent the evening mugging up on different types of clay and the firing processes producing earthenware, stoneware and porcelain. She realised it was Abe's opinion she sought, but she didn't want to appear a complete ignoramus.

They sped past Ipswich and over the elegant span of the Orwell Bridge, following the heavy traffic heading for the container port. She was trying to remember how majolica was made as they slowed to feed into a roundabout. 'Felixstowe already?' she murmured.

'OK, we come off at this roundabout and follow the signs to the town centre or station, not the ferry.'

Nick gave directions and soon they were driving past Edwardian and Victorian villas, built shoulder to shoulder for elegant residents and the seaside visitors of a past century.

'East Cliff Road. Hey, there's the sea. Wow.' It stretched out, blue grey, hardly a shade's difference between water and sky.

They turned onto smaller quieter roads and stopped outside what could have passed for a rundown guesthouse with stone steps leading up to a heavy front door. Chrissie was surprised. She'd expected an antiquated office on an old high street with maybe some figurines and plates displayed in a window. This was altogether different, understated.

'Well this is number four. We'd better go in,' Nick said.

While Nick struggled with his seat belt, Chrissie opened the boot and lifted out the box with its precious contents. They climbed the five steps to the front door and pressed the doorbell.

'There's a security camera,' Nick said under his breath.

The door opened slowly and an elderly man wearing rimless glasses looked them up and down before saying, 'Good afternoon. You must be....'

Chrissie understood the pause. It was a test. 'Chrissie Jax and this is a colleague, Nick Cowley. Good afternoon, Mr Pawcett. We've spoken on the phone.'

His watery eyes flicked from her face to the box. She got the impression he was no longer listening to her, his attention seemed focussed solely on what might be inside the bubble wrap.

He led the way into a room. An Edwardian bay window stretched up to the ceiling. It seemed light and airy, almost devoid of furniture apart from a desk with a computer, a large illuminated magnifying glass on a stand, and a microscope.

'Please,' he said, holding out his hands for the box.

They sat on straight backed wooden chairs and watched him examine the pot.

'Oh yes,' he murmured, turning it over, running his fingers across it and looking at it through the magnifying glass. 'This is typical of Saint-Porchaire ware. It's French, almost certainly made from the lightweight pale clay found near the village of Saint-Porchaire, hence the name, but the style – note how the design is almost like the metalwork of that date.'

'What date?' Chrissie asked.

'Sixteenth century.' Mr Pawcett stared at her through his glasses, before continuing, 'but the style suggests Bernard Palissy, or rather his workshop near Paris.'

'Ah,' she sighed. She knew the name. She'd already looked him up after the Snape Maltings Antiques & Fine Arts Fair organisers had wanted to photograph her pot. But she hadn't dared hope it was the real thing. 'So you think it's genuine?'

'Yes. If you leave it with me,' he turned his attention back to the pot, 'I'll look at it further and write a report. Valuation may be difficult. There aren't many of these around. As you can imagine, they don't turn up in auctions or for sale very often.'

A knot of excitement twisted in her stomach. It was like winning the lottery, but instead of elation she felt muted. Was it the Abe effect? She glanced at Nick, but she couldn't read his face. It was difficult to believe Ron and Abe had ever been friends. Could there be two more different characters? She tried to remember if Ron had actually said they were more than acquaintances. She guessed she must have jumped to conclusions again.

Five minutes later, she'd signed some papers authorising Abe to examine the pot further, with the understanding it would be kept secure and was covered by his insurance.

She hurried down his front steps, thankful to get back into her TR7.

'Well that didn't take long,' Nick muttered as he negotiated the seatbelt.

'He didn't even offer us a cup of tea.'

'We could go for one now. I can't say I followed all of that, but I guess from what he said, it's rare and valuable?'

'Yes, it is. Shit. I should be feeling excited, jubilant, but somehow I feel dismissed. I suppose Mr Pawcett wasn't how I'd expected him to be.'

'Will you keep it?'

She didn't answer. She hadn't thought that far ahead.

'Come on, let's find that cup of tea.'

They traced their way back onto the East Cliff Road and took the signs to Felixstowe Ferry. The road shadowed the coast, threading through a golf course. Wind caught the long wispy grass, bending and swaying it so that it rippled like water. A handful of resolute players pulled golf trollies, adding spots of colour to the cheerless winter fairways and greens. It was barely a mile and then they entered a tiny fishing village, scarcely more than a dozen houses.

'Felixstowe Ferry, I presume.'

'Did you see the Martello towers?' Nick asked, his voice suddenly alive.

'No. I was thinking about a cup of tea.'

She parked on the waterfront, near a short wooden jetty. Small fishing boats were beached on the pebble shore. A boat yard and a hut selling catches of the day caught her attention. She stood by the car and let the wind whip through her short hair, tussling and pulling at its roots.

'What's over there?' she asked.

'That's… well we're on the mouth of the estuary. Back up there is the river Deben and Woodbridge. Out there is the sea and Holland, and across over the estuary… I think Bawdsey Manor. It was something to do with radar research during the last war.'

She gazed at the shoreline on the others side of the mouth of the river. 'Can we drive to it from here?'

'No. There's only a foot ferry, and it doesn't run in the winter. At least that's what the notice on this jetty says.'

'Wow, just knowing there's no road and no ferry makes it feel kind of sinister. You can't help feeling it's concealing something from us, and at the same time, watching us.' She shivered and hugged her duffle coat close around her. 'Would you want a beach hut here?'

'What? A beach hut? What a funny thing to ask.'

'No, it just that Mr Kell said he had one somewhere here.'

'I suppose... well, maybe.'

'You said the Deben, right?' A thought struck her. If Woodbridge was at the head of the estuary, then Hemley was somewhere inland along the flat muddy tidal shoreline. If it felt as bleak and sinister and brooding as this–

'Those poor kids,' she said, breaking into her own train of thought.

'What?'

'Do you want to have a look at the Martello tower? I don't mind having a wander.' She read the visitors' notice near the jetty. 'Hey, did you know they built the tower, well really it's a fort, in the early 1800s using bricks shipped or barged all the way from London?'

'No wonder they look sort of grey,' Nick muttered.

'It was meant to stop a Napoleonic invasion,' she said as they headed into the tearooms near the jetty.

The light was starting to fade by the time they'd drunk their tea. Chrissie picked up the strained look on Nick's face and guessed his painkillers were wearing off. 'Come on, time to get you home.'

She thought he'd nodded off to sleep as she drove. His eyes were closed, so when he said, 'Chrissie?' she was surprised.

'I didn't want to ask earlier, but has Clive got any closer to finding whoever killed Graham? I mean, he thinks he was killed, right?'

'Yes, he thinks he was killed. And not an accident. The turkey breeder is the main suspect in the frame. Clive reckons he had opportunity and knowhow.'

'Mr Core? But....' Nick shifted in his seat. 'I suppose I got the impression he didn't like Graham. But then why employ the bloke, not only once but twice? He did the work in the turkey shed as well as the stable conversion. Ah, maybe I've just answered my own question. He wanted him back to... kill him?'

'It's not that straight forward, according to Clive. The argon / carbon dioxide mixture of gas that almost certainly killed him was bought over the phone and paid for with Graham's business credit card. The supplier remembers it was a man's voice making the order and he asked for it to be delivered to the turkey farm.'

'So what are you saying? Graham was planning to kill Mr Core?'

'I'm not saying anything.'

CHAPTER 29

Matt sat at a computer station in the library. He stretched and yawned. It had been a long day; first his Thursday morning tutorial, followed by a practical session in the computer lab. It had been on the topic of programming languages and the concept of virtual machines, and then combining the ideas to consider virtual machine programming language. And like all concepts, you either got it immediately, or you didn't. Matt suspected he was still getting it.

Rosie and Martine were talking together at the library assistant's table near the printer. His brain was aching from the morning's effort and he found himself watching, happy to be diverted. He guessed they were unaware of him. It was impossible not to be distracted by the way Rosie stood, leaning on the table, one hip at an angle, her legs cased in faded denim. He rubbed his eyes and turned his attention back to his screen.

It was time to put his course work to one side and refresh his mind by studying Nick's photo from the canoeing club again. He'd previously sent the email to himself from Chrissie's laptop, and he'd already played with it at home using Word to format the picture and size the image. It hadn't been easy, but he'd managed to cull some names. His plan was to use the Academy's Photoshop editing software. Aside from the names, he'd also be able to crop the faces, resize and improve the colours and definition, and produce images to a standard suitable for a reverse search on Google and Facebook. He'd borrow

Rowan's name and Photoshop password for an hour. The photography student owed him a favour for retrieving some files he thought he'd deleted.

'Frag!' Photoshop wouldn't let him in. '*Virus software installing?*' he muttered under his breath as the words popped up.

There was nothing else for it; he'd have to go through his list of names again. Some of the letters had been a complete scrawl, but so far he'd found Green, Keogh, Frostick, Denny, McKelvie, Cooper, Jonhson, Quinn.... He glanced up just as Rosie turned around and looked across the library. She caught his gaze and smiled.

'Hi,' he mouthed, grateful to be sidetracked. She wandered over.

'Are you OK?' she asked.

'I'm having trouble with makin' out some of these letters, Rosie.'

'And also having trouble volunteering to help with the Olympic flower bed, I see.'

'What?' A thought struck. 'Are you helpin' then?'

'Working out the letters or with the Olympic flower bed?'

'Both. Either. I don't know.' He scratched his beard, conscious she was watching.

'Well, yes, I'm helping with the flower bed.'

'In that case, course I'll help as well. You should've said.'

'Really?'

'I've got a part time job, so I aint much....'

She'd turned away and was already heading back to Martine.

'Spam,' he muttered. 'How'd that happen? I don't like gardening.'

It was no use. Short of wandering over to the library assistant's table, he'd have to get back to the task in hand. As he saw it, there was no one called Core, Tollington, Kell, Skylar, Pack or Haigh amongst the names he'd managed to decipher on the photo so far.

What would Damon do? How'd he go about making sense of the spidery writing, he wondered.

'Bet you his Photoshop programme'll be working.' Perhaps that was the solution.

He opened his email account and fired off the photo with a message to Damon. With any luck, Matt thought, he'd hear from him by the time he next saw his mates in the Nags Head.

Now he felt free to saunter over to Rosie. Try to look cool, he told himself as he asked her more about the flowerbed.

•

Nick opened the back door and stepped quietly into the kitchen. Chrissie had just that moment dropped him off on the way home from Felixstowe Ferry. He hoped his mother was somewhere upstairs or busy fussing over the air fresheners in the living room.

'It's that older woman with the fast car, isn't it?' she'd say in her disapproving voice if she heard the throaty engine.

It didn't seem to matter how many times he told her Chrissie was a work colleague with a steady boyfriend. She assumed all women fancied him. A flattering view only a mother could hold, and unbearably tedious. If he landed the Willows job, he might earn enough to afford his own place, at least to rent. And now he'd bust his, what was it? Olecranon. That's what the doctor had called it. God he felt bad. It could mess up his chances of getting the permanent job when his apprenticeship ended.

'Hello, Nick.' His mother stood, blending into the stainless steel worktops and the pale blue tiles of her over-styled kitchen. Her voice sounded kindly, concerned.

'Woa! I didn't see you there, Mum.'

'I was just about to start cooking super. How's the arm? You look a bit peaky.'

'I'm fine, Mum. In fact, I'm feeling great. Could you drop me off over at the Clegg workshop after my fracture clinic appointment, tomorrow? I'm going to help with some plan drawings for....' He couldn't think what the drawing might be, but he doubted his mother would notice he hadn't finished what he was saying. He just needed an excuse to get out of the house.

'Are you sure you'll be well enough, dear?'

'Of course, Mum. I haven't cracked my elbow on the side I write with. And if I'm off sick, they won't want me sitting around at Willows yet.'

•

When Maisie phoned Matt later on Thursday evening, he felt deflated when she asked him about his day.

'What you mean, you volunteered? A flowerbed? Digging up soil? Don't sound your kind of thing, Matt.'

'Yeah, I know. Don't suppose you want to help too? Could be fun, Mais.' He wasn't sure how wheedling should sound, so he went for a small voice.

'You are joking, right?'

'Yeah, an' I aint got anywhere with the Word and Photoshop programmes. I dunno, maybe I should've worn me lucky tee-shirt.'

'The one with the colour written in HTM…?'

'L,' he finished for her.

'Yeah, the grey-green one. So if today wasn't brilliant, why don't you wear your lucky tee tomorrow? Then it's got to be better. It makes sense.'

'If you say so, Mais.' He wasn't convinced.

•

Chrissie didn't check her emails until nearly ten o'clock at night. She'd been too excited about her Saint-Porchaire pot. The implications had only sunk in when she'd phoned Clive earlier to tell him the news. Butterflies started exploding in her stomach and she couldn't settle to anything for hours.

'You mean it's almost five hundred years old? To think I carried it around Paris in my backpack all day. It was only wrapped it scraps of newspaper.' He'd sounded surprised as well as incredulous.

'I know, and I tripped over it in the hallway and nearly broke it.'

'So how much is it worth? Five thousand?'

'More.'

'Ten?'

'And multiply by five.'

'My God. Fifty thousand pounds?' Shock and disbelief echoed in his voice.

'Possibly. Mr Pawcett was very guarded about the price, but the insurance value on the form I signed was for that amount.' She'd dropped her voice, 'I know, I can't take it in either.'

Eventually the accountant in her remembered saleroom prices were often lower than insurance valuations. And there'd be percentage cuts to deduct for whoever took on the task of selling it. After all, the cut was the incentive to get the best price. It brought the money for Clive and her down to sums she could get her head around without making her eyes water. Finally she felt calm enough to look at her emails, but there was another surprise.

Chrissie, I've thought about what you said – and it's not a silly idea. A display cabinet in my kitchen is exactly what I want. So please would you come and measure up. I'd like oak for the one in the tasting room and beech for the one in the kitchen. Regards, Strad.

'Yes,' she said, punching the air. 'Another commission.'

Great, she typed into the reply box. *I'll drop in at 8:00 tomorrow (Friday) morning to measure up. Let me know if inconvenient. Chrissie.* She pressed send before savouring the last few drops of her celebratory glass of Chablis.

•

Ping! Matt reached for his mobile. He was in bed and almost asleep, his thoughts drifting on flying carpets, hundreds of names hidden in the weave. If he laid his head down on the pile, the letters would be pretty much decipherable. All he had to do was close his eyes and–

Ping! There it went again. 'Spam,' he muttered and groped for the switch on his bedside lamp. He rolled onto his back and screwed up his eyes, struggling to shut out the glare of light and focus on the text message.

'Maisie?' What was she doing sending texts so late?

He opened her message. 'Frag. How's that goin' to help? You're goin' to do what?'

He read it a second time to be sure. *Got 2morrow morning off. Decided to get photo of Skylar. Thought might help to cheer you up. xxx.*

Was he unhappy, he wondered. He certainly hadn't been aware he needed cheering up a few moments earlier when her text dragged him from the brink of sleep.

Don't. I'll wear the T, he texted, and then as an afterthought, *How are you getting photo?*

Ping! *I'll ring the bistro wine shop 2morrow am. If she's there I'll get bus to Rattlesden. Cool, yeah? Snap her in the shop.*

'She's crazy,' he groaned. *Be careful. Don't let her nick your phone. x.* He pressed send and let his lids drop. He needed to shut out the light. Drift back onto the carpet. Lay his head on the pile. And sleep.

CHAPTER 30

Damn, Chrissie thought. Is that the time? Half the morning's gone. She'd only just drawn away from Strad Kell's cottage and had barely covered fifty yards. I shouldn't have lingered so long over a coffee with him. I'd better phone Ron. She braked and fished her mobile out of her bag.

'Come on, come on,' she muttered. 'Pick up the phone, Ron.' She knew he'd be wondering what'd happened to her. It didn't usually take so long measuring up.

Ahead, the doors of the store unit, where she'd seen the delivery vans the other evening, were firmly closed. A padlock hung from a large bolt, and what had looked in the dark like a long low unit, was really a series of sheds. She glanced in her rear view mirror. 'Oh God, now Strad is wandering over. He probably thinks my car has broken down.' She lowered her window.

'Everything OK, Chrissie?'

'Yes fine, thanks. Just need to touch base with Mr Clegg,' she said, still holding her mobile to her ear. 'Isn't that where you keep your delivery vans?' She nodded toward the shed.

'Yes. Why do you ask?'

The ringtone cut out as a voice said, 'Hello?'

'Hi, Mr Clegg.' *Sorry*, she mouthed to Strad.

'I let the phone go on ringing, Mr Clegg. I reckoned that way you'd know it was me and not a customer.' She listened to Ron's concerned enquiry.

'Yes, all good, Mr Clegg. I've been at the vineyard. All measured up, but this one'll be for the kitchen, and in beech. I'm on my way now. Bye.'

'Sorry about that,' she said, realising Strad was still looking at her.

'No, that's OK. But, why the interest in where the vans are kept?'

'What?' Talking to Ron had momentarily distracted her.

'Oh yes, the other evening the doors were open and my headlights caught the motif on the side of your vans. I was thinking we could carve it on a wooden plaque. Maybe put it above the door to the tasting room?'

'Really? Can you do that sort of thing?'

'Well yes, but I wondered if I could have a look at it more closely to be sure. Would that be a problem for you?'

'Not at all.'

She watched as he drew a bunch of keys from his fleecy stowaway jacket. 'Take a look,' he said as he walked over and pulled the doors open.

'Thanks.' A breeze chilled her face as she hurried to the shed. February daylight bathed the rear and sides of a couple of green vans. The rest of the space was empty.

'Are these the same vans?' she asked, confused.

The other evening her headlights had picked out a pyramid of round, almost iridescent shapes on the side of a van. She'd guessed it was an image of a stack of wine bottles or a bunch of grapes, but the sides of these vans had nothing like that on them. They were busy with a picture of a man striding out of a vineyard and carrying something over his shoulder.

'But they had....' She gaped at Strad and looked again, this time searching the picture for something triangular.

And then she saw it. Bunches of grapes in a cloth were slung over the man's shoulder. If she ignored everything else, that's all she saw. A triangular shape. So was there something about the pigments in the paint? Did the colour of the grapes reflect the light differently, making the rest of the design seem invisible? Not in natural light of course, but when headlights caught it at a particular angle in darkness?

'What's the matter, Chrissie? You look puzzled. What did you think you'd seen? I've always had this logo of a man on my delivery vans. Right from the start.'

An echo of something Clive had told her weeks earlier stirred in the depths of her mind. What was it? She tried not to frown.

'Nothing. I was thinking the man in the picture means the plaque will have to be an oval portrait shape, rather than landscape. Ah, that's lucky,' she murmured, feeling her phone in her coat pocket. She must have slipped it there after she finished the call to Ron.

'What are you doing?' he asked as she took a quick photo.

'If you want the plaque to look like this, then I need a picture to work from.'

'Of course, but you should have said. Why not take an unused bottle label? There are plenty in the tasting room. Have as many as you need.' He smiled at her, before adding, 'I expect you'll want to measure up for the size of the plaque.'

'Yes, if you'd like one. But I must be quick. I'm really running late now.'

She left him to close and lock the shed while she scooped her bag from the passenger seat and hurried to the winery's rear entrance. I'll get it done on a computerised laser carving machine, she decided.

The sound of a familiar two litre engine drifted through the winery door as she let it swing closed behind her. 'Funny, I thought the vans would be diesel,' she said under her breath.

•

Matt waited for the computer to boot and scratched his beard. A dusting of sugar fell onto the keyboard.

'Frag,' he muttered, and tried to brush the tell-tale grains to one side. There were often fresh doughnuts in the canteen on a Friday morning. It was like a celebration of the end of the week. And he'd naturally followed his nose after the morning's lecture.

The subject matter had been on representing numeric data, and had covered range, precision and rounding errors. It was essentially maths and it had been a doddle. He felt good, buzzing with a sugar high.

Specks of sweetness sparkled on the front of his lucky tee-shirt. He smoothed the cotton, running his hand over the HTML lettering design and spreading a blob of jam into a smear. He licked his fingers and keyed in his password.

He grinned at Martine, busy with a stack of books on the far side of the library. She ignored him, but nothing could deflate his mood. He was flying. He logged into his email account.

'Wicked,' he murmured. Damon had sent him something.

He clicked on the message. *Hi, I've attached the expanded image of a teenager from your photo. Reverse searching matches photos of Strad Kell, but name on canoe club photo - S McKelvie. Interesting, don't you think? None of the other expanded images and reverse searches came up with names on your list. Damon.*

'Spammin' hell. The bloke must've changed his name.' Matt fired off a text message to Chrissie.

•

'Hmm, there should be enough space,' Chrissie murmured as she gazed at the wall above the lintel. 'On the other hand, the plaque might look better on the door.'

She stepped back to view it from a couple of yards away. The vastness of the winery dwarfed the section of wall above the tasting room door. She'd need to ask Strad.

'Yes, something like a twelve by eight oval,' she said, thinking in inches and rummaging in her bag for her retractable steel tape measure.

Ping! A text message arrived. She let her bag slide to the ground and reached for her phone. 'Now what?'

'Hey, Chrissie. How about this?'

'Aaah!' Chrissie spun around, startled by Strad's voice. 'I didn't hear you behind me. You gave me a–'

'I know. How about this?' He raised his arm, a bottle of the vineyard's finest 2010 in his hand.

She flinched. She knew he'd seen her spark of fear.

'What's the matter, Chrissie? I thought I'd give you a bottle with the label on. Nicer, that way, wouldn't you say? I've got some unused labels in here.' He seemed amused.

She realised she'd overreacted. It must be obvious even to Strad, she thought. Her face flamed as she followed him into the tasting room. 'Damn,' she muttered, catching her foot on a large section of loose carpet, left like a protective mat on the new floor covering.

Ping! Her phone almost sprang from her hand as the text reminder sounded.

'You're in demand today, Chrissie. You'd better read it. It may be important.' His tone was rich, his manner relaxed.

Automatically she turned away from him and tapped in her passcode. Strad seemed very close. Too close. Was he reading her text message? She shielded her phone's screen and focused on Matt's words. S McKelvie? It was difficult to take in.

Something in her peripheral vision skimmed towards her. Thump.

'Ughh.' Chrissie stumbled forwards. Her focus blurred. She buckled onto the oak counter. Something caught under her shoulder. She heard it scrape as she slid to the ground. Everything went black.

•

Matt waited, his mobile close at hand and the computer screen still displaying Damon's email. Why hadn't Chrissie got back to him? If he discounted the spicier communiqués from Maisie, then the Kell / McKelvie combo was hard to beat. This was his hottest bit of news in ages.

'Phishin' hell. Why aint she texting back?'

His excitement and frustration racked up another notch. He drummed his fingers and scratched his beard. It was no use; he couldn't contain it any longer. He decided to phone the Clegg workshop.

CHAPTER 31

'Thanks, Mum. Bye.' Nick raised his good arm in a half wave as he watched his mother drive out of the Clegg's courtyard. The yellow TR7 wasn't parked outside the old barn, but that didn't matter, Ron's decrepit van was there.

'Hi, Mr Clegg,' he said as he stepped into the old fashioned workshop. Scents of wood, beeswax and linseed oil hung in the air, slowing time and turning back the clock.

'Hello, Nick. What brings you out this way?' Ron smiled and then turned his attention back to the cramp he was tightening. 'I'll be with you in a moment. I just need to clamp the sides of this drawer before the glue in the joints starts to set.'

'Do you want a hand?'

'Thanks. Can you just slip these bits of hardboard under the metal cramp heads here?'

'Sure.'

Ron glanced up. 'Hey, your arm's in a sling.'

'I know. It's only my elbow, a hairline crack. But it hurt like hell at the time. Stupid really. Did it on Tuesday.'

'But shouldn't you be....'

'It's OK, Mr Clegg. I've been to the fracture clinic this morning. Apparently I've got strong triceps. They'll pull on the hairline if I straighten my arm, so I'm in this lightweight cast for a few weeks. They didn't say anything about not using my other arm though.'

'Come on then, if you're sure. How long will you be off work?'

'Six weeks. Possibly less. So where's Chrissie?'

'Over in Rattlesden. Measuring up another display cabinet, this time for Strad Kell's kitchen.'

'Really? She didn't say anything about it yesterday.' Nick was puzzled.

The workshop phone erupted with a shrill ring, killing further thought.

'Can you get that, Nick? It'll probably be Chrissie again.'

'Sure.' He hurried to answer the call before he was deafened.

'Clegg's Furniture Restorers and–'

'Nick? Is that you?'

'Matt? How are you, mate?'

'Is Chrissie there? I want to tell her something.'

'Chrissie? Afraid not. I guess she's still at Strad Kell's winery, measuring up. Why?'

'Cos Strad Kell aint really his name. At least it's his name now, but his photos match someone on the canoeing club wall called S McKelvie. I just wanted to tell her. I texted but she aint got back to me. Hot news, yeah?'

'Wow. Cool bit of tracing, Matt. I'll get her to call you as soon as she gets back, OK? Bye.'

'Everything all right?' Ron asked.

'I don't know, Mr Clegg.'

•

Matt felt restless with excitement and too hyped for course work. It was such an awesome way of tracing someone, and he, with Damon's help had nailed it. Street cred was running sky-high and he wanted someone to pat him on the back, tell him he was brilliant and appreciate him. He'd tried to pass the info to Chrissie, and now he'd told Nick.

'Maisie?' he murmured.

It was obvious. Why hadn't he thought of her before? He'd scooter over to Rattlesden and meet up with her. Save her a bus trip home, and if she'd taken a photo of Skylar, then he'd try another reverse search. 'Epic.'

•

'What did you say, Nick?' Ron asked.

'I said I don't know if everything's OK, Mr Clegg.' He caught Ron's frown.

'It's Chrissie, isn't it? You're worried about her. Try ringing her.'

Nick didn't argue. He knew it was the sensible thing to do, but he also knew if Chrissie had read Matt's text, it would be just like her to ask Strad about his name change. This time Chrissie might have bitten off more than she could chew. He pulled his phone from his pocket and pressed her number. No answer.

'I've got a bad feeling about this, Mr Clegg.' He flicked into his phone's directory, found Clive's number and pressed ring. He watched Ron's concerned face as he waited and listened to the ring tones, each one tightening the knot in his stomach.

'Hello, DI Merry speaking.'

'Clive? Thank God I've managed to get you.'

'Nick? It's Nick isn't it? What's up?'

'It's Chrissie. She went to measure up another display cabinet at Strad Kell's winery this morning. She should be back at the Clegg workshop by now and she's not, and she's not answering her phone.'

'What are you trying to tell me, Nick?' His voice had an edge.

'Matt matched the face of S McKelvie, a canoeist on the canoeing club's photo display, with someone we know as Strad Kell. Matt texted the info to her while she might have still been there. You know what she's like. She probably asked him about it, or–'

'What the hell are you all playing at?'

'Nothing. You know Matt does people tracing. It's what he does.'

'Yes, I know. He's almost as fast as our team.'

'So who was S McKelvie, Clive? Is he someone Chrissie should be worried about?'

'I don't know, but the canoeing club still had records of past race winners, and it seems he lived at the....'

'It was Hemley, wasn't it? He was one of the kids at the children's home, wasn't he?'

Nick listened to the silence. Clive had as good as said yes.

'Did you know Graham Tollington had been a member of the Woodbridge canoeing club before he joined the Ipswich club? Dave, one of the carpenters at Willows told me.'

'Oh God, that makes sense now. He'll have seen those photos. I bet he'd worked out who Kell was. I'll send a patrol car over to the winery straightaway. Don't do anything, Nick. Stay where you are, and if you drive over to Rattlesden I'll arrest you. Do you understand?'

'I can't drive at the moment. I've bust my elbow.'

'Good.'

•

Chrissie became aware of noises around her. She didn't know how long she'd been hearing them but it was slowly dawning on her, she'd been out for the count and was coming round. Coarse-weave carpet pressed against one side of her face. She tried to move, but her neck ached and the back of her head throbbed. Where was she? What had happened? She opened her eyes. Memories seeped back. The tasting room. Of course, she'd been talking to Strad, looking at her phone. And then what? Had she had a stroke?

'Please God, not a stroke.'

She tried to focus. She had feeling in her legs, she could move her fingers, feel pressure from the carpet against her stomach and chest, and she'd formed words. Not a stroke then.

She heard footsteps and inwardly froze. Someone approached. Was it Strad? She closed her eyes.

'Still out cold? Or are you pretending, Chrissie?' the mellow voice purred.

Oh God, it was Strad. She knew his voice, heard his words, felt the toe of his shoe push at her ribs. It was a kind of rocking movement trying to roll her over. He must have hit her. But why? Don't move, she told herself, as a pulse thumped in her head. She made a split-second decision. She was safer lying on her front and playing as good as dead.

'You can't fool me. I had too much practice as a kid - faking sleep, slowing my breathing, holding my breath, hoping he'd go away. At least it made me good at canoe rolls, though. Gave me the lungs of a pearl diver.' The half laugh, it was so typical.

She heard him step away from her. 'Must've hit harder than I thought,' he muttered.

Her hearing seemed hyper acute as blood sashayed through her ears. She listened to him walk from the room and the door close. She caught the unmistakable sound of a key turning in the lock.

Shit, what do I do? He knocked me out, the bastard. And then she understood. The pieces of puzzle finally collided, striking her like a thunderbolt. He was S McKelvie, hardly more than a kid when the photo had been taken all those years ago. In a panic she raised her head and groped for her phone. Nowhere. And her bag? Gone as well. Shit! Her eyes saw something but her brain didn't register. What had she been lying on? Dark coiled metal with a wooden handle? Then she recognised it.

Stupid, stupid, stupid, she thought as fear gripped her throat. Stay still. Play dead. He'll have put security cameras in here. She needed to pretend, swaying and collapsing back onto the carpet to hide the corkscrew. At least that way she could get her arms into a more comfortable position and slip her hand into her.... Of course, the retractable steel tape measure.

Her heart pounded but her mind entered a colder zone. She had one chance and she couldn't afford to blow it. She had to get out of the tasting room and into the winery proper. That way she had some hope of escape. If she was to get Strad off guard, she had to play her part convincingly. She must focus and wait for the right moment, but for now she'd play dead and plan.

CHAPTER 32

Matt slowed as he rode the Piaggio into Rattlesden. Maisie had said to take the lower road into the village.

'Keep your eyes skinned for Kell's wine shop and restaurant. It's a barn conversion. It's got weatherboarding all over it and it's painted black,' she'd said.

'Yeah, you said a barn, Mais. Reckon I'll be there in fifteen minutes. OK?'

Weak sunshine played on the houses as he coasted the last hundred yards, glancing to the right and left. He spotted her, wrapped in a black down-filled jacket and skinny jeans, and standing on the gravelled parking in front of Kell's barn emporium. She waved and he swung onto the gravel.

'Hi,' she squealed, flipping his visor up and giving him a kiss.

He gave her a hug. With his Alpine Monsters on, it felt as if he was cuddling a duvet.

'Are you OK, Mais?'

'Yeah, why shouldn't I be?'

'An' Skylar?'

'She's quite sweet, really. She remembered me from Frasers in Bury. I don't think she's all there, mind.' She tapped the side of her head. 'I asked her about her job, said I was looking for part time out this way. She even gave me a coffee.'

'And the photo?'

'I took a selfie of us together and then I got one of her, but she don't know about that one.'

He gave her a kiss and tasted the coffee. 'There's a spare helmet stowed. Come on let's get back to Stowmarket.'

'Can we have a peak at the vineyard on the way? She told me about it. I aint seen one before.'

'Yeah, and Kell aint Kell. His name's McKelvie. Least it used to be. Found that out this mornin'.'

'Fancy that. O-o-o-h you're s-o-o clever,' she squeaked. 'Skylar said the winery's as good as closed down at the moment. It's their slow season, apart from wine deliveries. Otherwise we could have asked for a tour. Cool yeah?' The duvet gave him an excited hug.

•

Chrissie went over her plan again. She had two weapons; her steel tape measure in her pocket and an antique corkscrew. She was going to push herself up from the ground and launch into a racing sprint, but she needed the tasting room door open and Strad unsuspecting.

Her joints were getting stiff and she wanted to move her arm. She'd been lying on it for too long. If she left it much longer she wouldn't be able to feel the handle of the corkscrew in her palm. It was time to put her plan into action.

She'd worked out there were security cameras in the tasting room. If she wanted the door opened for her then it was time to get Strad's attention. She moved her shoulder and then one leg. She pumped her fist, hidden by the way she was lying on her hands, and pulled out a length of the retractable steel measure.

'Come on, come on,' she muttered, half to her numb hand and half to Strad, wherever he was watching.

The key grated in the lock and the door swished open. She braced herself as his footsteps crossed the room.

'It's time,' he said smoothly, and pushed at her ribs with the sole of his shoe again. She lay on the carpet playing barely conscious.

'It's all set up now, Chrissie. You and I need to make a little trip out into the winery.' He drove his foot harder.

'OK, have it your own way. I'll take you on the carpet.'

She watched him through half closed eyes. He stepped somewhere beyond her head. What now? Her pulse raced. Was this her moment to spring up and run?

Without warning the carpet moved, and with it, her head and shoulders. She tried to scream but her throat constricted. The surface curled, tilting her face, rolling it into the harsh fibres as he lifted one end. She tensed her neck and started to twist, but the carpet shifted again. This time it kept moving. She was being transported. She heard it slide with her, felt the strain in the coarse weave as he dragged it across the room.

'I hope I'm not disturbing your sleep,' he said as he hauled it through the doorway, 'but I reckon you're awake enough to appreciate this. We can't have forensics discovering you've been dragged. This way there'll be no grazes. It'll look as if you've walked, no duress.' He sounded pleased, as if he needed someone to appreciate his skills.

The swishing changed as the carpet trailed with her across the concrete. She was out in the winery but he was picking up pace. She started to roll. The carpet stopped. Her head plunged with the coarse weave back onto the ground.

'This is the end of the line, I'm afraid. This is where you get off, Chrissie.'

Her stomach twisted. Now was her moment. She spun onto her side, bent her knees, dug her toes into the carpet, and pushed up from the ground. In a coiling, squirming movement she sprang to her feet. Surprise was her weapon, but her stiff joints failed. She lost balance. She flung out her arms to steady herself. The steel tape flashed through the air. She felt a resistance as Strad grasped it. She pulled back, holding onto the casing, jerking it towards her. The catch held.

He screamed. The steel slid across his skin, the sharp edges slicing into his fingers.

She turned to run, but he still held on. Desperate, she tugged again, hoping he'd grip harder and cut through his tendons. The catch gave way and the tape reeled out. He staggered back into a cylinder. She lurched in the opposite direction. The cylinder smashed into the side of the fermentation tank.

She saw it in a flash - the cylinder was a carbon dioxide one. She recognised it from the bottling machine. And now it lay on its side, a hose leading into the fermentation tank through the hatchway near its base.

•

'Left here,' Maisie squealed as she tapped Matt's shoulder.

He slowed, almost overshooting the roughly tarmacked track. He turned hard left and rode across the rutted surface, watching out for nails and dreading another puncture.

'Are you sure it's this way?'

'Yeah, Skylar gave me directions. Keep drivin' down here till we see vines.'

He caught the sound of sirens wailing somewhere behind him, back along the main road. He instinctively slowed, churning muddy water as his wheels bumped through a pothole. The wailing got louder, closer.

'What you stopping for?' Maisie yelled.

He turned to answer, but his voice was drowned as one, and then another police car sped past, almost overbalancing him and tipping him off the track. Tyres spat gravel and lights flashed a relay of warning colours.

'Frag!'

'What's goin' on? Let's follow them, Matt.'

'You said the vines, Mais. I thought you wanted to see vines.'

'I know, but….'

'There's a turkey farm somewhere here. I bet that's where they're headed.'

'What? You think someone's stealing turkeys?'

'No, Mais. There's already been… someone died there, about ten days ago.'

'Oh yeah, I heard somethin' about that.'

He started the Piaggio. He didn't want to tangle with the police. This was meant to be about Maisie and him. He drove further along the gravel and tarmac, enjoying the duvet holding onto him around his waist.

'Left here,' Maisie shouted, pointing at the sign as they reached where the track forked.

'Vines,' Matt said and slowed to a halt twenty yards on.

They leaned against the wooden rail fencing and gazed at the vines. Row upon row striped the gentle hillside to the side of the track. Hundreds of short wizened trunks fed knobbly branches along wires linking one vine to the next. No leaves, no hint of the fruit they'd bear come the summer.

'Awesome,' Maisie whispered.

CHAPTER 33

Chrissie knew exactly what Strad had planned for her. The carbon dioxide cylinder and tubing said it all. Terror galvanised her legs. The front entrance was close, but she'd have to get past him to reach it. Instinct propelled her in the opposite direction, away from Strad and towards the rear of the winery.

'No-o-o-o,' he yelled and launched himself at her.

One stride, two strides – on she pounded, accelerating as she ran. She thought her lungs would burst with the effort. She dared not look back.

'Ughh!'

He grabbed her shoulder, wrenching her off balance. She started to fall, but her momentum kept her moving. Somehow she righted herself. Strad held on.

A siren wailed in the distance.

She sensed he'd heard it too. His pull slackened for a moment and her coat began to slip. She dragged her arm from the sleeve as she struggled to run, but his hold swung her off course. The bottle opener almost flew from her hand as she freed her other arm.

The siren wailed louder.

'Stop, you've got it all wrong,' he shouted.

She didn't care if she'd got it wrong. She had to get away. Tripping, and stumbling, she blundered on, leaving him with her coat.

Sirens shrieked outside, but Strad still came at her. She heard his footsteps closing. Ahead she saw the bottling machine, and beyond it, the packing line and roller-topped tables. She darted to one side. He cut around the other side of the bottling machine. And then he was facing her. Air rasped in her throat.

Hammering on the front entrance door sounded in the distance.

'Hello? Is someone there?' a gruff voice boomed from beyond the nearer delivery bay exit.

Strad eyed her up. 'No one knows we're in here. And the door's locked,' he said softly. Blood dripped from his hand.

In a lightning move, he hurled the coat at her. Like a blanket, it swathed her head, obscuring her view, and knocking her backwards off her feet.

'A-a-a-h,' she yelled and flung out her arm, still gripping the corkscrew. It drove through air and into his flesh.

A stifled groan chilled the winery.

'This is the police. We know someone's there. Open the door, or we'll use force.' Pounding resounded on the door as, at the same time, hammering echoed from the front entrance.

She clawed at the material, desperate to yank it away from her face. Terror seized her throat. Half suffocated, half blinded, every fibre in her body strained to detect his next move, hear his footsteps. A lock turned.

'What's going on? Why the urgency?' his mellow tones floated on the air from the rear exit.

'Good morning, sir. We're looking for a Mrs Jax. We have reason to believe she may be here.'

In the background a walky-talky crackled into life; *'No cars found parked anywhere to the front of the building....'*

'Mrs Jax, you said? She left hours ago. But why are you asking? Has something happened to her?'

'Just following inquiries. Could you give us your name, sir?'

'I'm Mr Kell and this is my winery. It's our quiet season so you were lucky to find anyone here,' he soothed. His mellow words, so reasonable, jolted like an electric shock. She tried to cry out.

'Is everything all right, sir?'

'Of course. Why shouldn't it be?'

'There's blood on your hand, sir.'

The walky-talky crackled; '*Outbuildings all locked, no cars....*'

'Your hand... are you sure you're OK? And your leg... you've been stabbed, sir. We need to check inside.'

Sound burst from her throat as she finally tore the coat away.

•

Matt leaned against his scooter, and gazed at the vines. Maisie stood, huddled next to him, his arm encircling the duvet jacket and holding her close.

'Aint it peaceful,' she murmured.

'Yeah, but I reckon it's a bit spooky with them sirens still wailin' somewhere over there.'

'Yeah, but it's kinda different though. Aint the turkey farm in the other direction?' She waved vaguely to the right.

He let her query float for a moment. 'Yeah, Mais.'

'I thought you said they'd be headin' for the turkey farm. Do you think the police went the wrong way?'

'Then they'll be comin' back in a moment.'

He took in the vista with the police soundtrack in the background. It was like watching a film, and just as in a film, it needed a hero, a villain and a plot. A thought struck. Frag, was it all about Chrissie? The police? The drama?

'She was at Kell's winery this mornin', measurin' up. I've just remembered,' he said, more to himself than Maisie. Angst gripped his guts.

'Who are you talkin' about?'

'Chrissie. That's what Nick said when I rang. Thought I'd be talkin' to her and I got Nick.'

'Why'd you want to talk to Chrissie?' Her tone sharpened.

'Cos she'd asked me to find out about Kell and Skylar. I fancied she'd want to know Kell had changed his name.'

'Yeah, you're real clever at tracing.' She kissed him.

'Thing is, do you reckon....' He let his voice drift as he picked up the sound of someone moving between the rows of vines.

'What's that?' Maisie whispered. 'Did you hear it?'

They listened, scanning the vineyard. A stooping figure came into view.

'There! Over there.'

Matt instantly recognised the man's bald head. He'd stared at his photo for too many hours not to be sure. Fascinated, he watched as Strad hurried past, no more than fifty yards away.

'Hiya!' Maisie squealed and then waved. 'He's in a rush.'

Her voice seemed to strike like a bullet. Strad's head dropped and with a crouching lollop, he dashed between the lines of branches and wire, and away in the direction of the turkey farm.

'Who was–'

A car engine drowned Maisie's question as a black Ford Mondeo sped into view from the main track and hurtled towards them. Gravel scrunched on tarmac. The car braked hard, almost skidding to a halt. The window wound down.

'Scammin' hell,' Matt muttered under his breath.

'Matt? What the hell are you doing here?' The voice was stern, impatient.

'I was lookin' at the vines. What's goin' on, Clive?'

'Have you seen Chrissie or Strad Kell?'

'Yeah, just seen him running through the vines, that way.' He pointed in the direction of the turkey farm. 'Least I reckon it must've been him.'

'Really?' Maisie squeaked. 'Was that Strad Kell?'

'Was he alone?'

'Yeah.' Matt's innards twisted as the significance struck home.

Clive didn't ask more. He spoke into the car's hands free system. Matt heard it crackling and spitting interference as the names Mrs Jax and Mr Kell bandied around. 'Get a car over to the turkey farm now. Call the dog unit. Where's DS Stickley? Get him over here ASAP. We need a road block. And alert the helicopter, we may need it to help with the search….'

Matt stopped listening. It sounded as if half the police force in Suffolk was being mobilised. But the one thing he'd definitely picked up was that Chrissie was OK. The relief was overwhelming.

'Come on, Mais. Let's go to the winery and see what's goin' on. I think we'll find Chrissie there.' He heard the muffled squeak of excitement as she climbed onto the scooter and sat behind him.

'To the winery,' she squealed.

They rode slowly along the track skirting the gentle slope of the vineyard. Clive's black Mondeo caught up and overtook, almost pushing them onto the rough grassy verge as a patrol car with reflective orange and white warning markings raced towards them. Matt kept moving. He guessed the patrol car had more important things to worry about than stopping a Piaggio scooter travelling in the opposite direction.

He accelerated to keep up and tailed Clive's car into the winery forecourt.

•

Chrissie sat, wrapped in her duffle coat on some wooden steps just inside the rear loading bay. She felt mentally numbed. Clive had offered her a more comfortable seat in his Mondeo or the patrol car, its doors still thrown open and the roof lights even now flashing outside the rear entrance. If she'd had her way, she'd have preferred to sit in her own car, but they'd found it in the shed with the delivery vans. When Clive explained the TR7 was evidence and therefore off limits for the moment, she'd nearly broken down.

'I'm really sorry, Chrissie, but we'll have to let the SOCO team go over it first. And we want to keep your coat, I'm afraid.'

She'd understood, guessed it would tell its own story.

'But do I have to go to hospital?'

'Yes. An ambulance is already on its way.'

'But–'

'Of course the medics need to check you over. Make sure you're OK. You know that.'

A uniformed policeman poked his head through the door. 'Back up's on the way sir.'

'Send them straight to the turkey farm,' Clive said decisively. 'And find something of Mr Kell's with his scent on for the dog handlers. Scramble the helicopter. We need to coordinate this from the air.'

It was obvious he was concentrating his energies on heading up the search for Kell, but his concern for her was clear. She could read it in the strained lines across his face. She guessed she was a distraction.

'You know I want to go with you to the hospital, Chrissie, don't you?'

'But you're needed here. I'll be OK. Really I will.'

'I know. But I've got an idea. I was wondering what to do with him, but he might just be what you need. Our very own bearded scootering wonder and his squealing companion.'

'Bearded scootering wonder?' she echoed, trying to make sense of it. Any more conundrums and her brain would burst. She'd been on high alert and overdosing on adrenaline for too long.

'Matt.'

'What about him? Are you saying he's here?'

'Yes, as it happens. He can keep you company while you're waiting for the ambulance. I'll OK it with the uniforms. Sorry, Chrissie, I'm going to have to leave you now. I'll catch up as soon as I can. We have to get Kell.'

'I know,' she said softly as he turned to hurry away.

Everything was moving so fast she was having trouble taking it in. Had he just said Matt was here? At least if it was Matt, he'd have his own take on what had happened and be a distraction; much better than a professionally sympathetic policewoman.

'Chriss-i-e,' a voice squealed.

She listened to her name squalling through the loading bay. Of course, that's what Clive had meant. 'Maisie!'

'Are you OK?' The voice climbed another octave, as a black down-filled jacket on skinny jeans ran screeching towards her.

'Hi, did you get my message?' Matt asked, following close behind.

'What message?' She hoped Matt hadn't sent concerned texts. It wasn't his style. Maisie's reaction was more than enough.

'About Kell being McKelvie. There was a photo of an S McKelvie on the canoein' club wall. Same face as Kell on reverse searchin', but much younger. Yeah, I reckoned you'd be impressed.'

'Yes sorry, of course, your text. Kell saw it too. I've been so stupid,' she groaned. 'I just hadn't suspected... didn't make the connections in time. So the photo was taken years ago when the club was at Waldringfield? Near the children's home in Hemley?'

'Yeah, I guess it must've been, Chrissie.'

'We saw him, you know. The Kell geezer. He was runnin' through the vineyard. That Clive bloke was right pleased we spotted him,' Maisie chipped in.

'Yeah, reckon he was in a hurry.'

'And he aint got no hair. Weird.'

Chrissie's mind went into a spin as Maisie's words summoned an image. For a moment she heard Strad's footsteps pounding after her, rekindling the fear. She whispered, hardly aware she was speaking out loud, 'When the police burst in... he crashed through the fire exit over there. He was like bloody greased lightning. I never knew anyone could move so fast.'

'Awesome. Look, Matt. There's blood on the door.'

'No, Mais. Don't go over there. Frag, Chrissie, what's been goin' on in here?'

'He tried to kill me.'

'Spammin' hell. Are you sure?'

CHAPTER 34

Nick hadn't been to Clive's house in Lavenham before. He instinctively liked it. Eighties build. No fussy female touches, no overly sweet scented air fresheners, everything a little tired and slightly worn. He rested back in the armchair and drank slowly from his can of beer. The sound of Clive working the barbecue drifted through the open patio doors. It was going to be lunch chez Chrissie and Clive. The smell of burning charcoal and the first half-decent sunny day in April had tempted Matt into the garden.

'What's Matt doing?' he murmured.

'What? I didn't catch that,' Chrissie said as she walked in from the kitchen carrying a bowl of cheesy crisps.

'Matt, he's out in the garden poking around with his foot.'

'Oh no. You must've heard about his latest knotweed coup. Volunteered to help with the millennium flowerbed and found knotweed rhizomes. Quite the horticultural expert, you know. Thinks he'll find it everywhere.'

'He only volunteered because Rosie was involved. You know he's always trying to chat her up. Hey look, the gardening toe of his horticultural boot is being applied to something green.'

'If it's knotweed,' Chrissie shouted, 'don't throw it on the barbecue. If it's an ordinary weed, just leave it in the ground.' She shook her head. 'He'll have all the flowers up.'

Nick watched as Chrissie set the crisps on a low table. It was barely two months since Kell had tried to kill her, but no one would have guessed by looking at her today. She appeared to have taken it in her stride.

'Are you OK, Chrissie? I mean really OK?'

'How's your elbow? Fully healed?'

'You know my elbow's OK now. You had me humping a sack of charcoal around less than half an hour ago. Come on, Chrissie. I want to know. This is me, Nick asking.'

'I try not to think about it. The important thing is that Clive caught the bloke. A bit of a cross-country chase. What with the dogs and the helicopter, they flushed him out of Birds Wood, then Great Wood and finally got him in Woolpit Wood before he reached the A14.'

'Yeah, you said he could run.'

'Hmm… you see, I haven't told Clive, but part of me still kind of likes him, respects what he's achieved.'

'But he's a killer, Chrissie.'

'I know. But he didn't kill me.'

'He tried to. He killed to revenge the abuse in the children's home and then to hide his past. You'd realised it was his van the witness saw near the Needham Market railway bridge. You would have been next.'

She sat down opposite him. 'Nick, you know me. I'm nosy. I thrive on challenging brainteasers. I hear stuff from Clive I probably shouldn't hear. If I let what happened eat away at me, Clive will know. He'll shut off his work from me. It'll alter our dynamics. I don't want to lose him and I'm too stuck in my ways to alter.'

'So you see yourself as a kind of investigator?' He was starting to understand.

'Kind of. I was stupid with Strad because I was blinded by his achievements. I wasn't being objective. But I've learnt my lesson.'

'Then you should take some self-defence classes.'

'Self-defence classes?' Clive said as he stepped in from the garden. His face had the flush of an enthusiastic barbecue handler. 'Thirty minutes and I can put the sausages on, Chrissie.'

'Potatoes are baking in the oven and the kebabs are marinating. I'll part cook them in the oven and you can finish them off on the barbecue. More drinks anyone?'

While Clive refilled his beer glass and took a can of lager out for Matt, Nick let his mind drift. He could still hear Kell's persuasive voice coaxing him to talk about Graham Tollington. 'Skylar always tells the truth,' he'd said. And no doubt she'd proved true to form and told him she'd lifted Graham's business visa card during the week he'd worked at the winery. Would they ever know more about her? Maisie's photo certainly hadn't shed any light. Was she just a vulnerable, light-fingered teenager?

He pictured Kell easing a confession out of her, asking for the card on the pretext he'd return it and smooth over the theft. And then he'd used it to order the argon / carbon dioxide mixture of gas, as if for some welding work at the turkey farm. Graham had paid for his own death. You had to hand it to him, Kell had style. No wonder Chrissie had flown too close to the flame. She'd always been attracted by style. Take the Saint-Porchaire pot.

'A penny for them,' Chrissie said as she came back in from the kitchen again.

'What?'

'Your thoughts. You looked as if you were miles away.'

'I was thinking about your French flea market pot.'

'Ah, Abe Pawcett finally came back with a massive valuation. It's unbelievable. Never in my wildest dreams had I ever thought anything like this could happen to me. I mean my share of the money will give me, after all the deductions... I reckon about twenty-five thousand. I'll have enough money to catapult the Clegg's business into the twenty-first century.'

'That's fantastic.'

'I know. We've got to sell the pot first, but it's so exciting. And now I've got a taste for undiscovered treasures.'

'Please not metal detecting. What will Clive do with his share?'

'I don't know. I suppose he's got to decide what to do with this house. He spends most of his time at mine. But this is good for the garden and barbecue. You know we're off to Centre Parks tomorrow? Thetford.'

'No. Doesn't sound quite your thing.'

'Not really, but it's only for a couple of days, and then we've got the time to ourselves. His ex and her two kids are there for the week with her new bloke, sorry, third husband. They reckoned Ellenor and Josie would like to see Clive. He was their step dad, after all. So in the spirit of the modern extended family, we're doing our duty.'

'Shit.'

'I've not met Mary before. She's his ex. Makes Strad trying to kill me seem quite tame, don't you think?'

Before he could think of a suitable reply, Matt appeared at the patio door.

'Clive says the charcoal's nearly up to heat.'

'Oops, better get the kebabs in the oven,' Chrissie said and hurried into the kitchen.

'Maisie not able to come today?' Nick asked.

'Yeah, she's workin'. I'll see her this evenin'. She'd of liked this.'

'Come on, let's go outside. Enjoy the sunshine.' Nick stood up and led the way through the patio doors. He guessed the garden was about thirty yards long. An abandoned vegetable patch had been taken over by weeds, and a child's plastic sand pit lay broken and half lost to wild grass. It looked unloved, as if time had stood still, probably since Mary had upped and left. He doubted Clive had ever had time to garden. The only nod to the day's barbecue was the mown turf and the swept paving stones.

'Are you really playing at being apes and zip wiring in Thetford Forest, Clive?'

'Why? Do either of you want to join us?'

'Me, a flyin' fox? You must be jokin',' Matt wailed.

Nick coughed on his beer. 'Maisie'd like it. You'd be able to hear her ten miles aw–'

'I know. Let's shelve that thought, shall we? I heard you talking to Chrissie about self-defence. They run martial arts taster sessions. I thought she might….' Clive turned his attention back to the barbecue.

'Oh Yeah?'

'Chrissie doesn't know yet, but we drive straight to Norwich airport from Thetford and spend the rest of the week in Amsterdam.'

'Just the two of you?'

'Yes, but let's just pretend the highlight of the trip is the martial arts in Thetford, shall we?'

Nick laughed. 'She'll like that. Do you know, Matt, I could see you in a tee printed with, *Have we descended from Apps or Apes?* and a picture of you doing a flying fox.'

'Wicked! Mais wants me to wear a tee advertisin' me Utterly Olympic Silver App. Did I say Mr Smith is pretty impressed with it?'

'Really? Well done.' Chrissie appeared carrying a tray of uncooked sausages.

'Damon says it's rubbish.'

'Ah, well I expect he can see your potential. He'll be egging you on,' Clive said quietly.

'There's just one thing I don't get,' Matt said.

'What's that?'

'Well, Strad Kell was called McKelvie. I looked up tartans and there aint one. Least not one I could find for McKelvie. I reckon he was from Ireland. So why the tartan anorak?'

'When we interviewed Strad, he told us Victor Pack used to call him Scott. It was a kind of nickname taunt, labelling him as Scottish when in fact he was Irish,' Clive said.

Matt turned to Chrissie. 'I still don't get it. So was the tartan anorak some kind of irony?'

'Maybe, Matt. I'd say it was all part of the tragedy.'

The End.

Made in the USA
Charleston, SC
22 October 2015